A
BESTSELLER

By

WALTER M. MALONEY

Dedication

This book is dedicated to Bob Holland of Virginia Beach, Virginia. Who had faith in me when I'm not sure I had any in myself. A waterman who taught me integrity, and how to dance on the waves.

Basic registration TXu 2-002-323

Supplementary Registration TXu 1-373-916

ISBN 0692747230

Cover by Brian Rylas

I would like to thank the many friends and family members who have helped in this endeavor. Special thanks to Charles and Ginny Crone, Frank and Missy Deaner, Mike and Debi Wood and Don and Gail Fentress.

Contents

Advanced reviews of a "A BESTSELLER"

Absolutely delightful! It is indeed a page turner with great characters and a very happy ending.
> Hazel Horton – San Diego, California

It's a great read mate. By the time I finished the second chapter, you had me hooked. You had me laughing through each chapter while looking forward to the next.
> Ed Barry - Virginia Beach, Va.

It was a great holiday read, especially as I was sitting on the beach. It was actually hard to put down as I was really keen to know the end. It has everything, romance, suspense and humor.
> Adrienne Lees – Sydney Australia

G'day Mate! Well you certainly achieved your goal of writing "A BESTSELLER" I think you're on a winner. It had me engaged right until the very end. Great storyline. Well done.
> Bob Lees – Sydney Australia

I have read it cover to cover and wanted to tell you, I laughed, I cried, I mind surfed and I almost peed in my pants! I might add that I agree with Ross' friends that 'He has a way with words" . . . as do you!
> Bill Frierson – Virginia Beach, Va.

QUEENSLAND, AUSTRALIA

This wave is big. Bigger by far than any wave that has come through all morning. At first, I'm trying to escape from it; now I am trying to catch it. The reversal is instinctive. I go from paddling hard in one direction to spinning my board around 180 degrees and heading in the exact opposite one. Stroking, then lunging down and forward on my board, I hang motionless in the air for a heartbeat. Free-falling, I cascade down the face of this speeding wall of water.

I can feel the wind on my face, and the salt spray is stinging my eyes. I hear the bottom of the board slapping down the chop as it skitters down the vertical face of the wave — both of us fighting for control. Reaching the bottom, I regain my balance, and make an arching bottom turn back up into the pocket. Once there I take two quick steps and get trimmed up. I'm locked in. I'm locked in to the perfect spot, in the curl, where every surfer wants to be.

The lip, which is now still a foot higher than my head, begins to feather down the line in front of me. This means I have to squat down to avoid getting knocked off my board. When I do, the wave loops over me like a convertible top springing up. There is only one place that's better to be in than being in the curl, and that is in the barrel; inside the wave itself. Call it the tube, the green room, the womb, whatever you like. It is the ultimate in surfing.

Inside the tube there is complete silence. Here, in this self-imposed cave there is only a small porthole of light and there is no concept of time. Finally, Mother Nature allows me to escape from the squeezing collapse of the tunnel. I see that I'm close to the beach and I kick out over the wave.

1

I sit on my board in a daydream of pleasant thoughts until honking horns from the car park jar me out of my reverie. It takes a minute, but I realize they are honking in appreciation of my ride. I raise both arms in a double fisted salute.

**

The Noosa Courtyard Motel is typical of the type built in the '50s and '60s. It has an office in the middle with small rooms fanning out in opposite directions. The only courtyard I can see is some scruffy dead grass between the highway and the asphalt parking places in front of each room. I still have a buzzing high from my wave, which I thought might last all the way back to Coffs Harbour. The only concern I have is to check out within the two minutes I have left until 11:00. a.m.

The sight of my door being slightly ajar stops my key in mid jab. Maybe it's the maid? A call of "Anyone in there?" goes unanswered. I poke the door the rest of the way open with my key. Instantly, my high is extinguished by a cold spray of dread that implodes deep in my gut. The cold spreads into my throat as I survey the room. My suitcase and clothes are gone. Which means that my wallet, brilliantly hidden under the suitcase, is also history. That meant all my cash and both my credit cards have also gone missing.

A hopeful flash! Maybe I'm in the wrong room. That idea is dashed when the key fob and the door both agreed on the number 12. Think, Ross. Think. A quick check with the desk makes it certain that the room has not been emptied by accident.

All right, first limit the damage. Call the credit card companies and tell them your cards have been stolen.

After numerous inane questions about parents and pets, both cards are canceled and I am off the hook for any new charges. The new cards will be delivered to my friend

John's flat in five business days. I feel better but still I'm penniless and pissed.

The owner of the motel looks up as I enter. "G'day mate, checking out are we?"

"Yes, Sheehan number 12," I say, handing him the key.

"Right, that will be one thirty-five US for the three nights. Would you like to use the same card you used to check in with?"

The cold returned to the pit of my stomach. "Sure, you've already run that card, right?"

"I made a copy of it; that's all. I'll still need your card in order to get the money put into my account."

"Yes sir, you see that's why I called a few minutes ago. Someone just stole everything I had in the room, cash and credit cards included."

"Have you canceled them?"

"Yes," I say," looking sheepishly at the floor. "Didn't think it through, I should have let you run my card and then canceled them. The lady said they'll send me the new ones in Coffs Harbour, in five business days."

"Fine, then you bring me a good card back in five days and I'll return your passport."

"No! I mean — I need my passport."

"And I need me 135 US. Look mate, that beast you call a car is out of rego. Plus, now you have no money; how are you going to buy enough petrol to get you to Coffs?"

I'm silent as my head dropped in defeat.

"Mr. Sheehan tell you what I'll do. Your surfboard stays with me as collateral, and you get your passport back. Then take that thing you call a car to the wreckers, and sell it. Hitch back down to Coffs, come back in five days and retrieve your board. If you can't make it back right away call me with the new card number and expiration date. Once we're square we'll keep your board in storage for 10 dollars a month. That's the best I can do for you, mate."

Minutes later I pull into the wrecker's yard. The plan was to park next to a car that looked worse than mine. Not finding one, I stop in front of the office. There, a man is just leaving and has hung a sign on the door which says, "BACK AT ONE."

"Ross Sheehan," I say grinning at him. "Looks like I got here just in time."

Robert, according to his name patch, tilts his head sideways at me and gives me a look. "Really, taking me to lunch, are you yank? Because that's what the time is mate, it's lunch time."

"No, not lunch. I only need a minute of your time. That's all just, one minute."

"Right then, you've got exactly one minute; you better make it good, mate."

In the next 60 seconds the air is pregnant with a sad but true story with more begging, cajoling and beseeching than a one-minute gestation period should allow.

Robert stares at me for a full ten seconds. Then he announces that if I keep my mouth shut, he'll give me 40 dollars for the car.

Realizing the premium Robert places on silence; I keep my mouth shut until I have the 40 dollars safely in my pocket. Quietly I ask, "Bob, there's just one more thing."

"Ah shit!" explodes Robert, placing both palms over his eyes. "I knew it; I just knew."

"Hang on Robert. I'm just talking about a ride to the beach. You're probably going that way for lunch anyway, aye?"

Not a word is spoken until we enter the town. Robert turns to me and says, "You know, Ross, we're a lot alike. Like friends, or mates as we Aussies say, except for one small difference."

"Really? What's that?" I ask.

"You've got a much better mate than I do." Robert says.

4

It takes me more than half a kilometer to catch the underlying meaning of that statement. The fact that it fits is what makes it hard to swallow. I nod my acceptance.

Unlike the décor in American pubs, there are no stools at the bar here in the hotel. You drink standing up, like a man. A voice from behind me says, "Getting stuck into it are we mate?" The question, which isn't really a question, comes from a guy I recognize from surfing. He was out in the water yesterday, and back out again this morning.

"No, I'm not really getting stuck into it. Just having a beer to pass the time. Got all my gear and money knocked off, so I'm looking for a ride back to Coffs."

"Two schooners, mate," he says to the barman. Then turns to me and offers me his hand, saying, "Daniel O'Hare, I was wondering what happened; how you arrived back here in a wrecker's limousine. I have a mate that asked me to offer you a hundred bucks for those sport wheel covers on your Holden."

"Perfect, my day just keeps getting better. Tell him he should be able to get a good deal on them from the wrecker's. I just now sold him the whole car for forty bucks."

Soon we are joined by two mates of Daniel, who in turn, each buy a round of beer. We are now in a "shout": regaling each other with surfing stories, past and present, some true some not. All no doubt somewhat exaggerated. Time and beers fly by. I learn three things about a shout. First, you are honor bound to reciprocate in kind when an Aussie shouts (buys) a round of beers for the group you're in, or buys (shouts) you a single beer. Two, you are not allowed to quit until it's your turn, and then you have to buy your way out by purchasing another round. Three, you will end up legless with the brains of a turnip.

This is no way to prepare for the most amazing and stress packed two days of my life. There being no way to see the future or change the past, I have to play the chips as they fall. My journey begins first thing the next morning, when the earth has spun far enough around for Cape Byron Australia to catch the first rays of the day.

*****

THE JOURNEY

There is a place in time in which you are neither awake nor asleep. It is neither a good nor a bad place to be. You don't necessarily want to stay or leave there. While lounging in this neutral zone, I am nudged closer to wakefulness by the voice of a radio announcer. "You're listening to WAVE radio 1330 on your dial, Coffs Harbour, the best address on the Mid North Coast. In cricket, Australia has won its one day match against..."

I'm surfacing, becoming aware of vibrations and intermittent bumps. It's dawning on me that I'm riding in a car. Either the road, or the car I'm riding in, or maybe both are in rough shape. More consciousness means more awareness. I realize I have a stifling hangover and nothing is working right. My tongue is stuck to the roof of my mouth. My eyes have been glued shut by a mysterious fluid that is secreted only when one ingests copious amounts of alcohol.

I pry open one eye and its retina is immediately speared shut by a laser of sunlight reflected off the car's hood. I squeeze it tight, which scrunches up my face and painfully informs me that I am also extremely sunburned. I use my left hand as a visor and the fingers of my right hand to pry open the other eye.

I try to reboot my brain and hope that any damage is only temporary. I look at the driver who looks familiar, but whose name escapes me. Underneath his backward facing baseball cap, spokes of blond hair stalks spray out in all directions. When he turns and faces me, I see that his eyes wear a raccoon's mask of freckles. He turns off the radio, fires me a goofy grin and says "Morning Yank."

"Water." I croak.

The driver motions with a nod of his head towards the back. In turning around, I see that we're traveling in a pickup truck or a "Ute" (utility truck) as the Aussies call them. The truck bed contains two surfboards, neither of which is mine. I twist the top off a warm but still greatly appreciated bottle of water. I chug down a third of it—then slowly release a loud medicinal burp. The other two thirds of the water follow quickly, and like a cloud burst over a burnt-out lawn. Life returns. Then the memory of the recent past creeps in.

"Shit! My board is a hostage at the motel." I slap my front pockets then check my back ones. "They took everything—my cash, credit cards, my clothes, everything." I check my back right pocket again and retrieve my passport. "Well, not every- thing. The guy at the motel said he'll give me back my board when I pay him a ransom of $135 US for my room. My car shit itself, no rego, no petrol. Had to sell that bastard to the wreckers for forty bucks and it looks like I used every bit of that to get wasted. Now, I got nothing, nothing, not a damn thing."

"Well, there you go mate, free as a bird you are now. Unencumbered by the material things that weigh the rest of us poor bastards down," says the driver.

"Well, Sigmund Freud, thank you so much for that compassionate observation."

"Well, mate that's about the fifth time you've told me the same story, and I reckon I'm all out of compassion."

"Ah man, I'm sorry." I say. "You're like a good Samaritan, giving me a ride, water and all; then I go and repay you by acting like a complete wanker."

"Kelvin!" I blurt, out overjoyed to have finally remembered his name.

"Yeah that's right. You know, yank, you were doing good earlier in the night, chatting up the best-looking bird in the pub. We were all sure you were going to kick a goal for Queen and Country."

"How's that?" I ask.

"You know, score. Anyway, the next time I look over, the bird is history and you are face down in a plate of calamari."

"Jesus, I don't remember any of that. What I do remember: man, that was some great surf. My first trip to Noosa. Main Beach was like Malibu and Tea Tree—man what a wave."

"The name's Ross, is it? (I nod) So, Ross you lucked out and caught a great swell?"

"Yeah, great swell, but I didn't luck out Kelvin. I knew there was every chance a swell would hit Noosa two days ago. I can read a weather map that shows a tropical cyclone three hundred kilometers off the coast as well as the next guy. I've been tracking hurricane waves on the east coast of the U S for more than twenty years. It's the same set up as here, only different."

"Different how?" asks Kelvin.

"Backwards really. Above the equator hurricanes usually come from the east across the open Atlantic or Pacific then turn north when they approach any significant land mass. These storms seem to almost sense land. Sometimes they whack us, sometimes not".

"Here, the whole process is pretty much back to front, as you would say. Results are the same though, the winds go off shore after the storms pass and we both get great waves. Maybe God's a surfer!" I smile at the thought, but shut it down quickly as the smile threatens to split my sunburnt lip open.

"Right mate," says Kelvin. "We just passed a hundred-foot long yellow banana, and that means Coffs Harbour. Now I need directions to the place where you're staying."

"Go straight through the roundabout to the other side of town. Then, it's only a block off the highway. I'll let you know when to turn. So, where do you live, Kelvin?"

"Ballina."

"Ballina, by Byron Bay, that Ballina?" I ask.

"The very same, mate."

"That's more than two hours out of your way, four if you count going back. And me, too screwed up to help with the driving, and too broke to help with the gas. I swear, I'll send you gas money when I get right — get my cards back, or when I get home, I swear it."

"No worries mate. You don't owe me a thing, well maybe a wave the next time I see you in the lineup."

"Got no choice now Kelvin. I swore, can't break a promise you know. One of my credit cards is maxed out, and the other had just enough for a ticket home left on it. They said it would only take a few days to get new ones. If I can find some cash before I leave, I'll send it to you straight away. More likely, it'll be a check from the states." Kelvin starts to protest but I stop him with "No! I insist. Now I need a pen and some paper."

"Might be a bit of a chewed-up golf pencil in the glove box." Kelvin says. "Could be an old receipt or some such in there too."

I open the glove compartment. "No paper, but what's this, a pint of Bundaberg Rum."

"Never leave home without it mate," smiles Kelvin.

I look under the seats and behind them, nothing, no paper of any sort. Grabbing my passport, I say. "I wonder if they would miss a page?" As I flip through the pages to see how many empty ones I have left, a small square of paper falls out. "Ah, just what we need."

Using my knee and the passport as a writing table I sound out and print KELVIN. "How do you spell your last name?" He slowly spells out Butterworth. As I look up to ask for his address, I see that we are only a block away from my turn.

"Next right, then second building on your left. I'll finish this when we stop." After writing down Kelvin's address and phone number, I tuck the piece of paper back inside my passport. Giving Kelvin my heartfelt thanks, I back out of the wheezing blue/black ute. I stand and watch as it smokes and shudders off down the road.

*****

JOHN

I step away from the exhaust smoke and start up the foot path. John, my flat mate, startles me as he steps out from the shadow of the car port. Although John is only an inch taller than my six-foot self, he seems to loom. Especially now, with his arms held out in a winged formation, he hovers motionless like a giant bat. "Where's me bloody car?" he screeches.

"It shit itself, and it isn't your car anyway, John"

"It's registered in my name," says John.

"John for God's sake, I paid for the car. I paid to have it registered and insured. It's only in your name because you saved me seventy-five dollars by you being on the dole."

"Pension. I'm on a pension; I'm not on the dole."

"That's like trying to pick fly shit out of black pepper— telling those two apart."

John, never one to give up, "It's still in my name."

"Fine! It's yours John; I'll give it to you. Hitch your stubborn ass the 500 kilometers' backup to Noosa and tell the wrecker it's registered in your name and you want it back."

"Where's your board and your gear?"

"You noticed? Well, I got robbed mate. They took everything: suitcase, clothes, and my wallet. They came into my room while I was out—took everything. The motel is even holding my board hostage." I jam my hands into my pockets to turn them inside out to show John how broke I am. I feel a coin. "Whoa! Let me adjust my assets. Adding in this just found two-dollar gold coin makes my new net worth soar to the grand total of two dollars."

"Bad luck mate, but right now you need to call your sister," John says as he opens the screen door. Once inside I

12

check the fridge for a beer, but finding none I settle for cool tap water instead. "In the lounge mate, the phone's in here."

"I know where the phone is John, what's the rush?"

"The rush is, your sister has called five or six times at all hours of the night. Which not only stuffs up me sleep, they charge me phone balance two dollars fifty for each international connection. My account will be empty soon enough. Lucky, I've still got a dial tone," he says, as he replaces the receiver. "I told her every time she called that I have no way to reach you but as soon as I laid eyes on you, I'd have you call her. Didn't faze her in the least. She kept calling, says not to worry, that it's good news that she has."

John plonks the phone down on the table in front of me. He's hovering again and his arms are starting to elevate, going into the bat mode. "All right, John, I'll call her but first put your arms down; I'm having a Dracula moment."

John complies and then punches the speaker button. "Reckon we should share the good news since I'm the one paying for it. "Call her, but make it short."

"You're a regular sweetheart John, Thanks."

I punch in the numbers and after what seems a long time we hear it ringing. Even though I know that it's on speaker, I don't quite trust it, so I keep the phone to my ear. Four rings and John's arms are getting fidgety. I raise a calming hand.

"Hello," comes my sister's out of breath answer from ten thousand miles away.

"Andy. It's Ross."

"Listen Andy. I don't mean to be rude but John here only has a limited number of minutes left on his phone, so we need to be quick. First, you and Anna doing OK?"

"Yeah, we're great and you?

"I'm fine. Now what's so important that you keep waking John up?" I smile at him to try to calm the waters but he only gives me the winding motion to hurry up.

"OK. Here goes," says Andy sounding a bit tense." Did you play the lottery the week before you left back in March?"

"I'm sure I did. I play the same numbers every Sunday when I'm home. You know that."

"Those numbers are still the same six you always play? Your birthdates, 10 plus 23 = 33 and my birthdates, 12 + 15 equals 27?"

"Yeah sure, that's right, but why are you reciting our birthdates like we don't know them?"

"I'm not reciting them; I'm reading them. I'm reading the winning lottery numbers from an article printed in the paper two days ago. Anna, your niece, noticed the article; it says someone bought the winning ticket in Virginia Beach on March the 5th. As of now no one has come forward to claim it. It says they must present it to a Virginia Lottery Office by 5:00 p. m. Monday in order to collect the winnings. Now, the questions are: Ross, did you buy that ticket, more importantly do you have that ticket, and finally, can you get it back to Virginia two days?"

"I may have bought it. In fact, I'm pretty sure I did buy one before I left. But Andy, I've just been robbed, and they took everything — Five loud "blips" blast through the speaker and John makes a cutting motion across his throat just as Andy screams, "It's 78 million Ross!"

"Sorry, I got nothing I . . . wait. Wait, wait." I switch the phone to my other ear grab my passport and flip it open. The lottery ticket—the back of which I just used to write Kelvin's name and address on flutters out and rocks its way towards the floor.

John and I both grab for the ticket at the same instant. We almost crack heads while simultaneously lunging for it, and just avoid a catastrophic cranium collision. I make an unlikely grab at knee level. Strange how our protectiveness comes about so quickly after finding out that the ticket worth millions. It isn't like the ticket is going to break apart or even hurt itself by hitting the floor. Nevertheless, I carefully smooth it out on my passport and go back to the phone.

"Andy, you still there? I found it! I've got it! Andy?"

Silence. Then a series of beeps, clicks, rings, and then a recording. "This is Austelcomm. We appreciate your business. However, you have insufficient funds in your account to continue at this time. You may use a credit or debit card at our toll-free number to reestablish service." Flurries of profanities, plus the receiver slams down hard on the cradle of the phone base.

"All right, first thing John, let's make sure this is the right ticket." I scan the ticket. "OK, it says here the draw date is March 23rd, so in six months that would be . . ." I count on my fingers. "Yep, this is the winning ticket all right. Andy said it had to be presented by Monday. What's that date?"

"Monday is September the 19th," says John, eyeing the calendar.

"And today is?" I ask.

"Saturday the 17th, replies John.

"First, I've got to get to Sydney by one o'clock this afternoon. All the flights to the US leave before three. I've no money for air fare; a car is way too slow. You're the clued-in guy, John. How can we make that happen? I'll make it worth your while."

"Know a bloke, Storkie, might be able to get his hands on a plane. Have to go to the flat upstairs and use Izzy's phone to call him. If that's a go, I'll see about borrowing Izzy's car. While I'm tending to the transportation end, you can figure how big my 'worthwhile' will be."

15

I get busy with a pen and paper figuring out John's worth and then how much time I actually have to get to Virginia. The fifteen-hour difference is at least in my favor.

John returns, "Can't swing it mate. Everyone in the bloody world must be broke today. Storkie, me plane guy, needs 40 dollars for petrol. Says he can't make it back from Sydney without extra petrol. Not even after I promised him a million dollars of your winnings. And Izzy, Izzy would only give us the loan of his car if we fill it up before we return it. It's most of a 3-hour round trip to the cattle station where Storkie and the plane are. That's another 25 or 30 dollars in petrol. I might can swing one but not both."

"John, I know you keep a 50 dollar note as a last resort."

"Right, but that's all I've got; me emergency money, to be used only in an emergency."

"Does this," I show John the figure I had worked out. "Does three and a half million dollars' sound like an emergency, cause that's your 10% if I make it back to Virginia in time."

"Never heard of anything that sounded more like an emergency in me life mate! I'll grab the keys from Izzy, but what about his petrol?"

"I've got that worked out," I say, putting the ticket inside my passport and buttoning it down in my back pocket. "You can keep your word and we'll still have forty bucks for the plane. It's not completely straight forward, but it's necessary. You can make it up to him later from your winnings."

We left, and hadn't gone three or four miles down the highway when I see a BP station. I tell John to pull over. "It's over half full," says John.

"That's the whole point, John. You told Izzy you would fill the car up before you returned it, and so you will. Pull the front wheel up on the island curb a bit just to be sure that it will read full sooner.

'STORKIE'

"You talk about me picking fly shit out of pepper. How about you giving your word and what you just pulled on Izzy?" challenges John, shaking his head as we roar down the road.

"My word wasn't given to Izzy, John, it was yours. Look, you did fill his car up before you'll return it. Just not right before you return it. Which might have been when Izzy assumed it would be filled, but you know what they say about assumptions."

Forty minutes west of town and it's like another country, an uninhabited one. As a flat lander, sand dunes are considered hills to me, so what we're in now qualifies as mountains. Like many roads in Australia this one has three lanes. Two lanes are apparently used to race past trucks uphill, and then you squeeze back into one lane at the top so you can get wedged in behind a truck before crawling back to the bottom.

Another forty minutes and I'm getting antsy and the roads are now a two-lane mixture of concrete and asphalt. Like they paved it with concrete for three miles, ran out, used asphalt for two miles, and then found more concrete.

"How much further before I meet, what'd you say his name is? Storkie?"

"Right, Storkie, and we're close now. The turn off is just round the next bend. You know, Ross, you got just about no hope of making it back to Virginia in time."

"Your right, John. Let's forget it. Turn around, we can drive back and fill Izzy's car up, properly on the way."

John shoots me an evil grin. "Not a chance mate, not a chance!"

"Hang on," John says as he yanks a hard left onto an unmarked dirt road. No signs are necessary to tell you to slow down as the whole road is one continuous speed bump. A hundred yards further up a timber goal post frames the rain rutted road for as far as you can see. The sign hanging from the crossbar read "Big Hat Station." I chuckle, remembering the quote about braggarts, "Big hat, no cattle." Several minutes later we come to a stop as a gate blocks the road. "Mind the gate, Ross."

I let John through, close the gate and jump back in the car. I repeat this drill twice more before we enter a stand of what John calls gum trees. Once clear of this sudden forest, a single-story house appears. It rests on three foot pilings with a roof that covers the wrap around porch. "A Queenslander," John informs me. Behind the house are several out buildings and a large barn.

As we come to a stop and get out the dust that has been trailing the car envelops us like fog. "Give it a minute," says John. As the dust settles, a tall stick figure emerges. He wears work boots, shorts, and a tank top t-shirt. Everything except his stark green eyes are dust colored. His clothes, his skin, even his hair. If he stepped back three feet and shut his eyes, he would have been invisible.

"G'day Storkie," says John. Storkie nods at the typical Aussie greeting and then looking at me says, "You must be the yank who needs to get back to Ameriker spit quick to collect millions, aye? Then, after successfully grabbing the gold, you plan to share some of it with us. Is that the story?"

"The name's Ross, and it's no story; it's the truth. I've got the winning lottery ticket right here in my back pocket. If I can present it to the lottery officials in Virginia by 5:00 Monday afternoon, they'll present me with a check for about 35 million. Ten percent of which is yours—if I make it."

"I'll be hanging everything out over the edge if I take this on. Me job, me career, such as it is. I might even be looking at goal time for stealing the plane. Tell you what John, I'd sure like to know the fellow I'm doing business with is fair dinkum." says Storkie.

"Ross is straight up fair dinkum, Storkie. Known him for what, four years now. Never known him to stone anybody; never heard of him lying or cheating. Know he don't cheat at golf; he ain't good enough. I've put up every last cent of mine to back this too, me emergency fund. I wouldn't be here if I didn't think Ross was fair dinkum."

"Righto, thanks for that, John. Now Ross, give us your watch."

"What?" I frown.

"Give us your watch." says Storkie

"You want this watch? It's a Timex. Why would you want a Timex?" I ask.

"Beats what I'm wearing, don't it?" says Storkie, flashing a naked wrist. It's a matter of trust, don't you see. Ross, I trust John 'cause he's got some skin in the game, his emergency fund. I got my ass hung out here seven ways from Sunday. That's my skin in the game. You've got to have some skin in the game too, to earn that trust."

After handing my watch over, Storkie buckles up the battered Timex and says, "Good, now that you've got some skin in the game. I'll tell you what yank, shortly after I cash me three-million-dollar check, I'll hop my ass on one of those 747's and personally bring this watch back to you."

"Here's the forty dollars for petrol Stork," says John.

"Thanks mate, wouldn't have left home without it. Now let's walk around back and check out this wonderful flying machine." Reaching the side of the barn, Storkie pulls on a thick manila rope, which opens the front doors by pulling them on their tracks in opposite directions.

19

The barn is spacious, well illuminated and clean. Sitting on the hard-packed clay surface is a plane. I hope it isn't the plane we are going up in, but seeing the proud, almost adoring look Storkie is giving it, I fear that it is.

"Isn't she a beauty?" says Storkie, looking at me for approval.

"Well, I've never seen anything like it." I answer honestly.

"You wouldn't have," says Storkie. "This here is a Ryan PT-22 recruit, built in the U S of A."

"How did it get here?" I ask.

"By ship of course," replies Storkie.

"You sure this can get us to Sydney?"

"Mate, this guy Ryan who built this plane, he's the same bloke built the first plane ever to fly nonstop across the Atlantic. The pilot, you know the guy, the famous guy with the cheese name?"

"Lindbergh?"

"The very same mate, and he kept The Spirit of St Louie in the air for more than thirty hours straight. Reckon we can stay airborne for the three hours it will take us to get to Sydney."

It does look somewhat like the pictures I'd seen of The Spirit of Saint Louis. I look the plane over with conflicting emotions. First off, it has a wooden propeller. Really 'wooden' in the year 2000. Then it has five or six pistons or carburetors or whatevers that stick out of the engine hood or cowling. Finally, it has two seats one right behind the other with no canopy—just two tiny wind screens, one for the pilot, and one behind for the obliging idiot.

"Noticing my skittish behavior, Storkie says, "Maybe we are lacking something a little more substantial than skin in the game, aye?"

"Waiting on you "Slick." I say. "Hope you fly as well as you bullshit."

"Even better," says Storkie. Now, if you blokes will give us a hand we'll push her out then turn her right 90 degrees." With that, he goes to the rear of the plane and lifts up the tail section. John and I each settle in behind a wing and begin pushing. The plane rolls surprisingly easy and in no time we have her pointed straight down the paddock with parallel fences bordering the runway on either side. This leaves a clearing 50 yards wide on fairly level ground for as far as you can see.

"I'll grab you the envelope you wanted to write me name, address and number on. You mentioned you also needed it for your ticket and passport; then I'll get us some water and we'll be off." Storkie trots back towards the house, while John, looking at the plane, shakes his head from side to side. "Not me mate, not for quids."

Storkie returns carrying two bottles of water, a tube of sun screen, and I kid you not, an old leather aviator's helmet and goggles that sit on his head. No one seems to think that his attire is the joke that I hoped it was. I don't comment.

"Lather up son," Storkie says as he hands me the sun screen. "You'd best have the loan of John's sunnies too; there'll be a lot of wind up there. Here's the envelope you wanted."

John reluctantly gives up his sunglasses. Finished with the sun screen, I follow the pilot's instructions by climbing onto the wing and then into the back seat. It is a little cramped, but not much worse than middle row, middle seat in economy. Storkie pops into his seat and then asks John to come around and give the prop a crank. John doesn't look too happy about that but he complies anyway.

"Grab this end of the prop, points Storkie, and pull it hard towards the ground when I say so." Then he turns on a switch that makes a humming noise. "All right John, when I say so; give it a burl. Set. . . Go!"

A whirling sound is followed by a barking cough—or it could have been a coughing bark. Then a loud backfire which sends clouds of thick dark smoke covering us and the plane. I duck but to no avail, and end up with a barking cough of my own.

Silence. The propeller has stopped spinning. Storkie turns to me; only his teeth and wiped goggles are not covered in carbon dust.

"No worries mate, she'll be right."

For no good reason, other than his confidence, Storkie's words make me feel better about leaving terra firma.

Thirty seconds later, and John gives the prop another hard pull. The same barking, coughing, and smoke, but less of each. Two minutes of idling and revving bring the engine to a happier place. It isn't exactly smooth, but it doesn't seem like it is going to stall out either. Storkie flips some flaps and gives a thumbs up to John, who does likewise and then drops a pretend flag. We are off!

The engine revs and then I feel the brakes release as we totter off down the paddock. The field is not nearly as flat as it looked from the barn. As we near 60 miles an hour, we find an amiable mogul and become airborne. The plane seems much more comfortable in the air than on the ground. Maybe because it is built to fly and not bounce along on some uneven cow pasture. We apparently reach cruising altitude and level off.

I can see the ocean off to our left, where the sun's rays dart off the surface straight into my eyes. Thanks for sunnies, John.

"Hey mate, want to check the surf?" Storkie's crackly voice comes from an until now unknown speaker. It hangs by my knee and looks just like an old drive-in movie speaker.

It feels silly, talking to a speaker, when the back of the person's head you want to speak to is only two feet in front of you. However, when you find yourself in the idiot seat of a 1940's pilot trainer plane you are obviously already certifiably nuts. I say, "Sure thing," into the speaker. That brings a thumbs-up from Storkie, and we bank left smoothly and head down towards the Pacific. We cruise the coast low enough to pick out individual surfers enjoying head high waves with a slight off shore wind. Any other day I would have dropped whatever I was doing and been in the water too.

Below there is an endless train of cupped beaches each bracketed by a pair of guardian headlands at either end, each one supporting its own community of surfers, fishermen and beach lovers. The idea of Australians traveling anywhere else for a vacation has always baffled me. We travel right along the coast line, gaining a bit of elevation for most headlands but having to flare out over the ocean for some of the larger ones.

"Look at the pelicans down there," says Storkie through the speaker. "We should join them surfing." Sure enough, a line of about a dozen pelicans right below us are using the lift from the walls of moving water to glide or surf for long distances. Just before the waves brake, one after the other the pelicans pull up and out of harm's way, like a surfer riding and kicking out of a wave. We drop down to an uncomfortable distance above the ocean. I feel like I can almost reach out and drag my hand in the water. There aren't many surfers on this stretch of the beach, probably because from the looks of them, most of the waves are closing out.

Storkie is now mirroring the pelicans, paralleling the beach gliding just in front of the curl of the wave. Using the movement of the waves along with the off shores for lift, we are able to glide up and over the waves before they brake. Cool! Pelican surfing!

Suddenly, a huge wave looms outside the impact zone and fun is replaced by fear. This random wave is much larger than the previous ones, and its white feathering crest is forecasting our demise. It is amazing how much information we can process in the blink of an eye. I take into consideration the distance and speed of the wave coming towards us, as well as the speed, trajectory and altitude of the plane. Now, I factor in the distance between the plane and the upcoming headland. All this information is instantly downloaded into my brain's computer. No suitable answer is forthcoming.

Storkie, concentrating on staying ahead of the curl of the wave is not aware of our impending danger. My scream at the speaker increases in both volume and panic. "Outside. Outside!" (then switching to my second language, Australian)"OUT THE BACK!!" finally the universal "WAVE! WAVE!!"

Once aware, Storkie is cool enough to realize that any sudden turn at this level means disaster. He throttles up a bit turning slightly to the right. This raises the left wing, which I hope is enough for the wave to pass underneath us. Just as I am about to breathe a sigh of relief, I hear a slap and feel the plane shudder and tilt violently in the opposite direction. The lip of the wave has hit the left wheel, which more than counterbalances our previous move. This brings our left wing-tip perilously close to dipping into the ocean and cartwheeling us into eternity.

Slowly leveling out, we seem to be out of immediate danger, only to have the lip's spray from the off-shore winds blow back over us and drench both us and the plane. I am momentarily blinded and soaked. But I can hear, and what I hear I don't like: cursing from Storkie, and the hissing and popping sounds from the engine. It begins to misfire and we are dropping precious feet we cannot afford to lose.

Storkie throttles up and we almost stall out, dropping the last few feet. Literally only inches above the Pacific, the engine catches hold and fires back up on all cylinders. To make sure we stay focused, nature has placed a large headland right in front of us. "Left turn Clyde," I scream. Resurrecting a line from a twenty-year-old chimp movie is a sure sign of panic. Storkie banks the plane hard left, as we barely clear the headland. We climb to a more suitable altitude, and stay well away from any more waves or headlands.

Not much is said for the next hour or so. I'm sure both of us are thanking our chosen deities for saving our separate asses. Then I think, maybe this is like fate, like karma or—then I reconsider, realizing that the universe has better things to do than save our asses.

"Thanks for the heads up back there, mate. Lesson learned. From here on out, I'm leaving surfing to you and the pelicans," says Storkie.

"Probably a good idea, but all up I think you handled the situation pretty well back there."

"Maybe, but I never should have put us in that situation."

Another period of silence is broken by the speaker, "That is Newcastle we just passed; won't be long now."

We are higher now, and the skyline of Sydney is in sight. Soon we are over the northern beaches and the harbour is straight ahead.

"There's the old 'Coathanger.'" says Storkie, using the Aussie nickname for the Sydney Harbour Bridge. "You know, mate, if you have a couple hundred dollars and three and a half hours to spare, they will allow you to climb over the top of that beast."

"Thanks, I'll pass." I say.

"Well then buckle up and put your tray table back in the upright position; the stewardess will be by to pick up any remaining items you may wish to discard."

"The airport's just there on the right. You see it?"

"Yeah I see it, so what?"

"Wanted you to know where it is so you'd have your bearings and all." says Storkie.

"Why would I need bearings? I don't have a compass and aren't we going to the airport anyway?" I ask.

"Can't go to the airport, mate. They would have to see the papers and the licenses I don't have. Check the flight plan that I didn't make. See that me safety inspection is up to date which it isn't. No. No mate, we're not going to the airport."

"Then where the hell are we going?" I demand.

"There's an open track just south of here— used to be used for gliders, but nobody uses it now. Once there, I'll spin around so the plane will take off going south—you need to go north—opposite the direction I take off. You go north. Not two miles ahead there's houses and people. With your line of bullshit, it should be an easy slide from there to the airport."

"I feel like I just had a fast one pulled on me," I pout. "Said you'd take me to the airport."

"Never said airport mate, said Sydney. When we land, you will be in Sydney, the suburbs, but Sydney none the less. That is my part of the deal. If you make it in time, you'll still write my name on the envelope still keep your part of the deal, right?"

"Right. I'll put your information on the envelope, and you will be a rich man if I make it in time. I feel like you tricked me a bit. 'No worries' as you say, I'm a man of my word."

"It was necessary mate. Haven't you ever done anything like bending or skipping part of the truth so someone else would make an assumption that would help you achieve an objective?"

I chuckle, as the whole John, Izzy, petrol trick flashes before me. "Yes, I sure have mate. Guess I'm just a little ticked off that you beat me at my own game."

"Right. OK, Ross, once we land there'll be no time for any emotional good byes so get out quick and stay clear of the plane. I'll be coming in from the south. After I drop you off, I'll chuck a Yewy and take off back in the direction that we landed. I need to take off into this southerly and I don't want to stay on the ground any longer than I have to."

The landing is manageable except for running into a rut which shoots us up and airborne again for about 20 feet. The second landing is smooth. Storkie is quick and hard after the brakes, while reversing the propeller. The plane is still rolling as I step out on the wing. When I grab the side of Storkie's cockpit, he stuffs a card into my pocket, gives me a big grin and a thumbs up.

As I hit the ground I realize how unprepared my legs are for standing, much less running. Being cramped and almost immobile for three hours they are half asleep and wobbly. Running, however, is needed as Storkie has completed his Yewy and is fish tailing back towards me. I duck under the wing, but then have to dive out of the way of the vertical stabilizer. I land hard on my chest and feel something give way. I roll away trying to escape from the stinging sand the prop wash is pelting me with. Not good, I feel a warm liquid soaking my shirt.

As Storkie roars off into the sky I check the hand that had been clutching my soaked chest. Water! I dropped my half full bottle of water down my shirt, needing to be hands free as I exited the plane. The plastic bottle suffered a blowout during my personal crash landing. The card Storkie stuffed in my pocket is wet, but still legible — Big Hat Station, Manager, Norbert Krauthiennie. What a name; no wonder he goes by Storkie. PH 61-66-340161. Under this he scribbled, "call when we're rich."

*****

ROSE

I stand up and wait a moment for my legs to wake up and un-cramp. They score well on the walking test and then slowly, with some loud cracking I barely get a D in deep knee bends. I start walking north towards the airport. Once the old glider field ends, the land is pretty much sandy dirt with a few clumps of wild grasses. There is an elevated ridge line a hundred yards to my left. It's dotted with telephone poles and they parallel my northerly track. My legs felt stronger now so I angle left and climb the gentle slope to the top.

The view is better from here: miles and miles of expansive nothingness. My old surfing buddy, Rob Hollander, said that if you were ever lost, to follow the telephone poles. They have to lead to a phone somewhere down the line. Makes sense.

Some twenty minutes later I notice a rather large block of shade trees down the ridge and farther to the left. Unremarkable, except for the fact that a long black wire loops down from a telephone pole and into those trees. Stretching my deductive reasoning powers to their limits, I figure: phone line to phone — phone in house — house in trees. What a mind. After slip sliding down the ridge I can see flashes of a house behind the waving branches of the trees.

As I get closer I see a driveway coming in from the other side of the house. I use that as my entrance, so as not to appear to be sneaking up on anyone. A maintenance free yard fronts a porch, which itself fronts a small house. The bad news is no car in the driveway, and no garage either. Three steps lead up to the veranda, and once there, I knock on the screen door. The response that follows is loud yet soft, feminine, but muffled and unintelligible. Through the screen door I see an indistinct figure march down the hall way; she speaking as she comes. "How can you possibly be here that quick? I just now put the call through?" She cracks the door enough to see who it is. She peers over my shoulder at the empty driveway and says, "Sorry, I thought you were the driver of taxi I just called."

The door is opened by a fit woman who is looking at middle age in the rear-view mirror. Silver has battled her natural brown hair to a draw in her Beatle's type haircut. However, her fluid movements and her impish facial characteristics are solid youthful pluses. All up, she must have been a stunner when she was young and isn't a bad sort now. She holds the door about a third of the way open, not hostile, but not overly welcome either.

"Hello," I say lamely.

"Well, stone the crows" she says, "Didn't the romance gods get my wish all stuffed up? I've order up a knight in shining armor and what did I get? A surfer covered in filth."

"Sorry, it's not really filth; I just got out of a plane; rolled away from it really and onto my water bottle." Both of us look down at my mud-caked chest. "Then, I got blasted by sand and dirt from the prop wash." I throw my hands up in surrender. "Sorry, name's Ross Sheehan; I'm from the US and I need. . ."

"Know where you're from Yank and what you need is a bath and a change of clothes. Rose is my name by the way."

"Well Rose, what I really need is a ride to the airport so I can get a buddy pass back to the states. Then I can cash in (I pat my back pocket) this winning lottery ticket. I didn't see a car." A negative shake of her head is my answer. "Well, if there's any way you can help get me to the airport and I make it back to Virginia in time, I'll cut you in for 10%, around three and a half million dollars. How does that sound, Rose?"

"That sounds like I might not have to sack my romance gods after all. Still, you need a bath and a change of clothes."

"Can't. I don't have time. I need to get to the airport and get a buddy pass."

"Look Ross, even if you manage to get to the airport and were lucky enough to score one; they would never let you on a plane using a buddy pass looking like that."

The truth of what Rose says finally hits me, and my shoulders slump in surrender.

"Come round to the back door. The bath's just there."

When I get to the back of the house we are again speaking through a screen door. "I'm drawing you a nice hot bath, won't be a moment. There's a chair by the door; leave your clothes on it and I'll chuck them in the tip later. There's plenty of clean clothes to pick from—got a wardrobe full. You can choose clothes from any of my three x-husbands."

"Three?" I exclaim.

"Yep, married three times. The first time was for love, the second for sex, and the third was for money. Next time, I'll be settling for nothing short of the trifecta. Right, tub's ready. I'll leave by the door in here."

Naked, I enter the room and close the door behind me. I am surprised by a stand-alone claw foot tub with the plumbing fixtures coming out of the floor. I gently step into it. Rose said it is going to be hot, but this is scalding. Immediately, I put my hands on either side of the tub, and balancing there, I jerk my burning feet out of that liquid fire. Within seconds my arms start shaking so I put my feet on the tub rails further up. Spread eagled, I feel extremely vulnerable. I decide to test the water again. The only means available is by dipping my ass into it.

This proves to be even more painful and propels me up into a naked, pelvic arching spread eagle. Precisely at that instant the inside door opens and Rose and I are face to face. At least, I hope it is face to face. I drop like a stone into the scalding water, only to surface and see Rose toss a towel onto the dresser and say: "You Yanks sure got a funny way of getting into a tub."

Later, I meet Rose in the hallway wearing only a towel; that seems modest considering our history. "There." She points. "On the bed are some clothes and shoes from husband number two. He is a surfer like you, and a golfer; he just couldn't seem to find time for work."

Having secured my passport and ticket in my new khaki pants, I peek in the mirror at my navy-blue golf shirt, and comb my hair. The boat shoes are a bit loose but they're a significant improvement on my old beaten-up tennis shoes.

Walking down the hall I hear, "In here, Ross." In the kitchen Rose has her back to me and is pouring drinks from a pitcher. "Hope you like lemonade."

"I see you've changed clothes also." I say, noticing that her blouse and Bermudas have been replaced by dark shorts and a white tank top.

She turns her head and says, "Looks like you've moved up a class to decent while I've dropped down into the working class. While you were washing up I decided to take a chance on your proposition. You know, I was going down to the hotel to fling a flying fifty at the poker machines, but your unlikely trek sounds more exciting. No doubt, the odds of winning on your gamble are worse than odds on the "pokies, but I've decided to give you the fifty anyway. Though I've probably no chance of collecting, just the thought of winning millions gives me a rush. Plus, I had already called a taxi before you even came to the door. The fifty dollars should just see you to the airport. It's like fate or something."

She turns around and brings our drinks to the table where I am sitting. It is impossible not to notice that she doesn't have a bra on. The globes underneath her t-shirt are bobbing, and weaving, bouncing, and jiggling. Unpredictable and mesmerizing! Obviously, she notices my noticing. Sitting down, she says, "Do they not have tits in Ameriker?"

"Yes, yes they do," I mumble.

"Good. Because I'm trying to have a serious conversation here and I need you to keep your eyes above my chin. OK?" That question is apparently rhetorical as she never even slows down. "Now this lottery ticket, mind if I see it before I hand over me fifty-dollar note? It's not that I don't trust you, Ross, it's just that I don't trust you."

"Sure, I understand; and don't blame you a bit," I say. "I need you to write your full name, address, and phone number on this envelope. I give it to her after taking my passport out. She leans back and stretches to reach a pen on the counter.

She glances back at me, and barks, "eyes above the chin!"

"Sorry."

"No you're not. If it wasn't for the situation I might be flattered."

Making sure my eyes are level with hers, I say, "Here's the ticket and my passport. You'll see that my birthdate digits, 10 &23 added together = 33. They are three of the numbers on the ticket; the other three are my sister's birthdate: 12 &15 which = 27. I play our birthdates every week; I have for years. Till now, the best we've done is 75 bucks once and about 5 or 6 free tickets."

"All right, you've convinced me. Here's the fifty-dollar note. Just in time too. I think that's the taxi's dust I see."

"Thanks Rose — not just the for fifty, but for everything. I really hope I make it in time for both our sakes, but if I don't, I'll send back you your fifty."

The taxi's horn beeps as Rose stands and gives Ross a hug.

There must be an unwritten law that a person born in a certain country, cannot drive a cab in that same country. Here, you might be chauffeured by an Asian, European or even an American, but here I've never been cabbed by a native born Australian. My driver today is of unknown origins. Australia, not being one of them. Our conversations are limited.

As I slide into the back seat, I say "Airport," and he nods. With not much else to do, I try to decide if "Nanook" (my made-up name for him) is bald. He wears a multi-colored pill box hat that would have made Jackie Kennedy jealous. I still haven't a clue as to his baldness when I see the landing strip fingers of the airport jutting out into Botany Bay.

I speak up and say, "International Departures." In reply, I'm given a double nod which exudes a total understanding and a complete confidence. As we come to the top of the ramp where passengers are dropped off, I announce "United." Once we stop, Nanook says something I can't understand and then straightens up the meter flag. Squinting, I read $44.75 on the meter. That seems high but it has been no short trip from Rose's house. Plus, petrol in Australia is three times more expensive than gas in the US. Although, to my knowledge they are exactly the same thing.

After a small moral debate, I hand him the fifty-dollar note and then say generously, "Keep the change." Again, I can't understand exactly what "Nanook" says, but it sounds an awful lot like, "Bite me."

****

SYDNEY AIRPORT

Being dropped off at United airlines doesn't mean I'm necessarily going to fly them. All of the US airlines ticketing counters are in the same area, and I am certainly in no position to be picky. Checking the departure boards, I see that two of the US carriers going back to the states have already left.

Walking up and down the aisles of ticketing counters, I imagine that I see people who represent every continent and most of the ethnicities in the world. Truly. And that's just the people working behind the counters. Clocks abound in airports and that's a good thing, since I no longer have a watch. I see that there is an hour and five minutes before the Delta flight leaves. The stewardesses for that flight have probably already been dropped off and are now safely tucked away behind the "Staff Only" door.

Wrong again. As I trip the automatic doors to the outside I'm met by a covey of Delta flight attendants. The responses I get range from: "Pardon me I'm late and excuse me," to serious down cast looks. And finally, from the only male member of the crew, "Piss off ya mug." He is either an Aussie, or possibly a Yank who picks up languages quickly.

The only remaining carrier is Eastern National, a relative new airline, started by an iconic business man. He started the airline when his own flight was canceled. Needing to get to his destination in a hurry, he chartered a plane. Then, he filled it with the passengers of his flight that had just been canceled. He and his friend ended up flying for free, plus making a little money from the other passengers. Seemed like a good idea and, voilà — Eastern National Airlines.

Back inside—a departure board informs me that the last flight for the US that day is leaving Sydney in an hour and thirty-four minutes. I know that the flight attendants disembark from their shuttle busses at the very south end of the drop-off area. I know this area well from the past, and it still smells of nicotine. As a former smoker, I have ruined many precious tiny air sacks sitting on this very bench.

Waiting on the bench, I feel rather like a vulture must feel awaiting his prey. Rather than committing a vicious act, though, I only want to enrich my own and someone else's life. Rather than a "Kick Me" sign slapped on my back, my sign would read "Pick Me." In a sports stadium filled with thousands, a lost soul needing a pint of blood for his ailing mother, or a prosthesis for his parakeet, would walk straight up to me. I would already be unconsciously nodding in agreement while he was still steps away. Now, I am looking for just such an empathetic, gullible, trustworthy soul as myself.

Time is a funny bugger. Not having a watch, I have to go back inside to check. The Delta crew pulled up about one hour before their departure time. The Eastern National team will likely have a similar time schedule. I feel it is getting close, as my mind tells me that 20 or 25 minutes have passed since I parked myself on the bench.

I duck back inside to find out that nine whole minutes has lapsed. First, I feel silly, then better, (more time), then worse, my timing sucks. What if the Eastern flight crew have a different pre-flight schedule. Maybe they arrived two hours ahead of their departure time. Possibly they are already ensconced in the bowels of the airport, and I will never see them. All these bad scenarios pin-balling around in my head are testing my somewhat fragile sanity. When stress tested, I always rely on the most trusted of all mottos, "Screw it."

"If none of this works out, so what? Nobody gets hurt or dies. A lot of 'would of, could of' dreams get shattered. Every-one who would have benefitted has previously lived their lives up to now without being millionaires, so buckle up; reality awaits. We must all play the cards Ms. Yin and Mr. Yang choose to deal us.

A contingency plan is forming. Call Visa on their eight hundred number and secure replacement cards; repay John and Rose each their $50.00. Meanwhile, I am trying to think of any bad things that can happen by becoming too rich, too quick. I can't think of a thing.

I'm so self-absorbed in day dreams that I don't notice the van until it stops. All of the van doors open and the Eastern crew escapes; everyone is decked out in their blue and grey attire with the distinctive red piping. How to choose the one most likely to help me? Once all the wheelies have been claimed by their owners, they head for the doors. Last chance.

"Who wants to be a millionaire?"

This brilliant question is rewarded by seven out of ten zeros. There's not even a flinch as the covey continues toward the doors. Two eye rollers briefly hesitate and then move on. Finally, a cute woman about my age, glances over and says, "That's original, but not very clever."

"It wasn't meant to be clever." It was just meant to be the truth."

"Fine, but I'll have to take a pass; I have to get to work." She starts walking.

"I can explain the situation by the time you get to the staff door if you'll let me?"

She stops and looks directly into my eyes. She's searching I imagine, for danger, insanity and no doubt, bullshit. Apparently finding none of the above she says, "Make it quick."

"In here," I say showing her my envelope, "is a winning lottery ticket, and if I make it to any lottery office in Virginia by five o'clock Monday, the all cash prize would be about thirty-five million. At the moment, I don't have any money or credit cards; due to the fact that yesterday everything I had got stolen except my passport and this lottery ticket. If you'll front me buddy passes to DC, or anywhere in Virginia, and I make it back in time, I'll happily give you ten percent. The total prize is seventy-eight million; all cash would half that. Your share would be about three and a half million dollars."

"I didn't catch your name; I'm Marylyn. Tell me, why I should I believe you?"

"Ross, name's Ross. You think this is a stunt, a con, look I just found out this morning, by phone from my sister, that I had the winning ticket. Now, I'm scrambling around like a goanna on a hot griddle. Is this the last flight to the states today?"

"Yes, at least we're the last U S carrier out today."

"Well then this flight is definitely my last chance. Tomorrow's flight wouldn't get me to California until mid-morning Monday. It's three hours later on the east coast and there's not a plane fast enough. . ."

The Staff door we stopped in front of were pushed open and a young stewardess stuck her head out. "The crew chief says we're boarding now, Marylyn, and he says that means you."

"I'm sorry," says Marylyn as she squeezes my arm, "I have to go." She turns away and says over her shoulder, "I believe you Ross, really I do."

*****

MARYLYN

I feel like I did when Cindy Hawthorne turned me down for the seventh-grade cotillion. I knew then that I was doomed to a life of misery and loneliness. Two days later when Susan Green accepted my invitation, that proved that to be a complete fallacy. However, in this case, I have no one to ask for a second chance. I check for flights to Hawaii but they have all already taken off, except one, which is in the process of final boarding.

I return to my bench outside to mourn. Done, finished, toast. Have the fates taunted me? Why spark the hopes and dreams of people only to dash them? Are Mr. and Ms. Yin & Yang dancing around a Maypole in celebration? Maybe they have something against John, or Storkie, or even Rose. Nonsense, I'm just trying to ease the pain by finding someone or something else to blame. But no one is to blame; no one is being picked on. Things just happen, no reason, just chance. Now all I have to do is to make myself believe that.

A slight soapy smell eases the tartness of the nicotine, and I breath in deeply trying to savor only the soapy scent. A familiar voice says, "Thinking about having a cigarette?"

"No," I say defensively even before I look up. I'm shocked to see that it's Marylyn who is behind the voice and the scent.

"What happened? Did you get fired?"

"No, nothing like that; some warning light won't go off so the plane never boarded. The flights been delayed an hour and fifteen minutes while the techies check it out. The fifteen minutes is for the addicts." Proving her point, the door opens and four of her crew members came out searching purses and pockets for their cigarettes. "Let's talk inside."

"Here's good," she says indicating chairs at the end of a row. "From here I can see my friends. When they head back, I will too, that way I won't be late." We sit and Marylyn continues, "Ross, I know I said I believed you and I do. Here's the situation; if I arrange to get you companion passes from here to DC; they take that money right out of my next pay check. It's not near the full fare that they deduct, but It's enough to make me choose between eating and paying rent next month."

"All right. Look, if I use the passes and don't make it in time, I'll pay you back whatever they take out of your pay. I have a surfboard. They, actually Greg Noll made only 250 of the Mickey Dora, Da Cat model surfboards. They were made back in the 60's and are now a collector's items. I have a standing offer of twenty-five hundred dollars for my Dora Cat. If I don't make it, I'll sell it, and send you the money I owe you."

"Here," I say taking my passport out and handing her the envelope. I need your name, address, and phone number." When she hands it back, I show her the winning ticket. "You see," I say opening my passport, "my birth date 10-23, added together, you get 33, which are the numbers right there on the ticket."

"And the other three numbers?" asks Marylyn.

"My sister's birth date 12+15 = 27," I rattle off as Marylyn checks the ticket.

"I guess that if I'm going to believe this lottery tale, I might as well believe in a twenty-five-hundred-dollar surfboard. Give me your passport, I'll go to the ticket counter and try to get some buddy passes for my new best buddy," she smiles.

Marylyn is walking back a few moments later when she notices her friends have returned inside and are walking to the staff door. She makes a quick ninety-degree turn towards them and sends me a low hand signal to hurry up and catch up. Which I do in short order.

As I come up alongside her, she casually slides me my passport. There is a ticket jutting out of it giving me a jolt of optimism. Marylyn dims that light by halves by saying, "That's not a ticket or a boarding pass. It just registers you for standby. It still depends on the loads, the number of people in each class, and the seniority of the sponsor—me. You go to gate sixteen and hope you hear your name called."

We have drawn abreast of her crew as they start through the "staff only" door. Stopping and turning to face me, Marylyn gives me a quick hug and a little kiss: half lips, half cheek. "Hope I see you on the plane."

The staff door shuts and I still stand there in a warm glow. There is a distinct scent of soap lingering on my cheek. I'm wondering if the kiss was aimed at my mouth and missed, or aimed at my cheek and then misfired. I'm standing there like a stunned mullet, when the public-address system announces: "This is the final boarding call for Eastern National Airlines, Flight 861 to Los Angeles."

A forced marched stride puts me at gate sixteen in time to hear that flight 861 is now boarding passengers in group one. Out of habit, I look at my ticket and of course there is no group. I sit down quickly hoping that no one notices that I am group-less. Finally, the last remnants of group three pass into the tunnel.

Now the only people left are the scavengers, the parasites, and the groupless. We all know what the others are and yet I, for one, try to maintain some dignity. There are only four of us left, and after a demoralizingly long time a couple are called and admitted into the tunnel.

Now it looks to be a standoff between me and a middle-aged woman whose clothes and jewelry indicate that she can buy a plane, never mind a first-class ticket.

I was hoping to give her a smile that would have say — "Golly whiz, I sure hope we both make the flight." However, she won't make eye contact. Rather she looks down her imposing nose, focusing somewhat disapprovingly on my apparel. I immediately decide to wipe the "golly whiz" off my face and in fact, not give her a smile at all.

The crew member who is announcing names cleared his throat over the intercom. That brings the remaining two of us to full alert status.

"Winthrop, G. Winthrop."

The woman stands and, with another disdainful look at me drags a huge wheelie towards the magic tunnel.

"That closes the standby seat availability for flight 861."

The gate keeper announces.

Somehow, even after that soul jarring body punch, I manage to rise and begin to walk away. Then I hear voices being raised from the podium near the tunnel. I stop behind a cement pillar and listen. The woman is screeching . . . "do you know who I am? I measured it at home." Then there's a lull, which is probably the response from the crew member that I can't hear. The woman carries on: "stupid, asinine, ridiculous . . . report you to . . ."

Finally, I heard the crewman's voice loud and clear. "Have a seat lady."

"Well, I never, you . . . you have no idea . . ."

"I have the idea that you are leaving the area right now, or I will have security remove you." Louder and clearer.

I duck back behind the pillar as the woman and her oversized wheelie careen past.

Peeking around the pillar I make eye contact with the crew man. "You." He points. He gives me a wave to come forward. Halfway to the podium he looked up and questions me, "Sheehan?" I nod. We trade, my standby ticket for a boarding pass. "Here, quick get on board."

I had hopes of gliding through this tunnel, with the prospect of fulfilling my dreams on the other side. No time for enjoyment or gliding now. Moving at just under a sprint, my mantra now is "Don't shut the door." I bank around the corner and there is the door, it's open and manned by a lady. The flight attendant takes my boarding pass.

"2-K," she says.

2-K? I turn to the right and started walking. I don't ever remember ever being in a seat K. An impatient "Sir" stops me in mid-step, not now, not this close, the fates can't be this cruel, can they?

When I look back, the stewardess points to her left and says, "Up the stairs, sir."

"Right, thanks," acting like I'd been preoccupied. Upstairs, really? Like up the steps. So, that's where the mysterious seat K is, up the sacred stairs.

I'm turning towards the stairs when Marylyn pops her head through a half-closed curtain. She looks as harried as I feel. She is just ducking out of a yellow life vest and, after a shake of her hair, she whispers, "Just relax. Try an act like you've been here before, and I'll get up to see you after we serve dinner."

Corkscrewing my way up the stairs I emerge into a different plane. I don't mean a different airplane. I mean a different plane: a different level of existence. Room, lots of room. The aisle is wider. There are only two seats on either side; each one the size of a 'Lazy Boy.' There is a counter on my left sporting bananas, pears, apples, and any number of other crispy treats. Before I can grab at least one of each a voice says "Good afternoon sir. 2-K will be the aisle seat up front on your left." She isn't physic; 2-K is the only seat left in this new and roomy wonderland.

Not wanting to upset the ambience of first class, I sashay down the aisle empty handed. I sit down next to a chubby adolescent boy who has seemingly pocketed one of everything from the snack counter. The protective crouch he has formed over his booty tells me that he is in no mood to share. He also proves to be ambidextrous, and a bit of a glutton. I may act like I belong in first class, but my stomach is singing the economy class blues.

When the flight attendant comes by offering drinks, I settle for water as I don't want to start something with alcohol that I can't finish. The plane increases speed down the tarmac leading to a smooth takeoff that has us banking left over the beaches of Sydney in no time. Soon the whole world below is covered by the blue-green waters of the Pacific.

As soon as we level off and are free to roam about the cabin, I'm heading back to the snack counter and load up. With visions of bananas, and sugar plums dancing in my head, I fall sound asleep.

"Ross?" The voice is soft, but it wakes me just the same.

"Hi Marylyn, how you doing?"

"I'm fine but I must say you've turned into a regular Rip Van Winkle, sleeping through dinner and a movie. I stopped by several times but didn't want to wake you."

"Thanks for that, and this too," I say as I bunch up the blanket and pull it off me.

"Oh, I didn't cover you up; another stu must have, and now I can see why she did." She says looking at my lap.

I look down and to my embarrassment, "Damn, a traveler, sorry," and I quickly pull the blanket back over my lap.

Rather than share in the embarrassment, Marylyn muffles a laugh, or at least a chuckle. "I've heard them called lots of things but never heard of a "traveler." Is that what you call it?"

I nod. "It's an Aussie term. It's a situation that happens when you're traveling. You could be going to work, or school, or anywhere. You can be traveling by train, car, bus, and also apparently, an airplane. It presents itself, even though you're not having any thoughts about sex. Still, up pops a "traveler."

"Well I think it's cute — the word I mean — not the traveler itself. "Yikes! Would you listen to me? I'd better get us both a cool drink of water."

Marylyn returns with a cup of ice and a bottle of water, plus a bag of peanuts. She must have downed her water in the galley. You know, I have never seen a stewardess take a drink or eat anything while he or she is working. Might be a rule. Might be food for thought.

My seat mate is blanketed in a fetal position with his seat in the fully reclined mode. Marylyn is crouching in the aisle, so we are more or less on the same level. I want to ask her which of the seventeen buttons, switches, and nobs I should push, pull, or twist to get my seat into the laid-back position. However, considering our previous conversation about "travelers" I think it might not be the appropriate time to ask.

"What time should we arrive in Los Angeles now, after the delay and everything?"

"DING! Dong . . . DING! Dong! Passengers, please return to your seats as the Captain has turned on the seat belt sign. Flight attendants, check your sections to be sure all seat belts are buckled. We are expecting some moderate turbulence so please remove all items from your tray table and return it to the upright position. Thank you."

As if on cue, the plane experiences a slight drop followed by a bucking lift which gives everyone a hint of what is to come. "Duty calls," says Marylyn. She stands, gives a half salute, and a smile, and walks away. Another flight attendant comes by and motions for me to return my tray table to the upright position. Having squirreled away my water bottle and secured my plastic cup between my feet, I dutifully preform the only business class task that I have mastered. My tray table is now secured tightly to the back of seat in front of me.

Then it starts. The bucking and the weaving, followed by the climbing and the dropping. Then the side-slipping — into a void of silent weightlessness, which is even more frightening. Each torque-twisting spasm of this flying mechanical bull snaps another one of my frazzled nerve endings.

I have made this round trip across the Pacific and the equator quite a few times. This, as a matter of fact, is my fourteenth crossing. The three hundred miles on either side of the equator is called the doldrums by ancient mariners. Today, it is known as the Intertropical Convergence Zone (ITCZ). It is a low-pressure area and the prevailing winds are calm. However, when the trade winds return, they cause more severe weather systems. It's here that squalls, depressions, thunderstorms and tropical cyclones are born and bred.

Being a surfer, you naturally become a student of the weather. After all, if we have no storms or high winds, then we would have very few, and very small waves. Except for the occasional tsunami, usually caused by an earth quake. As a surfer, I look forward to North-Easters, tropical lows, tropical depressions and even hurricanes. It is my considered opinion that this particular turbulence seems more than moderate, and it is lasting longer than any others have on previous trips.

It is also my opinion that, whether one is on earth or seven miles above it, it is always best not to piss and moan about Mother Nature. That includes: what she has done, what she is doing and what she may do in the future. Period.

With that in mind, I try to go back to sleep. Every time I reach a calm pattern and feel ready to drop off, another barometric burp rudely awakens me. It reminds me of trying to take a nap in the summer afternoon heat. Comfy, savoring a light breeze provided by an ever-vigilant ceiling fan that produces just enough cooling. Hours of surfing followed by a big lunch is the perfect recipe for an afternoon nap. Then would come the fly! I feel sure there is only one, just the one. It isn't possible that two or more such demonic pests exist on the earth at the same time. This single beast, whose flying ability and evasiveness, not only a match, but seem to surpass, his persistence and his determination.

The intermittent buzzing and biting would finally bring one's exasperation level to such a height that one would inevitably smack the shit out of one's self. Thus, bringing one to a painful awakening, and another victory to the fly. Slumber on this ruckus plane ride is as hard to come by as it was while fighting that fly for a peaceful summer's nap.

I took a chance earlier in the turbulence and escaped stealthily to the loo. That, however, was only a ruse in order to plunder the snack counter. Someone else had the same idea, and there were only three packs of peanuts remaining. Pocketing them, I return to my seat and eyed my chunky seat mate suspiciously. I don't know why, but on a plane, I tend to hoard food, and will eat things that would never pass my lips on the ground. Long ago now, the last peanut has been munched, crunched, savored and swallowed.

I must have nodded off because the next thing I know Marylyn is crouching in the aisle next to me. "Hey, sorry I took so long; the people downstairs are having issues. I wanted to tell them we have a new Captain and he only has a learner's permit, but they didn't seem in the mood for humor. "Oh here," she says, putting down a pack of peanuts. "That's all that was left on the snack table; I've never seen it that empty before."

I flick my eyes over at my rotund seat buddy.

You think? Her eyebrows question.

I give a noncommittal shrug and rip the corner off one of the bag of peanuts, thinking— "A banana, a banana, my kingdom for a banana!"

*****

THE GALLEY

"Look Ross, we need to speak privately for a few minutes so I've asked a friend for a favor. Wait about five minutes, then go all the way to the back, past the stairs, till you get to the curtain. Say "knock, knock" quietly, and one of us will let you in."

After counting slowly to three hundred (damn Storkie), I casually stroll back past the stairwell to the curtain. Before I can utter the magic words, Marylyn opens the curtain peeks around me, and gently pulls me inside. "Ross, this is Joanie; Joanie, Ross." A tall thin red-haired stewardess is also behind the curtain. Dual nods, and Joanie steps back outside the curtain. Marylyn tilts her head towards the curtain. "She'll keep watch."

Behind the curtain is a U-shaped galley with different sized metal drawers from floor to ceiling. There are two jump seats attached to the bulkhead on the right-hand side. Marylyn points to the one next to the window and says "Have a seat, and buckle up. You don't want to get launched from one of these; I can tell you that from personal experience."

The jump seat while not nearly as comfortable as the business class lazy-boy, becomes somewhat luxurious when Marylyn sits down next to me. "Cool, kind of like a little fort back here," I say, trying for a cuddly ambiance.

Marylyn sobers up the mood with, "Not if you're working. Ross, I need to be reassured that I'm not being scammed, or conned, and that we have a realistic chance of success.

Now we are going to play twenty questions, with me asking all of the questions."

"I don't get to ask any?"

"Not now, maybe later."

"That hardly seems fair."

"Well, as my granddaddy used to say: Since I'm paying the fiddler, I'm calling the tune.' "

"Good point. OK, fire away."

Marylyn settles back in the jump seat and takes a deep breath. "All right. First question. Ross, do you often lie?"

After thinking for a second, I reply, "Not often and not well, which is why I quit."

"What are the numbers of your sister's birth date?"

I shrug. "12+15, and remember, we add them together to get 27."

Marylyn holds out her hand. "Let me see the ticket again."

I give her a look of disappointment, but reach for the envelope.

"Trust," she says taking the ticket, "but verify, to quote Ronald Reagan."

That, I imagine, is in response to my hurt look. I'm stymied again by her logic. She takes the ticket, and compares it to the numbers I recited a moment ago; then uses my passport to check my birthdate. Satisfied with the numbers, she hands me back my passport and turns the ticket over in order to study the rules and regulations.

"Why is there a name and address written on the back of this ticket?"

"Oh, that's Kelvin's, he gave me a ride back to Coffs. I told him I'd send him some gas money; this was the only thing I had to write his address on." Marylyn squints at the small print; then is unbuckled, up and out through the curtains in a flash. I admire her nimbleness as well as other departing assets.

Returning to her seat, Marylyn slides on a pair of reading glasses and says, "How can they expect anyone to read this tiny print even in a good light?" After reading the back, she flips the ticket over. "The date stamp says you bought the ticket on March 5th with a draw date of March 23rd, and you have one hundred and eighty days from the draw date to redeem it."

"Right, I bought the ticket a few days before I left and forgot about it until yesterday. That's when my sister told me that her daughter saw our numbers printed in the paper. Andy said that if I have bought a lottery ticket before I left, with a March 23rd draw date, we had won the lottery. Andy knew I played the same numbers every week, our birth dates. The 180-day time limit; I worked that out with a calendar and a calculator at John's. I'm pretty good with numbers but I double checked them anyway. One hundred and eighty days from March 23rd is September the 19th, which is the day after tomorrow, if I'm not mistaken."

After glancing at her watch, Marylyn says, "You're not mistaken, but tomorrow arrives in forty-seven minutes. That's going to make it tight, really tight, time wise."

The 747's doorbell rings again. A voice follows, "This is the Captain speaking and first I'd like to apologize for the rough ride. The system we ran into was unexpected and too large to avoid. Secondly, because of the unforeseen head winds we encountered, we now do not meet the safety margins for fuel through to Los Angeles. Therefore, will be diverting to Honolulu for a short refueling stop and should be back in the air in less than two hours. If there's a silver lining, it's that you'll get to stretch your legs for a bit in Hawaii. It looks to be a smooth flight from here to Honolulu, with an estimated arrival in less than two hours."

Marylyn stood up. "Just when I had my mob settled down, another dilemma pops up on the radar. Give me a minute or two and then go back to your seat. 'I shall return,' to quote Slack Mac," Marylyn says as she disappears through the curtain.

Fortunately, they have great flight map diagrams in the back pages of the inflight magazine. Therefore, I know that Hawaii is not that far off the air route of Sydney to Los

Angeles. I am still considering this new "spanner in the works" when Marylyn crouches by my seat. "Looks like we need a new plan mate," she whispers.

*****

GALLEY HO!

Marylyn looks around to see if anyone is awake and listening. "Things are not always as they seem; hang on for a second." Returning a few minutes later, she leans down and says, "Follow me." Her voice is sexy, and another bouquet of honeysuckle and soap remain behind. Marylyn is standing in the aisle waiting, so I try to get up quickly. I say try, because my launch is abruptly stopped mid-liftoff. My ass is halted in mid-air at the dizzying height of three inches and from there, I plummet back down to my seat in ignominious failure. Stifling a laugh, Marylyn leans down and unbuckles my seat belt. "You fly often?"

I humbly follow her back past the stairwell where Joanie again stands, guarding the curtains like a sentry. We nod to one another as she draws the curtains aside, and Marylyn and I enter our little fort. Curtains closed, we settle into our seats.

"Remember what I said, about things not being as they seem?" I nod. "Well, the fuel safety margins may be close, but the real reason we're going to Hawaii is that the warning light came back on. That means a longer delay or maybe even a cancellation, so we should plan accordingly. It could mean that the only way for you to get to DC and Virginia on time, would be for me to spend more money—money that I don't have."

"So it's back to twenty questions. You say, you have a valuable surfboard that you would sell if you use the passes and still fail to make it in time. Would you sell it to repay me, if I have to buy you a ticket?"
"I would absolutely sell my "Mickey Dora" and repay you if I don't make it in time. I would like to keep the surfboard, but keeping my word is more important."

"OK, I guess. In for a penny, in for a surfboard."

Maybe it was the extra-long handshake to seal the deal; maybe it's because it is our second meeting in the cloistered "fort." Whatever the reason, we are like two magnets being drawn together by an invisible force. Our eyes lock with each other's, our parted lips only millimeters apart . . . "Knock, knock." Joanie's voice is soft yet strong.

A slightly flushed Marylyn, with another series of seamless moves is unbelted, up, and at the curtains straightaway. When she sits back down, she kind of leans into me and says "Joanie has to relieve another stewardess in twenty minutes, so where? — Ross! What are you looking at? God, my button came undone; why didn't you just tell me?"

I squirm uncomfortably in my seat, and Marylyn glancing down at my lap, says, "Jeez Louise! That can't be another, what did you call it, a "traveler?"

"Well, in point of fact, he is traveling," I say in a weak defense.

Marylyn sighs as she stands up and sticks her head through the curtain. It must have been short conversation with Joanie because she returns quickly and rummages through a steel drawer. When Marylyn sits back down, she has a towel in her hand. I have a strange fear that she is going to try to wash my mouth out with soap.

Those fears are quickly allayed when she says, "We need to get at least some of your blood going up to your brain, so you can concentrate on making it to Virginia in time." She looks directly into my eyes. "Don't make a sound." In a flash, the towel is over my lap belt unbuckled, and pants unzipped. "Commando," she smiles, "now that's helpful."

With matters well in hand, I spent the next thirty-eight seconds in pure ecstasy. The clean-up is just as efficient, and after disposing of the towel Marylyn sits back down.

"Ok. I just want you to know, 'that' is not a service that is offered on all Eastern flights."

"No, I'm sure it's not but I want to thank you for making an exception in my case. I appreciate the way you handled the situation, pun intended. Really, Marylyn, thanks. I mean that seriously; I owe you one. My mind does seem clearer now, and I think you're right about the need for a contingency plan. I don't imagine we have too many options."

"No, you're right. It has to be a plane to the US, and due to time constraints, you have to be on one quickly. We have planes that fly back to the states from Honolulu naturally, but also from Maui, and the Big Island, Hawaii. It's still two hours to landing so I'll have plenty of time to study the schedules and figure out our best options. Hopefully, they can fix the warning light, gas up, and we can continue on with this plane. My trip ends in Los Angeles, but if there's enough room left in standby, I could continue on with you to DC and keep an eye on my investment."

"That would be great. I look forward to having the pleasure of your company all the way to the finish line in Virginia."

Checking her watch, she says, "We still have ten minutes left and I have just about that many questions left from my twenty. So, Ross, number eleven, what do you do for a living?"

"Well, in Australia, I was on a tourist visa, so I really couldn't have a proper job. I did wait tables and bartend occasionally, but mostly, I gave personal and group surf lessons."

"And in the states, where you don't need a work visa, what type of work did you do for a living there?"

"Well, you caught me out. Yeah, I did pretty much the same type of jobs there, too."

54

"Changing the subject, have you ever been married?
"

"Yes, I was happily married for six days."

"That's all the marriage lasted, six days?"

"Oh no, the marriage lasted for 3 months; I said I was happily married for six days. It was like the person you went to sleep with was not the same person you woke up with."

"Over three months, goodness me, what brought that long relationship to a close?"

"Well, it was her house and she gave me an ultimatum; she said, either grow up or get out. I mean, she gave me no choice; you see?"

"Oh yes, I understand completely."

"Last question. If, you ever grow up, what kind of career would you like to pursue?"

"A writer, I'd like to be a writer."

"A writer, that sounds promising. What have you written, had anything published? Something I may have heard of?"

"No, no, nothing like that. The only thing I've have published are a couple of letters to the editor in the newspaper. I've started two books and several short stories but so far I have only finished one short story, and I never heard back from the contest I sent it off to."

"I don't mean to sound cruel, but your writing career sounds more like a wish or a dream.

"That sounds pretty cruel to me, Marylyn. I know you said I didn't get to ask any questions, but I'm breaking the rules. As a little girl, what did you want to be when you grew up."

"I always wanted to be a nurse."

"Nursing," I say." That sounds promising. How's that career going? Take any pre-med courses, volunteered at any hospitals, applied to any nursing schools? No? I thought not. Just because we have a dream, that doesn't mean we have to chase it immediately, or maybe even ever. Let me, more or less, quote you Marylyn, 'I don't mean to sound cruel, but—your nursing career doesn't seem to be any more promising than my writing career."

"I'm sorry, Ross. What I said was thoughtless, and I apologize. You know you strung those words together pretty well. It could be that you have a future in writing after all."

"Thanks. Truce?" I hold out my hand.

"Truce," says Marylyn, "But I don't think we should shake hands now—not after what happened the last time we shook hands. Maybe later, or maybe we'll never see each other again. You might go on alone from Honolulu, or LA, and maybe that's the end of us."

"Not a chance. One thing you should know by now, Marylyn, is that I'm a man of my word. I said I would repay you, and I will. I also said I owe you one, and that debt, can only be repaid in person. You can bet, I'll happily keep my word on that one, too."

*****

HONOLULU, HAWAII

This landing is the least exciting thing that has happened to me since I got out of Kelvin's car fifteen hours ago. The Captain says we can stretch our legs during the stop, but not to stretch them too far. He added that the refueling should be completed in less than an hour, and that we should stay in sight of gate eleven while in the terminal. Marylyn stopped by before the plane's final approach, and said she would meet me at gate eleven, where I am now.

I pick an empty row of seats far from the actual boarding area itself. Marylyn shows up twenty minutes later, explaining that the cleaning crew never showed up, so the flight attendants had to clean the plane themselves. I feel more empathetic when she says it is like cleaning the floor of a movie theater after a Saturday afternoon matinée double feature.

Marylyn opens a small notebook and says, "I've been checking the schedules and it looks like after LA, Chicago is the best bet, and then connecting to DC. The best arrival time possible for DC is 1:47 pm. However, I doubt you can get to Chicago in time for that flight. The next flight arrives in DC at 3:10 pm and a final one at 4:15 pm. It takes about 45 minutes to get to the Key Bridge from Dulles, so that last flight is out. Let's shoot for the 3:10 arrival."

After I signal my approval, she hands me her notebook. "Here, write down your passport and social security numbers so I can sign you up for these new flights."

Giving her back the notebook I say, "You know, there is a saying I saw on a t-shit concerning time: 'This is the earliest I've ever been late.' I'm reminded of that because, apparently, we've made great time, such great time in fact, that according to my memory and these clocks; we arrived here in Hawaii a few minutes before we left Australia."

"That's because Eastern is a very efficient airline, staffed with an exceptional and yet a humble crew." A peck on the cheek, a hint of soap and, "See you in the sky."

Not so fast. . . The clock over the podium registers 5:45. The screen below it reads flight 861, Los Angeles. Departure 6:00. Six o'clock comes and goes. No announcement, no crew personnel to answer questions, nothing. Everyone just playing visual ping pong between the clock and the screen. At 6:40, a collective moan signals that the screen has spoken. Departure 6:00 is replaced by "Delayed."

Seven o'clock ushers in two people from Eastern who stand stoically behind the podium, ready for the uprising. Before they can answer the first rant, the screen behind them switches from delayed to cancelled. The crowd is now in full mutiny mode and surging towards the desk. I back away, having no bargaining power and no ticket.

I catch a glimpse of the flight crew covertly exiting from another door at the far end of the boarding area. Most are moping along trying not to be noticed. Marylyn, though, is waving at me like a traffic cop hurrying people across the street. I slip away from the maddening crowd, and join her at the end of the line, with the rest of the retreating crew.

"First, they don't know what went wrong or how long it will take to fix. Second, they have ordered another plane but most likely it would be tomorrow before it gets here. That's too late, so we have to figure out something else. Now, though, we have to go through immigration since Hawaii is our new port of entry into the US."

The only place we can find that's open is a mini-bakery, and, graciously, Marylyn treats me to a giant sticky bun; it must weigh seven pounds.

After pouring over her schedules, and writing down stuff in her notebook, she finally looks up at me with what I would call a glimmer of hope. "Well, we've got a shot — a long shot — but a shot none the less. You have beat some heavy odds already: winning in the first place, then making it on the plane. Let's hope your good karma continues. The only way I can see you getting to the mainland in time is to catch the next flight to Maui. I'll have to buy a ticket because as soon as that mob (nods her head) figures out it's the only game in town, it'll be sold out quicker than a Rolling Stones concert. There's an Eastern flight that leaves Maui for the mainland in about two hours. If, you can get on it with a companion pass, and if, you arrive LA in time to catch the next flight to Chicago. Which, if you get on it, should get you to DC at 3:10 this afternoon. That's a lot of 'Ifs'. Any questions?"

I shake my head in the negative.

Marylyn returns shortly and hands me my ticket. "It's a round-trip, costs about the same as a one way. I hope not, but you may need it to get back here if you can't get on to LA. I have to get something at duty free, and then sign for these buddy passes. I'll see you at gate seventeen, straight that way. The plane leaves in twenty minutes."

Passengers are already boarding when Marylyn arrives at gate 17. I stand up and say, "Hey Marylyn." Exactly the same thing the guy in an Eastern uniform next to me stands up and says. We look at each other. Then we both look at Marylyn.

"Drew, uh, Captain Michaels, I'm surprised to see you," says Marylyn." This is my friend Ross Sheehan. Ross, this is Captain Michaels."

"Drew will do fine, thanks. Nice to meet you, Ross," he says shaking hands.

"Drew was our pilot on the flight from Sydney and now what? Maui?" asks Marylyn.

"Yes, I hope," says Drew, "and then Los Angeles. I received word over the radio-telephone during our flight that my wife had gone into labor. I checked with the office and they granted me personal leave. I missed the birth of our first, so there will be a special place under the dog house for me if I miss the arrival of this one.

We have been drifting closer to the actual ticket taker as we talked, and we are now next and also last in line. Drew, being a gentleman, goes first and disappears down the tunnel. Just as I hand my ticket to the attendant, Marylyn shrieks. "Your present!" and reaches into her handbag.

"Your ticket, sir. The plane is waiting on you."

I give him my ticket, and take the boarding pass in return. I had gotten to the arched opening of the tunnel, when I hear my name being shouted. I turn to see Marylyn throw a small white box towards me. It comes in slow motion (not quite rivaling Bo Derek in 10), ejecting its top ten feet away still tumbling on a great trajectory for success. I stretch high with every confidence in my ability to make the catch, being a sure handed receiver in high school.

Thwack! It hits the top of bulkhead. The bottom of the box flies off to the right. A battery and pieces of black plastic held together by wires smash to the floor on the other side of the door. Seconds earlier, that mass of plastic had apparently been a brand new cellular telephone. Still floating down is money; three or four bills of unknown denominations are just about to land. I start to dive back and retrieve the remains of the phone, and the money when a stern voice says. "You step back in here and try to pick that up; you're staying on Oahu." A Nano-second later, I am sprinting down the ramp.

Though informed of my row and seat number is 27-C, I am still escorted to my seat by a briskly strutting flight attendant. Apparently, the last tardy person getting on a plane is a real jerk, and requires special attention and supervision.

"Hey Ross," says a grinning Drew Michaels, "What took you so long."

I just shake my head and reply, "I'll tell you later."

There is no food or drink service; not even a dreaded bag of peanuts is dealt out.

*****

MAUI

Drew is quicker off the mark than me and is already waiting in the arrival area. "Let me buy you a cup of coffee; we have almost an hour before the flight is called."

"Make it a coke and you have a deal" I answer.

"You don't like coffee?"

"No, I don't, but basically I try not to drink anything that doesn't have bubbles in it."

"Water?"

"Only in cases of severe thirst or under duress."

"All right, a coke it is then."

Finding a table in an open area of a restaurant, Drew parks his wheelie and motions for me to sit. Returning, he sits and slides my coke over. "What held you up back there in Honolulu trying to get on the plane? I thought you were right behind me."

"I was, but at the last second, Marylyn remembers that she had bought me a cellular phone. She yelled, but by then I was already in the tunnel, so she threw it. It smacked into the top of the bulkhead and broke into pieces. I really feel sorry for Marylyn, spending money she can't afford and then see it turn into nothing. Like a hundred-dollar bill, or whatever they cost, going up in flames right before your eyes."

"OK look, hold that thought for a moment. I'm going to need an explanation about that; but right now, I need to call home and make sure that everything is going along smoothly."

When Drew returns, I ask if everybody is OK. He answers that everything is fine, but that his wife is still in labor, and still at home. He was under the impression from the radio message that she was already at the hospital. Now, she and Drew's sister are waiting for the contractions to get more frequent before leaving for the hospital. The mention of which makes both of us quiver.

"Where were we Ross? Some mystery about Marylyn throwing a Hail Mary pass with a cellular phone. Why did she do it? I mean why was it so important for her to get that cellular phone to you before you got on the plane?"

"I'll tell you why Drew. It's imperative that I get to Virginia by 5:00 tomorrow — excuse me, this afternoon — and Marylyn has a vested interest in seeing that I do. Since I am without funds, she rightly assumed that having a cellular phone would have been very helpful to me."

"Flight 914 to Los Angeles will be boarding in twenty minutes at gate six." That announcement interrupts our conversation.

"That's us," says Drew pushing himself away from the table. "I'll see you at boarding, and we can continue this conversation. I'm on standby too, so I'll check the loads on the way down to six, and hopefully, we'll both get on."

They were already starting to board when Drew sits down next to me in the waiting area for gate 6. Looking at the floor, he says, "Sorry Ross, but there's only one standby seat left. If Marylyn is your sponsor, then that seat will be awarded to me because of my seniority. I feel bad but it's family you know."

I take a minute to gather my thoughts. "You know Drew, I never did finish explaining the mystery with Marylyn and the phone. Come 5:00 o'clock on Monday afternoon, The Virginia Lottery will turn over 78 million dollars to the educational systems of Virginia. Minus taxes, and a penalty for all cash of course. That this will happen is inevitable, unless I produce this." Carefully I take the lottery ticket out of my passport. "The winning ticket. If I hand this ticket over before 5 o'clock this afternoon, the lottery will give me a check for about thirty-five million dollars."

Drew holds up his hand, "Stop. You're not going to talk me into giving up my seat."

"Fine, I understand, just allow me to finish. Marylyn, as you can see has written her address and phone number on this envelope, as have (I count as I show him) three friends in Australia. Each person on here has helped me get this far, and each one of them will get 10% if I make it in time. I will make the same offer to you. Write your name address and phone number on this envelope, Drew, and you could have three and half million dollars by this afternoon at five o'clock."

"Even if I believed you, which I'm not sure that I do, I can't."

"I think it was Maya Angelou who said, if you substitute the word 'unwilling' for the word 'can't'—you will be speaking the truth."

"She's an inspiration, she's brilliant and she's right. I am unwilling to give up my seat."

"How old is your first child, Drew?"

"She'll be two in three months' time."

"So let's see then, roughly eighteen years from now both kids will be ready for college. The question is, will you be ready? A school like Duke, Stanford, or any Ivy League University—man—I read where a full ride in the year 2018, about when your kids would be ready, would cost over fifty thousand dollars a year. Add in books, housing and food, you're talking a hundred and twenty-five thousand for two. That's a half a million gone in four years to six years. Hard for anyone to save up that much."

"Was your father there for your birth, Drew? I'll take your silence as a no, or maybe you just don't remember. Ever hear your mom complain about it? Now, what if next week, you give your wife a check for a million dollars. Then show her that your children's higher education is already paid for. After you put another million in the bank for yourself, do you think you would ever hear anything about you not being present for the birth of your children?

They have been calling out different row numbers to board while we are talking. Now, there is silence and only Drew and I remain in the boarding area. Drew takes the envelope from me, jots down his info, and hands it back.

"Ross, I'm beginning to think you could sell swim fins to mermaids. One thing about this is certain, if this doesn't work out in my favor, I surely won't need to consider that vasectomy my wife and I have been talking about. That wonderful part of my life will be over."

"Michaels — Michaels." The crew member looks directly at Drew.

Drew tears his ticket in half. "Have a safe and successful trip Ross," he says, as he stands up and walks away.

The crew member taking tickets is apparently aware of Captain Michaels' approaching parental situation and gives me a hard stare. Grudgingly he hands over a boarding pass, and when I reach the tunnel entrance, I turn and shout back at the counter man, "I told Captain Michaels it wasn't his child."

Fast walking down the tunnel, I realize what a stupid thing to do that was. I stop and cup my hands, like a megaphone, and holler back down the tube, "Just kidding!" He may not have thought it is funny but at least he didn't come running down the air bridge and confiscate my boarding pass. I need to rein in my mouth, which, as usual, is about three steps ahead of my brain and forever getting me into trouble.

When I arrive at my window seat in the back of the flying bus, the aisle seater stands to allow me access. However, the very small Asian man in the middle seat does not stand or even unbuckle; rather he smiles and gestures for me to slide between his knees and the seat in front — a generous opening of about seven and a half inches. With a stewardess pounding down the aisle to see what the holdup is, I side step to my seat with my ass no doubt inches from his face and me sort of dry humping the seat in front of him.

As I sit and buckle up, Mr. Middle Seat leans over and says, "Oh! You big one!" Not being a super large person, I guess the observation came from his perspective and hopefully not a sudden growth on my derrière. I sit back and take a deep breath, thanking the good fairies for seating me next to a non-English speaker. Smiling and nodding will suit me just fine.

As we roar away into the heavens, the sun has only its own length to drop, until darkness begins to have its turn at covering this half of the globe. Considering all of the near misses and pressure-packed incidents of the last day or so I'm sure sleep will be hard to come by.

Hence, I fall asleep immediately and am only barely conscious when the seat belt chime releases its captives to freely move about the cabin. Once again I have proven that I am not Pope material; that infallibility is not a trait that I'm endowed with. I awake some time later as the flight attendants are picking up the dinner trays. Missed another meal.

I flag down the nearest stewardess and ask for a coke and any kind of snack. She reacts as if I told her that upon landing she had to unload all the baggage herself. A half can of coke and a plastic cup with three ice chips arrived that very same evening along with, you guessed it, a bag of peanuts. The next ninety minutes I enjoy watching "The Green Mile". Spooky, but cool.

After coming to a halt at our arrival gate Mr. Middle Seat smiles, his eyes now magnified by oversized glasses. He is un—belted, but while still seated tries to wave me through the narrow channel again. Not a chance! I remain seated and attack the air with a scooting motion saying, "You go, you go". I say it so many times he probably thinks my name for him is Hugo.

As he waits in the aisle, I realized that this nice, overly polite young man doesn't increase his stature much by standing. We bow our good byes at the departure information board. I set out at a brisk pace. Sixteen minutes to get to gate B-9 and Chicago.

*****

Los Angeles to Chicago

It takes me a lot longer to get to concourse B than I anticipated. Turning left onto the concourse itself makes me feel better. That is until I pass a departure board which informs me that the flight is boarding on time and, according to the clock, I have less than ten minutes to make it. My already brisk pace becomes more lively as I motor past gate 15. Gate thirteen is an unlucky blur. Once abreast of gate eleven, my goal, gate nine, appears not forty feet away.

I arrive at the ticket podium and breathlessly announce, "Sheehan, on standby, hope there's a seat left."

Looking bored, the female attendant says, "Oh Yeah, there's a seat left; trouble is, the seat that's left — just left. It's on that plane; the one that's pushing back now," she says, pointing out the window.

"It can't be! I still have time. That flight isn't scheduled to leave until 7:35, and it's not even 7:30 yet."

"It can and it did. That plane, like all other planes, departs as soon as all the paying passengers are aboard."

Slammed, pummeled back into the reality of being a scavenger, a parasite, a groupless companion-pass-holding serf. Disbelief and despair fight for top billing on my mental marquee. Possibly in shock, I amble back down the concourse, depositing the useless Eastern Airline buddy passes into the next trash can. I actually feel weak, and crash in a chair, at an unoccupied boarding area.

Finally, all the wheels, gyros and gears slow enough for an actual clear thought. I call on every bit of what my granddaddy called "gumption" and talk myself into giving it another go. Airports all have their own personalities which seem to reflect the city they serve. Los Angeles, where the ordinary is unusual and the unusual is ordinary. The original brave and somewhat wacky adventurers may have settled here because they have no back up in them and this was as far as they could go. People in LA may have lost some of their adventurous spirit, but generations later the wackiness remains.

Here I am in the land of make believe, trying to make myself believe that I still have a chance: a chance to make it to Virginia in time to cash in my ticket. DC is the logical landing spot, and is, according to legend, only a silver dollar toss away from Virginia. The four time zones I'd pass through would erase three hours from my quickly draining hourglass. That means I have nine and a half hours to reach my destination, 2500 miles away with no physical or financial means of support. That seems to be an impossible task, until I realize that I have already come three times that far, 7500 miles, with no tickets and no money.

I walk down the concourse looking at the departure boards that list flights I can't afford, clocks I am unable to stop. I step around a janitor's cart and see an open doorway with a small sign next to it. "Chapel" it reads. I hesitate, not wanting to be a hypocrite, but going instead with two well-known slogans which have garnered mixed results in the past: "Any port in a storm," and "What have I got to lose?" Although these slogans were usually involved with late night decisions with beings of a less than a celestial nature.

Entering, I almost collide with a young Latino woman in a work uniform who is just finishing up the sign of the cross. We both step to the side to let the other pass and my "Excuse me," is followed instantly by her "Lo siento."

We each try to wave the other through in vain. Finally, she says, "It is more important that you come into His House than that I leave it." I can't fault her logic, but

I'm thinking maybe this is a bad idea. I take a step back and mutter, "Later, I'll go later," I say.

"Do you believe in God?"

The question surprises me so that I blurt out my answer: "Fervently, at least during takeoffs and landings." My mouth again, sprinting three steps ahead of my brain.

"An honest man," she smiles. "You should not delay in expressing your hope to Him."

"Hope? Why do you use that word?" I ask.

"Some call it praying, but they always hope that something good will happen, or that something bad will not happen. Is that not so with you?"

The Twilight Zone music theme instantly jingles through my mind, but she's right; pretty much all I have left is hope.

"Please," she says, imploring me with golden retriever eyes and sweeping her arm in a welcoming manner as she steps completely out of the doorway. I have no choice.

She is standing by her janitorial cart when I walk out a few minutes later. She greets me with, "my name is Simone," and holds out a small delicate hand.

"Ross Sheehan," I say trying to shake her small hand without completely enveloping it, resulting in my handshake being almost feminine, that is until Simone 'grips up' and gives my hand a powerful squeeze.

"I pray that your hopes, as well as mine, will come true," she says.

"I hope that all your prayers will also come true. I appreciate you convincing me to go inside. I feel, I don't know, somehow refreshed. Now, I better let you get back to work and get going myself. Thanks again, Simone."

Mr. Sun's forehead is just peeking over the hazy fence of the horizon as I look out the long narrow windows on the concourse. The most popular place at this hour is naturally the Cappuccino Cafe. Though not a coffee drinker myself, I know these types of eye openers are expensive. I stand by a table at the edge of the seated flock. The reason I pick this place is because of Willie Sutton's famous saying "Because that's where the money is." He was referring to banks, in answer to why he robbed them. but it is also true of over-priced coffee bars.

There are only a few patrons. I think I'll have to take a gamble on a stranger, a risky proposition, but time doesn't slow down for curves. Husband and wife choices are out; they never agree on anything. That whole goose and the gander story is total bullshit!

The only person close to a prospect would not have been my first choice, but due to time constraints, he seems the most likely of the last resorts. He is dressed in khakis, an open-collared shirt, and tennis shoes. As I approach his table I notice a small gold chain around his neck. I don't abide with bling. Even if it's Saint, "Whose it" hiding under the shirt, no saint worth his salt would hang from gold bling. Putting that thought aside, I ask for, and am given, permission to have a seat.

"Name's Ross Sheehan," I say without waiting for an introduction, "and this is coming from way deep in right field. Here's the deal I'm offering. You front me a ticket from here to DC, probably less than $300, and if I make it to my appointment in Virginia on time I'll repay you five times your investment. If unsuccessful, I'll repay you six hundred dollars within a week."

"I'm Rick," says the guy sitting across from me, "and I might be interested, but I would need something a little more substantial than just your word before I can agree to anything like that. Maybe some collateral or proof of what you're saying would be nice."

"I have a winning lottery ticket right here," I say, patting my back pocket.

"Where? I don't see any ticket. You know what they say, "No ticket, no laundry."

I have the envelope out, and my fingers are pinching the edge of my passport when I get a bad feeling, and decide to cancel the whole deal with Rick. I decide to return the envelope to my pocket, when it happens very quickly.

First his coffee cup tips over, spilling the dark liquid across the table towards me. I react by jumping up in a half crouch, staring at the stream of coffee. Next, I feel rather than see the envelope being snatched from my fingers. I look up to grab and throttle the thief, but have only the briefest look, at what seems to be, an asteroid on a leash hurtling towards my head.

When the hundreds of tiny golden fireflies quit exploding in my brain I pick myself up off the floor and begin a wobbly pursuit. The backpack which was launched at my head had apparently been under the table. Even if I had seen it, I doubt I would have thought of it as a weapon. Less wobbled, I am now keeping pace with the culprit. Following Rick is made easier by the monk-like bald patch on the top of his head. Still, some twenty or thirty yards separate us.

He turns down a corridor that turns out to be the main concourse, and heads towards the exit doors. Weaving through the crowds is easier for me since many have moved aside to avoid the fast-moving perp. The separation is down to twenty yards after turning another corner, but now there is only about forty yards left before he hits the exit doors. If he makes it outside my chances of catching him are gone.

The only other person between my lottery ticket and the exit doors is an old, bent over man, walking with the aid of a cane. "Stop! Thief!" I yell. "That man's a thief."

Rick is almost running as he approaches the exit doors and is paying no attention to the old man. The instant Rick is abreast of him; the old man jams his cane in between those fast churning legs of the assailant. The results are the same as they were many years ago, when my sister stuck a stick into the spokes of my bicycle. Ass and teacups everywhere.

In this instance, the backpack flies off to the left, and the cane whipsaws back towards its owner. The thief is down on the floor sliding towards the exit doors. Not giving up, Rick has gotten to his knees when I launch myself and land on his back. I hear a distinct crack, and the sound of air exploding out of him as his chest hits the floor; this is followed by a noisy smack, as his face finds marble.

My envelope is still clutched in the fingers of his right hand; however, they offer no resistance when I take back my property. The inability to resist was expected, since we all know how weak we are, when we get the wind knocked out of us. I am certainly not helping him regain it by kneeling on his back, but even after a pitiful moan, I am not in a sympathetic mood. A mood apparently shared by the older gentleman recently reunited with his cane. He comes up and 'knights' my shoulder with his cane, saying, "Well done young man, well done."

"All the credit belongs to you sir," I say. "You must be a fan of Teddy Roosevelt, you know, 'speak softly and carry a big stick'. "

The police show up and relive me of my containment duty. They cuff and then stand the fleeing felon up, leaving a smear of blood on the marble floor. The officers get both of our names and addresses, along with my statement. Winslow (the man wielding the cane) is eager to go to court and more than willing to testify.

As the policemen lead Rick away, the small crowd that had gathered also fades away. Only one small woman remains; she with golden retriever eyes and her tiny hands perched on the handle of her janitorial cart.

Simone smile exudes a calmness that I have never felt before. As I approach her she says, "We meet again, but much sooner than I expected. Surely, this is not what you hoped or wished for in the chapel?"

"No, this fiasco gets me no closer to my hope of getting to Virginia by 5:00 today. I'm still stuck; no money, no credit cards, and apparently, I'm also out of hope."

Simone startles me with, "I can get you to Chicago."

I guess my dumbfounded look asks for further information.

Simone complies. "Maintenance workers get 500 stand by miles for each month of work they complete. I have two thousand miles saved, and Chicago is only seventeen hundred and forty miles from here. My airline has a flight leaving for Chicago shortly. This way," she nods, pushing her cart down the concourse.

After a few hurried steps of my own, I catch up. Sensing my presence, she says, "The next flight on my airline leaves for Chicago in forty minutes. It is the earliest of our flights to Chicago and is seldom much more than half full. You should have no problem getting a seat.

When we get near the ticket counter she parks her cart next to a restroom and says, "Watch my cart please; also, I will need a picture ID to show the counter lady."

I give Simone only my passport carefully replacing the lottery ticket back in the envelope, and both of them in my buttoned up back pocket. A piece of paper half stuck on the back of my passport comes loose and floats to the ground. Simone picked it up glancing at it while handing it back to me. "Immigration receipt. Where are you coming from, Ross?"

"Australia." I answer.

"Australia." She says softly to herself. "Sydney's almost a fifteen-thousand-mile round trip. That would take two and a half years of work."

"How do you know all this stuff?"

"Each month I see how far I can go in all directions with my new mileage totals. I have a good memory and know most of the flight schedules. Every new month, in my dreams, I go to and explore each new city that my five hundred new miles allows me to travel to. Next month, in my dreams, I will explore Toronto, Canada."

"I can't take away your dreams," I say, reaching for my passport.

"No one can take away anyone's dreams, Ross. Dreams belong to the dreamers but this is real," Simone says as she turns and walks away towards the counter. She returns in less than ten minutes and gives me back my passport with a ticket sticking out of it. "Good luck on your journey, Ross, and God's speed."

She is pushing her cart away and I say, "Wait, Simone." Handing her the envelope I say, "Write your name, phone number, and address on this." When she hands the envelope back I say, "Simone, see this name, Marylyn, if you would please, copy her phone number down. Call her tomorrow or the next day. Tell her you sent me off to Chicago. Tell her, to let Captain Michaels know that everyone on the envelope is still in, with a chance. That list also includes you now, Simone.

She looks at me with a quizzical stare. "A chance for what?"

"Maybe, just maybe, a big win that might put a bit of reality into your dreams."

Head shaking in confusion, she points me in the opposite direction and says, "Gate 22."

Name called, boarding pass accepted and then surrendered, then an easy walk to the back of the plane. After what feels like a twenty-minute nap, the air hostess informs me it is four hours later and we are preparing to land in Chicago.

*****

Chicago to D C

Cold. The jet way bridge is a body slap of frigid air. Even in the terminal, it seems cold. I'll admit most people are better prepared, with sweaters and coats and stuff, but I have good excuses. No time to pack, no suitcase, and nothing to put in it. Those excuses, though true, produce the same result as all other excuses. Absolutely nothing—meaningless words that never change the facts. Ok. Now as a self-chastised goose bumped philosopher, I move on lemming-like going with the flow of crowd.

Back on the concourse after a bathroom break, I stop. I realize that I have nowhere to go. People give me impatient glares as they bang into and then step around me. Notably, I'm the odd lemming out. I walk over to an empty boarding area and sit.

Good news, bad news. I am closer to my objective than ever — six hundred and twelve miles according to Simone. Yet I feel farther away than when I started from Australia, almost ten thousand miles ago. Time is more the enemy now than distance. The forty some hours I had in the time bank when I left Coffs Harbour has dwindled down to four. Sitting still is hardly restful, as the Pac Men of doubt and worry begin snapping away at my resolve.

Since I have always been too proud to beg and too nervous to steal, only one option remains. The only chance that I have is to convince someone that I can make them rich for the price of a ticket to Washington, DC. The decision to make is whether to go to the boarding area for the next flight to DC or try to find a slightly intoxicated and gullible patron at the bar. Backed by a steely willpower and my unwavering indecision, I decide to flip a coin.

My entire net worth is tied up in this Australian two-dollar gold coin. As the coin is summersaulting down towards my palm, I hear "Tails!" When I look towards the source, the coin bounces off the heel of my hand and rolls across the floor. A husky young man marches after it, and stabs it still with the tip of his umbrella. Graceful for a big guy, he swoops down in one quick move picks it up and returns it to me.

"Sorry to make you miss. I guess I was trying to change my own luck. I'm Martin Maher; glad to make your acquaintance."

"Ross Sheehan; my pleasure," I say, as we shake.

"You play golf, Ross?" asks Martin.

"No, not really . . . oh, you mean my shirt," I reply, noticing where Martin is looking. "This? It's a loaner. I've never been to the . . ." I look down and pulled the pocket away, and read upside down— "The New South Wales Golf Club."

"I was hoping to find a golfer . . . a backer really, who would float me a ticket to San Diego. There, I could sell my car, and pay my entry fees for Q school, as in the qualifying school for the PGA tour. I would happily pay back my backer, two-fold, with my winnings. I'm just starting to feel it."

My laugh caught both of us by surprise. It is a little too loud and a little too long.

"What's so funny?" Martin asks testily.

"Sorry, no offense. It's just that asking me for money is like asking a gerbil to recite the Gettysburg Address. That two-dollar gold coin you just handed back to me is all the money I have in the world. It's Australian. It's not gold and it's a foreign coin, useless in the US."

Martin joins me in laughing now. "Aren't we a pair?" He says. "My total assets are this umbrella, thirty-eight cents and a Select Jets mileage card that won't get me past Des Moines, Iowa."

"Wait," I say, "what kind of card did you say you have?"

"A Select Jet Mileage Card. I won it as a prize for a hole in one on the Nike Tour, two years ago. The card had twenty-five hours of free flying time on it, but now, it's useless, down to, I don't know, how many hours away is Des Moines, Iowa?"

"I don't have a clue, but do you think that card could get me to Washington DC?"

"I'm not sure," says Martin. "We'd have to check with General Aviation. It's a long walk, I just came from there; and it would take fifteen or twenty minutes to walk back. Why? What's in DC?"

"It could be the end to all our financial problems, Martin. If I can make it to a lottery office in Virginia by five o'clock this afternoon, I'll be rich. And, if you're a part of helping me get there in time, then ten percent of the winnings of the lottery ticket I'm holding is yours. That ten percent is more money than you would get for winning The Masters."

Together, our attention turns towards a beeping noise, the sound like garbage and cement trucks makes in reverse. We see the culprit weaving towards us through the crowded concourse. Not a trash truck, but rather a three-seat golf cart with a large "COURTESY ASSISTANCE" decal across the windshield.

"Hang on," says Martin. "I got this."

Before I can question him, the golf cart whizzes by and Martin is limping after it using his umbrella as a cane shouting "Excuse me, excuse me!!" After a yard or two, the golf cart stops and Martin catches up. Then he slides into the shotgun seat, and he and the driver look to have what seems to be an earnest conversation. They beep off in the same direction the cart had been traveling. I feel another notch lower as I watch Martin and the golf cart disappear behind the curtain of the crowd.

Moments later, I hear a muffled beep from the direction the cart had gone. Then spearing through the concourse hordes, I see the alternate black and white pie slices of a huge umbrella parting a sea of travelers. Like the canopy above them alternate black and white grinning faces radiate through the wind screen. As they pass by I noticed an elderly lady in the third seat with a walker folded up next to her. The driver chucks a Yewy and comes to a stop right beside me.

Martin steps out, nods towards the back seat, "This is Miss Ida and we're taking her on a grand tour to gate twenty-six. Hop in mate; after that we're off to general aviation." After seeing Miss Ida safely to her boarding gate, we speed off. A sudden juke to the left and we're facing two solid looking metal doors. The driver points a remote at them and magically they whisk open. We sail through without slowing down and immediately we are frozen, zipping down the edge of the tarmac. I hold my breath and hug myself for the rest of the short ride.

Once inside the hallway to general aviation, I look at Martin who is now without his umbrella, and ask. "You got the driver to do all that for an umbrella?"

"Not just any umbrella" says Martin. "I explained to Herman, the driver, that I used that very umbrella to keep the rain off Tiger on the way to a limousine."

"Jesus, you shouldn't have lied to the man like that Martin," I say.

"I didn't lie; I may have embellished the facts a little. The person I sheltered with that umbrella was Tiger. I fudged a bit though; her name was really, Tiger Lily, of exotic dance fame. It was in Dallas, Texas, after a bachelor party. . ."

"All right, all right. I believe you enough to let it slide. We need to be serious now. This could well be the last chance either of us has to become a millionaire today."

A deep breath, and a nod to one another. We walk through the door and into the offices of Select Jets Aviation.

"Well, hello again," says the counter guy, "long time no see must have been what . . . almost an hour? Decided we liked Iowa after all, did we?" says the grinning young man behind the counter.

"Good to see you again too; Sidney, is it?" asked Martin. The clerk nods in the affirmative. "Well, Sidney, is this whole company staffed by out of work comedians, or is it just you?"

"Sorry," says Sidney "It's been a slow day."

"No problem. I was wondering if you can do me a favor and see if this card can get my friend here, Mr. Sheehan, to DC? It's really important and time, as usual, is of the essence. If you can give this card a nudge and he makes it to his destination in time, there would definitely be a handsome cash reward for an up and coming comedian."

"Let's see what we can do." says Sidney. After running the card and checking the computer, he says, "Sorry guys, but getting to DC would take more than a nudge. This card has less than an hour on it. At most, I could nudge that up to four hundred miles, but DC is over six. I'd really like to help but a nudge or fudge that big, would get me fired."

"I understand that" says Martin; "thanks for trying we . . ." The door opens cutting off Martin's words. A tall thin man with glistening dark curls, which seem to have sprouted up in random tufts, stands in the doorway. A series of glances flicker back and forth between all the players. Finally, the new man settles his gaze on Martin and says, "Are you two quite finished?"

Stunned, we stand riveted to the floor as the newcomer slides past, presenting his card to a likewise stunned Sidney. "R.W. Wankin, executive platinum member, and I require an immediate flight to Washington, DC."

"Yes sir," says Sidney swiping the card and checking his computer. Muttering all the right things the whole time he is searching the screen; "Yep . . . OK . . . and that flight crew is . . . Hum? Right, so, ah, Mr. Wankin, may I call you R.W.?"

"I prefer, Wankin."

Masking a laugh by coughing into his elbow, Sidney continues, "Mr. Wankin, do you see that 3800 Jet Commander out there on the tarmac?" he says, pointing out the window.

As Wankin glances out the window and mumbles "yes," Sidney gives Martin and me a conspiratorial wink.

"Sir, the bad news is that 3800 you see out there is already reserved. The good news is: that 3800 is reserved by Mr. Sheehan, who is standing right here," says Sidney, nodding at me. Despite the sour look on Wankin's face, Sidney continues, "More good news, Mr. Wankin, this gentleman, who has reserved that plane, is also traveling to DC. Mr. Sheehan might be willing to split the mileage with you."

"I prefer my own plane, when possible" says Wankin.

"In that case sir, let's see, we have a turbo-prop 440 and a crew can be here . . . in about . . ."

"Never mind, never mind. I'll share the 3800 with Mr. . . . him," says Wankin, nodding in my direction.

Martin and I can hardly contain ourselves. Sidney asks both Wankin and myself for our "Select Jet" cards, and I promptly hand him Martin's. Moments later returning our cards, Sidney says, "thank you both very much." Then, with a smug grin on his face, he says "Mr. Sheehan, you and Mr. Wankin can have a seat if you like, and I'll call you for boarding in a few minutes."

It took some self-restraint not to rush over and bear hug the breath out of Sidney. After borrowing a pen from the counter, I huddle with Martin on a sofa in front of a low coffee table. "This is the holy grail," I say, showing Martin the envelope. "This is the list of the people who have helped me get this far. If I make it in time, all of them will be millionaires, you included." I unfold and flatten out the envelope for Martin to write down his information.

"I'm more than happy to join this list," says Martin, writing down his information. Beaming surreptitiously at Sidney, I give him the OK sign. Martin and I agree that he will stay after the flight leaves and get Sidney's information so we can properly reward him, if I'm successful.

*****

THE FLIGHT

Wankin is ahead of me walking towards the plane carrying a briefcase that tilts him but doesn't slow him down. A pilot awaits us at the top of a short stairway. "Take any seat you like, on opposite sides of the aisle, if you don't mind." Wankin takes the second of the four seats on each side, and I take the one opposite. I didn't want to seem anti-social. After closing the door, the pilot or co-pilot says, "Buckle up gentlemen, we're cleared for takeoff and should be rolling in a minute."

It's less than two minutes later, and the pilot is standing on the brake. The plane is vibrating, shivering, like a horse in the starting gate. Bang! Rather like a pony being faster than a horse over a short distance, we are quicker than the larger jets. Fifteen seconds later, we are a quarter mile down the track, going over a hundred miles an hour and leaving the planet.

The co-pilot emerges after we have leveled off to offer us cold drinks and, what else but peanuts. "Short rations, for a short flight." He grins. That must be military humor, which I don't find funny, as peanuts have been my only sustenance for two days. "You may use electronics now, and the lavatory is in the rear."

Wankin pulls a fanny pack around from behind his coat, removes a phone, extends the antenna, and begins punching buttons. Seeing the phone reminds me that I need to call Andy, my sister. We haven't spoken since days ago in Australia, when the phone company abruptly cut us off for insufficient funds. No doubt she'll be worried by now; older sisters are that way. Apparently, no one is answering

Wankin's call; in any case, he clicks off and sets the phone down.

Even though we have not spoken, I know that Wankin and I are at opposite ends of the personality bell curve. I don't like being phony, but somehow I need to schmooze this arrogant twit so I can borrow his phone. I take a bite of humble pie, a deep breath and squirm on. "Hope we didn't get off on the wrong foot back there. I can see you're a busy man, and time is money, as they say. What line of work are you in, Mr. Wankin"?

Skeptically, he looks at my shoes. "Political consultant."

Those words just hang in the air between us, and I can't resist.

"You mean, like a lobbyist?"

Jesus. How could I? If there is a place for really stupid people in heaven, I'll be the one standing outside the pearly gates with his tongue stuck to the frozen metal flag pole.

"Political Consultant," he drags out at a lower pitch, and a higher volume.

So much for schmoozing. "Right," I say. "Would it be possible to borrow your phone for a moment? I need to call my sister, just for a minute, just to let her know that I'm OK."

In response, Wankin moves his gaze up from my shoes to my shirt and says, "Have you never flown privately before? No? If you had," Wankin says, "you would know that you have your own air phone in the side bin, and it's included in the fare."

"Yes, of course." I squeak. I pop the top of the side bin, and there sits an air phone, cradle an all. I take the phone out and lay it on the table in front of me. Then, placing the envelope next to it, I take my passport out, and finally from it, — the sacred one. 'The Ticket!'

Andy picks up on the third ring. The first minute is spent listening to her alternately thanking God that I'm alive, and then cursing me forever being born. While she's catching her breath, but before she starts another rant, I interject, "All right, enough, calm down, OK? . . . Good. Listen, I'm in a plane that just left Chicago, and should land at Reagan National in about an hour."

I glance over at Wankin, who now has one of those donut things around his neck; his head banked up against the window and his eyes closed. Safe enough.

I lower my voice anyway. "Do you still have a copy of the numbers? OK, great. I know it's going to be close, but if I do make it in time, I'd hate to run into the lottery office screaming Lotto or Bingo, or whatever, and have the wrong numbers." That earns more phone rage from her end.

"Andy!" I say much too loudly. Then stealthily, I look over at the still sleeping Wankin. Lowering my voice again, I say, "Listen. First, I didn't hang up on you in Australia. John's phone is a pay as you go phone, and it ran out of money, therefore I never heard you say the last two numbers. Now certainly, we know our own birth dates, and we know how to add. Just humor me, will you? Please, just read off the numbers one more time slowly and let me check them?"

I nod and mumble affirmative squeaks as each number matches up. I hold my breath for the last two but, of course, they match up as well. "OK, now let me read them back to you all right? . . . yes, I swear, this is the last time."

"Andy, I want to make sure I heard the amount correctly. Did you say seventy-eight million? All right, SEVENTY-EIGHT MILLION!" Inadvertently, the volume of my voice rises with excitement, and I timidly shoot one more glance over at the still immobile Wankin.

"I got to go now Andy; I'll call you back as soon as I know anything." After placing the phone back in its cradle, I carefully place the lottery ticket back inside my passport, then tuck my passport into the envelope. Glancing down at the scribbled list of names on it makes me smile, — makes me feel a bit like, John Beresford Tipton. I begin daydreaming, quietly tapping the envelope on the table in front of me. I'm thinking how happy and secure my sister and her young daughter, Anna will be. A reunion with Marylyn, man, the sparks and clothes will fly. I wonder, does this seat recline?

**

It is one of those dreams you feel like you can control. I'm on an airplane that's coming in for a landing. I feel the floating silence and see the ground rising up to meet us. Then, the wheel jarring skips are followed by full flaps, angry, hard breaking and the whine of engines in reverse. That combination forces everyone forward in their seats, only to be released seconds later as the pilot's soft touch glides us to the gate.

The noise of the door being opened in the front of the cabin wakes me. It isn't a dream after all. I see the back of Wankin's aerated head pass through the cabin door. Trying to fully roll out from under the dream cloud, and into reality, is taking longer than I thought. The sight of my envelope sitting on the table shocks me. I was sure that I had replaced it in my pocket. But then I remember—I finished talking to Andy, found out that the seat went way back, and then, immediate sleep. I pick up the envelope, feeling the reassuring bulge of my passport inside, and stuff it way down in my back pocket.

"Ready sir?" asks the pilot, who is standing by the door, waiting me.

"Sure, yeah!" I say. I try to pop up quickly, only to be jerked right back down by the seatbelt. "Houston, we have a problem." I say, then freeing open the clasp, "Belay that last transmission, Houston, all systems are go."

The pilot is still smiling as I walk out the door. "Nice recovery."

Wankin is already entering the terminal when I reach the bottom of the stairs. He is twenty yards ahead and motoring. I call out, but either he doesn't hear me or he doesn't want to. Walking at just under the speed of light I push through the exit doors of the terminal. Outside, Wankin is still twenty yards in front of me, hiking his briefcase into the backseat of a cab. In doing so, his suit jacket lifts up, and I see his fanny pack again. Isn't it funny, how we sometimes stereotype people by their accessories. And sometimes they deserve it.

"Wankin!" I scream. Wait up."

We almost make eye contact, but he slides into the back seat and leans away, out of sight. Two more long strides, and I'll be grabbing the door handle. Then, the cab's back wheels chirp and the exhaust pipe spews a blast of black smoke. I hurl accurate, but useless profanities at the retreating taxi. Now what?

No more cabs, no buses, no metro, no nothing. As I turn to go back into the terminal, I see that, in the all but deserted arrival lot, there is a single car. It's an older Cadillac with unreadable white writing on the side. More out of curiosity than hope, I step close enough to read the mud-spattered writing on the door panel.

Potomac Taxi
Independent Driver
Sampson S. Samuels

It's a good forty degrees warmer than Chicago and humid. As I lean in closer, I see that the windows are cracked a couple of inches. At least, if there is anybody in there, they might still be alive. Good news, bad news — no dead body, no body at all, it's empty.

*****

TAXI RIDE

Time is an incessant and inflexible trudger. It marches on regardless of its victim's pleas. Time is unstoppable and undefeated. I cannot worry about time, but I do.

Looking back towards the terminal I see a sign for a coffee shop. Now I am walking quickly although awkwardly. The clompy gait is caused by having my right hand stuffed deep down into my back pocket protecting my ticket. This makes me limp which makes me look like I'm riding an invisible hobby horse. So much for style.

I enter the door with a rush and attract the attention of the only patron, a huge man sitting at the counter. "Excuse me, sir, the time . . . can you tell me the time?"

Keeping his eyes on mine, he hitchhikes his thumb back over his shoulder towards the back wall. There, a large round clock tells me that my hopes are shattered. It reads 4:55.

More than just wind gets knocked out of my sails; it's like been demasted. I slide down on a counter stool and cup my hands over my eyes. I must be moaning out loud because the big guy says, "Can't be that bad."

"Really, I guess just missing out on seventy-eight million dollars may not seem bad to you; but it seems pretty goddamn bad to me," I say.

"What are you talking about, man?"

"The lottery! If I could have gotten to a lottery office in Virginia by five o'clock today, and given them this ticket," I say, smacking my back pocket. "Then I, and a lot of other people, would have become millionaires. One hour, I only needed one extra hour."

"Clock's wrong," says the huge coffee drinker.

"What?" I almost shout.

The big man's eyes dart from the clock to his wrist watch. "They didn't set the clock back. Day-light savings time ended yesterday, Sunday. You know, fall back. It's only four minutes to four."

"Oh my God! Oh man! Is that your cab outside?" Not waiting for a reply, I open the door and say, "Come on let's go! If you can get me to the nearest lottery office in under an hour, you'll be a millionaire too."

The big man doesn't move. "I'd like to help you, and believe me I'd like to be a millionaire, but I can't help you. Sorry, my transmission busted."

"No . . . really?" I moan.

"Really, I'm just waiting here for my brother-in-law to swing by and follow me to the garage, then give me a ride home."

"Follow you? You mean your cab runs?" I ask hopefully.

"Barely the tranny, the linkage, something is stuck. It's only got neutral and one forward gear, could be second gear, but you go past thirty, thirty-five, and man, she pitches a fit!"

"Look, 'Sampson' is it? I say," remembering the writing on the taxi door. He nods. "Look, Sampson, you're my last chance. Do you know where the closest lottery office is?"

"Sure, Woodbridge. Twenty miles south on I-95."

"How long would it take to get there?" I ask.

"If I could . . . which I can't, it would take about thirty minutes on I-95. I wouldn't last five minutes out there, going thirty-five miles an hour. I'd be arrested or more likely, road rage dead."

"There must be another way to get there besides the interstate?"

"You can get there on highway One, but that would take a lot longer, maybe forty-five, fifty minutes. I still wouldn't be able to keep up with the traffic, and trying to would probably blow up my car. No Sir. No Way." says Sampson.

I look at my empty wrist. "What's the time now?"

Sampson looks at his watch. "Two minutes to four. It doesn't matter; I'm not blowing up my transmission, period!"

"If it blows up, I'll buy you a new one."

"Sure, you some kind of underdressed tycoon, can't find a barber shop?"

"Ross, is the name and what? You don't think I'm honest?" I almost scream.

"Oh, I think you're honest," smiles Sampson, "I also think you're broke."

"All right . . . look you caught me out. You're right I am broke, and you're right again about me being honest. Inside this envelope, (I hold it up) is my passport and inside that is a lottery ticket worth seventy-eight million dollars. On the outside of this envelope are the names of the people who have helped get here from Australia. I started from there two days ago, when I found out I'd won."

"Let me see how many names? Four, five, I turn it over six . . . eight. Eight names. You Sampson, you would make nine and I would be ten. Perfect! Ten people each getting ten percent. Which, after taxes, is about half of the total or about thirty-nine million. Meaning about three and half million dollars for each person on this envelope. So, Sampson, if you like, I'll add your name to the list, and if you get me to the lottery by five, we'll both be rich, very rich."

"And Look Sampson, if your car blows up I'll buy you a new transmission. If I don't make it in time, I'll have other debts to pay off too. I would have to sell my 'Mickey, da cat Dora' surfboard. Selling that—I would have enough to pay off my debts, and buy you a new transmission."

It takes Sampson about six seconds to run through all the calculations, and logistics involved. "Must be some kind of fancy-ass surfboard! Get your butt in the car, surf dude, we're wasting daylight."

Gravel is flying from the back wheels before I can fully shut my door. We are off.

"Buckle up! Surf Dude!"

"The name's Ross." I say.

"Buckle up, Ross! Time to rock and roll." Moments later the engine begins to whine. Sampson lowers the windows as the odor of burnt motor oil seeps up through the floorboards.

The man can drive; I'll give him that. The big Caddy is slow but Sampson makes it seem smooth and agile. Cutting through gas stations, convenience stores and corner parking lots, we ignore traffic lights, and narrowly miss some miffed pedestrians. Sampson explains going up a one-way street the wrong way by saying, "Nobody uses this street much anymore."

"Well, OK then, no worries," I think, but don't say.

We merge into highway One, which is crowded, but traffic is moving along at a pace we can keep up with. When the speed limit is lower for road work, or even schools, Sampson takes it upon himself to leap frog as many cars as he can. The engine screams, horns blow, profanities abound and fingers fly. When we are safely tucked back in the right-hand lane, I find my breath again.

Even at this reckless pace, it seems to be taking forever. Then I see the sign:

Woodbridge 6

"Sampson, the time, how much time do we have left?"

He glances at his watch, then has to break sharply to avoid rear ending the car in front of us. "Never mind. You keep your eyes on the road. Just show me the watch. If we wreck, we're toast; we'll never make it." Sampson's wrist shoots in front of my face. "Quarter of, fifteen minutes' till. How fast we going?"

"Thirty—five, um, thirty-seven now" says Sampson.

"We'll make it thirty-six. Four into thirty-six is nine. So, we're covering nine miles every quarter of an hour. We only had six miles to go back there, so we should make it if we keep this speed up.

"You sure 'bout that Ross? That's awful quick figuring."

"I'm sure Sampson. I'm good with numbers, always have been."

We have several peeks and a balk before finally passing an overloaded, aging pickup truck. That last burst of acceleration adds a new voice to the engine and transmission choir. It sounds like metal grinding, backed up by a hard drum beat of tapping.

"Not good. Now we're smoking," says Sampson looking in the rear-view mirror.

"Sign! Two miles!" I squawk, "The watch, Sampson, let me see your watch. Six minutes, a little more actually," I say. I'm still holding onto Sampson's wrist, studying the second hand. "I don't want to jinx us but. . ."

"Then don't!" exclaims Sampson.

A new sound joined our mechanical choir, a siren. The sound of the siren is muffled by all the noise we are making, and the smoke makes it difficult to tell how far back the noise and the flashing lights are. However, there is little doubt as to whom they are pursuing.

"Woodbridge! That sign said Woodbridge!

"I know," says Sampson, who seems to be getting calmer as my nerves are splitting their infinitives. The siren is howling now, and a quick glance shows a State Police car pulling out from two cars behind us. We slow a bit, and just as the police car pulls level with us Sampson says, "Shortcut!"

A vicious, fish-tailing-ninety degree turn to the right leaves the police car hanging out in the passing lane, unable to follow us immediately. "It's just over this hill up here, no more than a minute away," says Sampson, as he shoots his watch under my chin again.

"Four minutes! Looking good!"

Just as we hit the top of the rise, a concussion blaring siren explodes from the driver's side. The charging State Police car pulls out and is abreast of us in seconds. A very irate looking policeman extends his arm across his front seat and points his index finger at Sampson. I watch dumbfounded as Sampson returned the gesture in full. The siren fades to silence, and the policeman uses his speaker to blast out, in a commanding voice, "RT, pull over God damn it!"

Sampson extends his left arm again and raises his index finger screaming "One minute!" The policeman flips the siren back on, and ratchets up the volume to where the pain level is unbearable. Sampson never flinches, saying, "When I stop, you get out, and go." The lottery is on the right: brick and glass, big sign, you can't miss it. Don't stop, don't listen, and don't look back. I'll take care of the policeman."

"You sure?" I ask.

"I'm sure. You just haul your ass up in there and get our money."

Tires screech from both cars as they slide to a halt, still parallel. I make it to the walkway of the building when I hear, "Halt! Police! Stop where you are!"

Naturally, I slow down but Sampson's voice rings out. "Keep going, Ross! — Just keep going." I close quickly on the solid glass door, and give its brass handle a mighty tug. I am rewarded with a metallic 'clunk.' Locked? Impossible. It can't be five o'clock. I'm sure that I still have minutes to spare. I cup my hands around my eyes, and press this finger visor against the glass, so I can see inside through the sun's glare.

Through this tunnel, I can see that there is a woman who is standing next to a security guard, but more importantly, a large clock on the wall behind them shows the time to be 4:57. I mime checking my empty wrist, and then point at the wall clock behind them. I simulate pulling on the door, and then throw up my hands in sign of questioning confusion.

"Sir." The voice comes from up high up on the wall, and with no warning. It so surprises me, that I actually duck. I look up to see a video camera mounted on a swivel, and next to it a speaker, which is inserted flush with the brick.

The wall speaks again: "Sir, I am Patricia Roberts, managing director of the Woodbridge, Virginia Lottery. I must inform you that you are being videotaped and voice recorded and that this can be used as evidence against you should the need arise."

"What are you talking about lady? Can you hear me?" I lean up to the glass again and fold my hands into the glare preventing tunnel again. The clock over her shoulder reads 4:58. The woman has a small microphone in her hand. She looks at me and says, "Yes, I can see and hear you just fine. Please step back from the door. The reason we are not allowing you inside is that we had a report that someone might come here falsely claiming to have the winning ticket."

"I'm not falsely claiming anything! I've got the winning ticket right here." I pull out the envelope and wave it at the glass. "Wait, will that recording show that I got here before 5:00; show that I got here in time and that you wouldn't let me in?"

"Yes sir, the time, the date, everything is being recorded. However, the winning ticket has already been claimed. Unless your ticket has those exact same numbers, and our records do not indicate any duplication of the winning numbers. May I see your ticket, sir?"

As I carefully take my passport out, I feel the presence of two people coming up on either side of me. Sampson's soothing voice says: "You got a problem, Ross?"

"No, no, just a misunderstanding. The ticket will straighten everything out." I say, opening up my passport.

Panic, fear, confusion, disbelief, all overwhelm me. What!! It can't be. I flutter the passport pages against my fingers, sure that it will fall out. Nothing. I search page by page; scouring the envelope, turn my back pocket inside out, peeking back, to make sure it's not there. I feel weak, disoriented.

"It's gone . . . I just had it. I've had it in my passport for more than a day, before I even left Australia. Hell, I had it for six months and didn't know I had it. I just saw it on the plane; I read the numbers off to my sister." I turn to Sampson. "Didn't I show it to you in the coffee shop? No, that's right, I only showed you the envelope."

"Sir, if there's nothing else, we're closing for the day and we need for everyone to clear the premises," says Patricia Roberts—via the wall.

I close my eyes and drop my head down, not in dejection but in recollection. The sun has settled down far enough so that most of the glare is off the glass. I can see both Ms. Roberts and the security guard; then someone moves casting a shadow behind them.

"WANKIN!! It was Wankin, wasn't it?" Both Roberts and the security guard glance quickly over their respective shoulders and then back. I follow their line of sight, and see a thinning head of sporadic hair divots, retreating behind a cubicle wall.

"You bastard, Wankin. You stole my ticket!" I try to scream through the glass.

"Easy Ross." Sampson says, as he and the policeman each hold an elbow for control. They have sidled up and grabbed me without my even being aware.

"Are you saying the winning ticket was obtained from you fraudulently?" says Ms. Roberts through the wall speaker.

"Yes, he must have stolen it from me while I was asleep on the plane. We were the only two passengers on the plane. That's why he rushed off and took a cab, leaving me stranded."

"If you wish to lodge a formal complaint under 'Possession by deceit or theft,' you are entitled to do so," says Ms. Roberts, sounding much less hostile. "If you wish to do so, a judge will be appointed and both parties must attend the arbitration hearing here tomorrow at ten a.m. Fair warning, the ticket has been validated, and possession of the ticket gives great leverage to the claimant in possession of the ticket. You must have clear, physical evidence that you have previously and legally possessed that ticket. If you can't, you may face fines, and possible incarceration. Considering that, do you wish to continue?"

"Yes Ma'am, I do."

"Very well then, if you all would step inside Mr. Roark here will assist you in filling out the form, and we'll need a copy of your identification Mr.?" Ms. Roberts tilts her head at me.

"Sheehan, ma'am, Ross Sheehan."

Once inside, we follow Mr. Roark to the reception area where he photo-copies my passport and I fill out the arbitration form. Ms. Roberts has gone into another cubicle, where the last Wankin sighting took place. Likely, she will have Wankin fill out the same forms. She returns quickly, and then join us, as we are leaving. "We'll see you tomorrow morning at ten then, Mr. Sheehan?"

She has a smile on her face and I return one to her. "Yes ma'am, you bet."

As we approach the taxi, it is in its death throes, hissing, clicking, and tapping. "She's gone," says Sampson, mostly to himself. "Say, Mike, could you get the police tow truck to haul my car up to the impound lot in Arlington? It sure would save me a lot in towing charges."

"What?" Says Mike incredulously. "I should be issuing you multiple citations, probably even arresting you, and you have the nerve to stand there and ask me for a favor?"

"Sure I do, RB, and while you're at it, Ross and I need a ride to Gran Nanna's."

"Jesus!" says Mike, looking up. "I know you hate hearing this again Lord, but why me?"

Receiving no answer Mike turns to us. "Both of you get in the car."

As soon as we are settled in Sampson introduces us. Mike reaches over the seat and shakes my hand saying, "Nice to meet you Ross, I think." He turns back around and starts his police cruiser. Looking straight ahead he says: "Now, both of you, buckle up, and shut up."

The silence lasted a good thirty or forty seconds, before Sampson starts reciting the many different makes and models of limousines he is going to purchase with his new-found wealth. Silence returns only after his list apparently tops out with a Rolls-Royce, Bentley Silver Cloud. We merged onto I-95, and slide through the traffic toward Gran Nanna's house in Nauck, Virginia. Nauck is a proud older community in Arlington that boasts its own zip code.

We pull into a long drive way with a detached garage at the end. Mike stops parallel to the walkway to the house. Shoving the car in park he says, "My apologies to Gran Nanna, but I've got dinner and a beautiful wife waiting. Hopefully, when I get home, both will be nice and warm. I'll be back here at nine in the morning, so you two be ready." The car is rolling backwards as our doors shut.

98

GRAN NANNA'S

We walk down a highly polished hardwood hallway and turn left into the den. Paying us no mind is a boy of about ten; he's on the sofa watching television. "Son," says Sampson.

"Hi Dad," comes a small voice from the still immobile head.

"Marcus, we have company; this is Mr. Ross Sheehan, a real surfer."

"Cool," says Marcus as he stands up and steps around the sofa. He offers his hand and says, "Marcus Samuels, nice to meet you, Mr. Sheehan."

"My pleasure. You can call me Ross." I say as we shake hands. "You know, Marcus, good manners never get old, and girls really dig that in a guy."

"Gran Nanna, set another plate for dinner; we have a guest," bellows Sampson.

"Gran Nanna? Nanna, are you in the kitchen?" Met with silence, Sampson walks into a room from which a bevy of enticing smells are emanating.

"How many times have I told you," commands a voice, a very loud yet feminine voice.

"I don't know Gran Nanna, lots," replies a meek Sampson. Marcus rolls over on the sofa covering up a snicker.

"And what did I tell you?"

"That if I want to speak with you—to come into the room you're in and then speak."

"All right. Now that we have that straight, I'd like to meet our dinner guest," says Gran Nanna as she plows past Sampson into the den.

"Hi," she beams. "Did I hear the name Ross mentioned?"

"Yes ma'am, Ross Sheehan." I nod.

"What a nice name, and what a nice looking young man," coos Gran Nanna. "Let me get you something to drink before dinner: sweet tea, a soda; we might even have a beer."

"A soda would be fine thanks, Gran . . ."

"Nan. You can call me Nan," she says returning to the kitchen.

Marcus and Sampson roll their eyes at "Nan" but wisely remain silent.

From the kitchen comes, "Hope you like chicken and dumplings Ross; dinner will be in ten minutes." Apparently, the 'only talk to a person when you're in the same room with them' rule does not apply to Gran Nanna.

The three of us men settle on the sofa, and Marcus turns the sound back up on the show that he had been watching. It is a B teenage romance movie; just now the young couple caught out in a rain storm find shelter in an abandoned cabin. They kiss and passionately embrace in clinging wet clothes — Marcus jumps up and shouts, "He's gonna get himself some!"

"Shut up Marcus. You got no idea what you're talking about," says Sampson.

"That's what Gran Nanna says when two people are rubbing on one another like that."

"Yeah, well just like you Marcus, sometimes Gran Nanna don't know what she's talking about," says Sampson.

Soundlessly, Gran Nanna has floated back into the den behind Sampson. Suddenly, "Thwack!" Gran Nanna's middle finger held back by her thumb, like a catapult, springs forth a stinging blow to the back of Sampson's ear.

"Jesus. . . Jesus, that hurt, Gran Nanna," wails a cringing Sampson.

"I told you never to use His name unless you're praying."

"I am praying," says Sampson; "I'm praying you never do that to me again."

Marcus can't contain his glee and a small chirping sound escapes from his partially covered mouth. Gran Nanna switches targets, re-cocks her catapult and zeroes in on Marcus. "Don't think I won't box those cute little ears of yours, Marcus Samuels."

Shortly after, we all sit down to dinner, which is even better than the aromas had forecasted. In between delicious mouthfuls of chicken and dumplings, I tell Marcus of my recent adventures from Australia through Hawaii and across the United States. I answer a multitude of questions from both Sampson and Marcus while Gran Nanna just sits and listens. Of course, the X-rated scenes and language are deleted.

The ride to the lottery, as told by Sampson, is almost a complete fabrication. Supposedly, we ran into Mike, who gives us an escort to the lottery. That allows for the limo to be dropped off at the auto shop for a tune-up and a state inspection. That's the reason Mike is picking us up in the morning, and taking us to the arbitration hearing. I explain to Gran Nanna that there is another claimant, but that the ticket really belongs to me and hopefully I can convince a judge of that tomorrow.

As the three of us not-so-wise men are getting ready to go upstairs to our bedrooms, Gran Nanna pulls me aside and says. "Ross, when you go to sleep tonight, I want you to be thinking about what it is that you need to remember, what's the one thing that will convince that judge that you're in the right. I want you to dream yourself a solution. It's strange, but it's true. Many a problem has been solved by just sleeping on it."

****

ARBITRATION

Breakfast the next morning is every bit as delicious as dinner had been the night before. After breakfast, but before leaving for school, Marcus bombards me with questions about surfing. Seems he has just passed his junior Red Cross swimming test and is ready to tackle the waves on the North Shore of Hawaii. I tried to explain that it requires a certain amount of knowledge and expertise to even survive in those waves. Finally, we settle on my promise to give him free surfing lessons, if he can make it south to Daytona Beach over the coming holidays.

"Mike is here!" Marcus yells back through the screen door as he is leaving.

Sampson and I are at the top of the porch steps when Marcus and Mike exchange high fives. "Let's go RT," Mike says, standing by the driver's door. "I got better things to do than chauffeur you two clowns around."

"You know, RB, you won't be so disrespectful towards me when I'm rich" replies Sampson.

"Yeah RT, and you won't be so rich when you pay me back all the money you owe me," answers Mike.

Once I'm buckled up in the back seat, and even though I am pretty sure I know the answer, I ask, "You guys been friends a long time? Right? I mean, you've got like secret initials for names and stuff."

"Those ain't no secret initials Ross," says Sampson. RT stands for right tackle, that's me. Behind the wheel is RB short for running back. We played the same positions, on the same teams, for about fifteen years. Yeah, I'd say we're friends."

"More like acquaintances," says Mike.

"Acquaintances yep, I guess that's what we are." says Sampson. "We got acquainted in Pop Warner football at age seven. I was a tiny-mite right tackle and (he pointing at Mike) was a tiny-mite running back. Every game, every play for seven years, all through Pop Warner football. Then, we stayed acquainted through four years of high school football, every play, every game. Then, two years at The University of Maryland. We also managed to stay acquainted while being best men at each other's weddings." That was enough to silence even Mike.

Sampson turns to me in the back seat. "Ross, you figure out how to prove that ticket really belongs to you?"

"Slept on it; I can almost see the answer. It's kind of like in the back of my mind. I can't quite get a hold of it."

"Well," says Mike "You better reach back down in there and pull it up to the surface, because here we are." We arrive at the parking lot just as Wankin and another man, both carrying briefcases, enter through the glass doors. "Early birds," says Mike, looking at his watch. "It's only quarter till."

"You guys go ahead," I say. "I need to retrace my steps one more time."

Their doors shut, and my mind travels back a little too far. There I am, surfing shoulder high waves in Queensland, Australia. It is helpful though, since these images help calm my mind. That gives my mind the peace it needs to move that elusive bit of proof closer to the surface. I can almost see it.

I meet the guys outside the glass doors; once inside we're met by Patricia Roberts. "Right this way, gentlemen," she says leading us to an elevator. We rapidly zip all the way to the summit and step out on the second floor. We follow Ms. Roberts down the hallway to a door whose frosted glass window has gold-leaf lettering declaring it a "Conference Room."

The room is set up like a little courtroom. A short podium is atop a large desk, which in turn, sits on a raised dais. Off to the side sits the typical court recorder. I say typical because she wears a long, full flowing skirt, her hair in a bun and her glasses are perched on the end of her nose. The aisle is wide, with each side having two rows of four folding chairs. Wankin and (I'm guessing) his attorney sit in the front row on the left. We sit in the back row, on the right.

According to his shoulder patch, it is a sheriff's deputy who walks in from a backdoor and says, "All rise!" He is followed almost immediately by the judge — a tall man with a no-nonsense stride and an old school, ice-gray flat top. The judge sits and the deputy tells us we can do likewise.

"I understand that Ms. Roberts has explained the situation to both parties. However, let me refresh. This is not a trial, this is an arbitration hearing; however, all the decisions rendered here are legally binding in the Commonwealth of Virginia. The gentlemen with you, whether they're friends or attorneys, may be consulted but cannot speak for you in any way. My ruling on this matter is final. There are no appeals. The rules of law in this arbitration hearing are similar to those in a regular court proceeding. The penalties for breaking these laws. such as perjury, are also the same. Understood?" Nodding heads from both sides of the aisle.

"In accordance with the rules of The Virginia State Lottery, I will now read the rules as written on the back of this, the ticket in question, and all Virginia Lottery tickets. "

"This ticket is valid only for the drawing date(s) shown. Prizes must be claimed within 180 days of the draw date(s) on the ticket. Ticket purchasers and winners must be at least 18 years old. Gifts of tickets to minors are prohibited. All tickets, purchases, transactions and winners are subject to lottery rules and state law. Tickets are void if stolen, misprinted, mutilated, incomplete, or cancelled or do not meet State Lottery Validation tests. Liability for void tickets if any, is limited to replacement of the ticket. This lottery ticket is bearer instrument unless signed. Knowingly presenting or transferring for payment an altered forged, or counterfeit ticket is a felony. To claim prizes over $800 you need a valid government-issued photo identification and proof of Social Security Number. Green card is also required if you are not a U. S. citizen."

Finishing with the rules the judge continues, "Now are all these rules understood by both parties? If so, I need vocal responses from both." 'Yes Sirs' erupts from both Wankin and myself. "Right then let the record show that both parties answer in the affirmative. Very well, now that that's been taken care of, are the two parties ready to proceed?"

The question was apparently being rhetorical, as the judge continues. "This is a serious matter with serious consequences, both legally and financially. Anyone found guilty of presenting false evidence or lying before the bench will face charges."

"Mr. Wankin, will you stand and be sworn in by the clerk?"

After Wankin is seated again, the judge addresses him. "Sir, is it your sworn testimony that the lottery ticket you presented to this office yesterday was purchased by you and has been in your possession or under your control since the time of said purchase?"

After a short consultation with his attorney, Wankin replies, "Yes, your Honor."

The judge stares at Wankin for an extra beat or two; he then turns his frozen face towards me. "Mr. Sheehan, will you stand and be sworn in please?"

After I sit down, the judge says, "Mr. Sheehan, it appears, that it is also 'your contention' that 'you' purchased said lottery ticket, and that 'you' retained possession of or control of it until very recently. Is that your sworn testimony?

"Yes sir, it is, Your Honor."

"I'm sure Ms. Roberts has explained to you that usually possession of the ticket is all that's necessary to claim the prize. Claiming to be the rightful owner of the ticket without actually having possession of it puts one at a huge disadvantage. As you might well understand Mr. Sheehan, the burden of proof for a non-ticket holder is set very high. The analogy that comes to mind is the National Football League's video replay challenge. In order to overturn the call on the field, there must be clear and indisputable evidence to the contrary. As it must be with your proof, Mr. Sheehan, in order to reverse the lottery's call."

"Staying with the football analogy the lottery's call on the field, so to speak, has Mr. Wankin scoring a touchdown on the final play and now winning the game by a point. The outcome of the game can be changed — but only by being able to provide indisputable evidence which is contrary to the call on the field."

"You may stand if you like Mr. Sheehan, and present your evidence."

As I stand, my proof dances past like a word or a name on the tip of your tongue. The answer flashes by, pin-balling around in my brain, but vanishes before I can grasp it. I know it's close. The elevator holding the answer has reached the top floor of my mind shaft, and the door is opening. I just need a little more of my old nemesis, time.

"Sir, uh, your Honor. My sister and I have played these same numbers every month for the last ten years, since the lottery started in Virginia. The six numbers are my sister's birthdates 12+15 which add up to 27 and mine 10 +23 which add up to 33— the winning numbers."

"A compelling coincidence if true," says the judge "but it doesn't prove your purchase, possession, or ownership. In fact, looking at the ticket now those are indeed the numbers. However, that proves only coincidence. I recently read some enlightening statistics about birthdays. In a room with 75 people in it there's a 99.9% chance that one of them will share the same birthday. However, this is a completely different situation, and the odds of getting all six numbers on this particular lottery ticket are well over a hundred million to one."

"We don't award lottery winnings to people because of their birthdates Mr. Sheehan; and in this case, we need verifiable and indisputable proof of ownership. If you are holding such proof, then please bring it forward; if not, the award goes to Mr. Wankin."

"Holding . . . Hold, — Holden, Kelvin's Holden truck, the pencil, the ticket— the answer!" I say softly to myself.

"Mr. Sheehan?" The judge says in a stern voice.

"Your Honor, did I understand correctly that Mr. Wankin swore under oath that the lottery ticket in question has been continually in his possession, or under his control since he supposedly purchased it?

"We can check the recorder for the exact wordage if necessary," says the judge, "but basically, yes, that's correct."

"Then Mr. Wankin would know what's written on the back of the ticket," I say, with what I hope is a smile and not a smirk. The answer has arrived!

The judge picks up the ticket and cups it behind both of his hands, like a card player.

"Mr. Wankin, there is indeed something written on the back of this ticket. Would you care to explain what it is and how it got there?"

Like a nervous bird, Wankin's beak flicks back and forth between his lawyer and the judge. Finally, he speaks. "May we have a moment, your Honor?"

"Fine. We will take a ten-minute break. The facilities are across the hall." Nodding towards the deputy, the judge says, "Ron, would you get everyone a bottle of water including me? Thanks."

Even though the judge doesn't tell us not to talk to one another, the three of us remain silent on our trip to the bathroom. No one spoke, even during the fake (at least on my part) peeing. Once we returned to our seats, Sampson leans over and says, "You got this, right Ross? You know what's written on the back of that ticket, right?"

I nod and open the water bottle that's been left on my seat. Taking a swallow, so I can speak, I say, "Yeah Sampson, I know some of it."

"Some?" he squeaks, just as the judge re-enters the room.

"Mr. Wankin, would care to tell us what is on the back of the ticket."

"Your Honor, I don't know what's written on the ticket, but it could have been done by the clerk who sold it to me. It's possible that I scribbled some name, address or note to myself on it. Whatever is written on there is certainly no proof that anyone else ever had possession, or control of that ticket."

"Mr. Sheehan?"

"Your Honor the name on the back of the ticket that I bought is Kelvin Butterworth, a friend who gave me ride in Australia two days ago. He drove through Ballina where he lives, and then two hours further south to drop me off in Coffs Harbour. Since I had no money at the time, I insisted on writing down his name, address, and phone number, so I could send him some gas money.

The only piece of paper available was that lottery ticket, which was in my passport. I wrote down Kelvin's information on the back. At the time, it didn't even dawn on me that it was a lottery ticket. I had no idea I had the winning numbers. It wasn't until after Kelvin dropped me off, that my flat mate told me of my sister's frantic phone calls. I called her immediately. She told me that her daughter saw a newspaper article in which our numbers (the winning numbers) had been picked back in March. She asked me if I had bought a ticket on that date — Thank God I had, because that ticket, and my passport were the only two things I had left."

"Mr. Wankin?"

After a short consult with his attorney: "That is a fine tale, your Honor, but there is still no proof, indisputable or otherwise. It's just as possible that, Mr. Sheehan took the ticket from me while I was asleep on the plane. That he wrote down, whatever it is that's written on the back and replaced it in my briefcase."

"Point taken. Mr. Sheehan? Last chance, anything?"

"Call him."

"Pardon?" squints the judge.

"Call him," I say. "Call Kelvin Butterworth."

A long moment of silence is broken by Wankin's lawyer. "Objection."

A flash of anger reddens the judges face. "There are no objections in this arbitration hearing. I explained the rules of protocol earlier. Another breach, and you sir will be removed
from these proceedings.

*****

THE RULING

The judge's face is still simmering when he turns
and confronts me. "Mr. Sheehan, if we did call Mr.
Butterworth in Australia, what could he say that would
convince the bench that you are the rightful owner of the
ticket?"

"Mr. Butterworth will say that two days ago in
Australia I wrote down his name and other information on a
small slip of paper. This happened just prior to him
dropping me off in Coffs Harbour, Australia. I have my
passport right here, your honor, (taking it out of the
envelope and holding it up) and it shows that I left
Australia about two days ago. If Wankin's passport puts
him in Coffs Harbour — hell if it puts him in Australia two
days ago, I'll forfeit the prize money."

"Mr. Sheehan, may I remind you that you have no
prize money to forfeit, far from it. You, Mr. Sheehan, are
not entitled to make any decisions or directives during this
arbitration. Is that clear?"

"Yes sir, sorry, I just kind of got . . ."

"Bailiff! Bring me a phone, and get me the country
code for Australia and the area code for . . . uh,"

"Ballina, sir, and if I may, the area code is 02.
Also, if it helps, the country code for Australia is 61."

"Unsolicited, but appreciated, Mr. Sheehan. Ron,
just bring the phone. Thanks."

The bailiff plugs a long phone cord into the back
wall and then places the phone in front of the judge.
"Would you happen to know the time difference, Mr.
Sheehan?"

"It ranges sir, from 14 to 16 hours, Australia being
ahead. It depends on which country is on or off daylight
savings time." I turn my head, to wink and smile at

Sampson. "We just went off daylight savings, so Australia could be . . . I don't know. If I'm not sure, I use 15 hours."

"It's almost eleven here" says the judge, "that would make it two in the morning there, give or take an hour. I'm putting this on speaker for the benefit of the court recorder." The phone must have been placed near the microphone because the number tones being punched in are really loud. Then two short trilling sounds brings a raised eyebrow question from the judge. I nod in the affirmative, indicating that yes, that is the normal ring tone in Australia.

I didn't count the number of rings, but there are a lot of them, and I'm getting nervous. Finally, the phone is picked up; then, it sounds like it gets dropped. After that, we hear a moan and then, "PISS OFF!" Clank! Silence. That brought out an involuntary chuckle from me, followed by communal laugher from most, and, even a smile from the judge.

"It seems Mr. Butterworth does not wish to speak to us," says the judge.

"Please try again, your honor. It is after all, the middle of the night there," I say quickly. "As soon as he answers say 'this is an overseas call'." Again, I needed one more, last chance.

The double trilling bursts stopped when the phone engages. "Right, who the hell is this?"

The judge responds as prompted. "This is an overseas call."

"Right, then who the hell is this calling me from overseas?" demands Kelvin.

"This is judge Lester Lambert calling from the United States. I am calling to verify the testimony of an American, he says that you gave him a ride to Coffs Harbor in Australia, two days ago —"

"The Yank, Ross, ah — don't tell me — he's got his self into trouble already."

"No, no, Mr. Sheehan isn't in any trouble yet. He did, however, swear that he wrote down your name, address, and phone number on a small piece of paper. Which he says he kept. He further testified that this all happened two days ago in Australia. Is all this true, Mr. Butterworth?"

"Technically, it's three days ago now. But yes, Ross wrote me info down on a small scrap of paper. It was about the size of a sticky note. He put it back in his passport and said he'd send me some money for petrol. I told him not to worry about it, but Ross insisted. Yeah, that's the truth; that's 'fair dinkum', as we say."

"Thank you for your time, Mr. Butterworth, sorry to have disturbed your sleep. I have a feeling that you'll be hearing from Mr. Sheehan again." The dial tone blasts us until the bailiff un-plugs the phone and takes it away.

"Now, Mr. Wankin, do you have your passport with you at this time?"

Wankin turns to his attorney, who is staring straight ahead, then back to the judge. "No. Your honor, I do not."

"If I were to call the pertinent authorities at immigration, would they confirm that you have recently been to Australia?" asked the judge.

"No, your honor." Wankin mumbles, never looking up from the table.

"Louder, Mr. Wankin, for the court recorder."

"No, your honor, I have never been to Australia," replies Wankin, not lifting his eyes.

"In that case," says the judge, "I am ready to render my decision."

"Mr. Sheehan, you are the plaintiff, the one who brought charges against Mr. Wankin. Your complaint contained allegations that Mr. Wankin stole, or unlawfully removed from your person or from your personal property, said lottery ticket. You were required to present irrefutable proof of this, in order to reverse the previous decision of

112

ownership. I see the evidence as overwhelming and irrefutable. Therefore, I find in favor of the plaintiff Ross Sheehan. This ruling grants Mr. Sheehan full rights and privileges of the Virginia Mega Lotto winning ticket drawn on March 23rd 2000. This includes, but is not limited to the cash prize; which I heard," smiles the judge, "is somewhere north of seventy million dollars."

"Ms. Roberts will be given the necessary paper work momentarily, and she will process it and you through to the presentation of the check. My congratulations, Mr. Sheehan."

"Mr. Wankin, you are to remain here under the purview of the bailiff, until such time as the authorities escort you to the Commonwealth Attorney's Office. At that time, they may add other charges to the perjury charges already being filed against you from this hearing."

*****

The Lawyer's Office

One hour later I float out of the lottery office building. My front right pocket explodes with endless possibilities and freedoms for myself and nine other lucky souls. Inside my pocket is my copy of the wire transfer — sending almost thirty-five million dollars into my newly opened bank account. Folded-up next to it, is a picture of me, holding an oversized check for seventy-eight million dollars. There's a grin on my face that I fear will likely become permanent. My mouth muscles ache and are locking up, but no matter, I can't stop grinning.

Sampson and Mike are waiting by the unmarked police car, beaming like proud parents. I show them copies of the wire transfer and the check; the result is a flurry of back slapping and grinning handshakes. Most of the slapping and shaking is done by Sampson. Mike's nature is naturally more quiet; plus, he won't directly benefit from any of this. Sampson starts asking me a second question before I can answer the first. "Let's talk in the car guys," says Mike, "You know there is one of us who is not a soon-to-be multimillionaire, and he has to go to work."

Probably because of my new-found status, Sampson insists that I ride up front. I buckle up after a small cough and an exaggerated demonstration from Mike. After which, he looks over at me, "Ross, I'm going to give you some advice that as a policeman, I seldom give. You need a to get yourself a lawyer."

"I'm listening."

"I know someone who is trustworthy and can help you. Sampson says you want to give a large percentage of the money to several different people. Is that right?" asks Mike.

"I'm not giving it away; each person on envelope earned their ten percent. Without the help of any of them, especially Parnelli Jones back there, I wouldn't have made it." I smile back over the seat at Sampson.

"Fair enough," says Mike. "Sampson, you remember that kid who played for us when we coached in Pop Warner football, named Tim Donald?"

"Sure," Sampson says, sticking his head in the gap between the front seats. "Wide receiver, good kid, great hands; eventually got a football scholarship to UVA, didn't he?"

"Right," says Mike, "but he got sophisticated and switched to lacrosse. Tim and I have exchanged Christmas cards over the years and stayed in touch. This past summer he graduated from law school at Virginia and got married. Tim has an office by the courthouse, and I have been meaning to drop in, but just like today, I don't have the time."

"I can take Ross by Tim's office," Sampson says.

"You don't have a car, remember? Look Sampson, I'll drop you at Gran Nanna's. Then I'll have just enough time on the way to work to slide by Tim's office and drop Ross off," says Mike.

"Sounds good to me," I say.

The rest of the trip up 95 and 395 Sampson entertains us with descriptions of the various makes and models of the limousines he is going to purchase for his new business. He even offers Mike a job at twice his present salary. Mike thanks him, but says he'll keep his badge job for the time being.

It is a good thing we get to Gran Nanna's as soon as we do because Sampson had already verbally spent a couple a million dollars and is continuing to spit out more expensive models of limousines with every new breath.

Ten minutes after we leave Gran Nanna's Mike pulls up in front of a single-family ranch. According to the sign, it had been converted into the law offices of "Timothy Donald." "Here," says Mike, handing me his card. "Give this to Tim and tell him I'll call in on him this week, without fail."

The sign on the door says "COME IN" and I do just that. As I enter a bell sounds; it's a necessary item I guess as no one is at the reception desk. "One minute," comes bellowing voice from down the hallway. The voice is followed shortly by a fit young man with his long sleeves rolled up and his tie untied. "Hey, sorry," he says nodding his head towards the empty desk. "Tara, my wife and temporary receptionist, stepped out for a moment. I'm Tim Donald, how can I be of service?"

"Ross Sheehan," I say as we shook hands. "Your old Pop Warner football coaches, Mike and Sampson, say you are the man who can help me out."

"Sure, absolutely, anything for those guys. Are they here?" asks Tim, squinting through the venetian blinds.

"No, Mike just dropped me off. He's on his way to work, but he told me to give you this." I hand him the card, "Mike said he would drop by this week, for sure."

"Great, then follow me," Tim says as he reverses himself and strolls back down the hallway. Once in his office, Tim points to a picture on a wall that is full of certificates, diplomas and photographs. "That," he says, "is a picture of the 1988 Arlington Sea Eagles, the undefeated Pop Warner, Mid-South Champions, coached, as you can see, by Mike and Sampson."

I squint. "Wow! Look at Sampson; he's almost svelte and is that you next to Mike?"

"Yeah. They were good coaches and even better role models. They drilled it into us that everyone is responsible for his or her own successes or failures. No social, ethnic, religious, or economic excuses were allowed on the football field or in the classroom., "Each of you, they told us, can practice and train as hard as you like. You

116

can study and read as much as you like. What you put into life is you get out of it, period. No one can stop you from trying hard enough to excel, on or off the field. That may sound corny, but I know for a fact that way more than half of the kids on that team received academic or athletic scholarships to college."

"Doesn't sound corny to me; makes me wish I had them for coaches myself." That subject being covered, we take chairs on opposite sides of Tim's desk.

"Tim, let me start with something that's probably going to be hard for you to believe. I've just won the largest cash prize in the history of the Virginia Lottery."

"Really?" says Tim looking through the venetian blinds again. He acts as though he thinks the coaches are out there hiding, waiting to spring a trick on him. "Amazing, I haven't heard or read a thing about it."

"You wouldn't have," I say. "The actual drawing was six months ago. We just finished up an arbitration hearing at the lottery office. The judge ruled in my favor, so I won."

"Fantastic," Tim says with a shallow grin. "And how much did you win?"

I'm feeling a lack of sincerity on Tim's part but carry on, "Seventy-eight million."

Arched eyebrows, but no comment from Tim.

"It ends up being under thirty-five million; since I took it as an all cash prize." I say this in order to make the amount sound more believable, but that seems to have backfired.

"Allow me to interject something here?" asks Tim. I nod, "Sure."

"Bullshit! Mike and Sampson put you up to this."

"No, look, I just got back from Australia Monday afternoon and . . . "

"Oh! Australia!" interrupts Tim, "Let me rephrase that then: Kangaroo shit!"

I start to get up and walk out, but think better of it, mostly because of my respect for Mike and Sampson.

Remaining in my seat I challenge Tim. "A hundred bucks says I'm telling the truth."

"Make it two hundred; that's what I charge an hour."

I stand, and extend my hand, "Deal."

Tim agrees, and we shake. "Prove it," he grins.

I pull out the copy of me holding the oversized check; I unfold it and hand it to Tim. Slowly, without looking back, he reaches around and finds his swivel back chair and sits down. His eyes never leave the photograph, but his Adam's apple is pulsing like a man standing in front of a firing squad. He croaks out an unconvincing, "You could have had this photo-shopped."

"Could I have faked this?" I ask, handing him a copy of the wire transfer from the Virginia Department of the Treasury depositing thirty-four point nine million dollars into a Capital National Bank account, in the name of Ross M. Sheehan.

"Capital National" mutters Tim, "That's where I bank; there's a branch only a block away. Kenny Mallard is the branch manager, and a good friend of mine. Maybe I should give him a call?" Tim challenges.

"Please do, I'm sure he'll be tickled that you're hanging out with one of his biggest depositors."

My confidence topples his doubt, and he looks me square in the eye. "Is this for real Ross, I mean really, for real?"

"Bet your ass it is," I grin, "Are you in?"

"IN? I'm in like Flynn! In like Errol Flynn."

***

"Tim, I need for you to disperse some checks. Two off the top and then ten percent of the remaining amount for each of my friends on this envelope. Poor me, guess I'll take what's left. We'll start with your check Tim; give us some paper and a pen and I'll try to figure out something that's a little better than fair."

"How's this?" Tim asks, as he slides a legal pad and a pen across the desk.

"Appropriate." I say. "This won't take long; I'm pretty good with numbers." Taking back the deposit slip, I flatten it out next to the legal pad. "I like working with percentages. How about you, Tim? Lawyers work a lot of cases on a percentage basis, don't they?"

"In some recovery cases and personal injury suits, yes."

"Well, this money has already been recovered and no one is suing anyone yet so the rate will be much lower."

A barely audible exhale suggests a negative response.

"Whoa! That's way too much," I say, as I cross out a tower of numbers. "Let's try another zero after the point, and . . ." I let that trail off and sneak a quick peek at Tim. He is staring at the floor, his head swaying back and forth.

"OK Tim", I say. "This should work; how does three thousandth of a percent sound?"

"Not promising, minuscule in fact" says Tim.

"You have a calculator handy?"

"Sure," says Tim as he slid one out his desk drawer and pushed the power button.

"Type in 34,903,600.00; multiply that by .003 or three thousandth of a percent. Now, what do you get?"

"I get, that's . . . that's, one hundred and four thousand seven hundred and ten dollars"— "and eighty-eight cents," I finish for him.

Tim slid the calculator aside, grabs another legal pad and begins crunching his own numbers. Less than a minute later he looks up at me in a dazed silence.

"Fair enough?" I ask.

"Fair! That's way more than fair Ross; as long as I don't have to kill anyone. Tara and I can pay off our student loans. She can quit being a receptionist; we might even have enough left over to put a down payment on a condo. Ross, I know I speak for both of us when I say you have changed our lives. Thank you."

"Glad to be of help. Now, let's see what you can do for me to make this process go forward quickly and smoothly."

"Well," says Tim, "federal and state taxes have already been taken out so we are in the clear tax-wise. Each individual will have to fend for him or herself as far as personal income taxes go. If you want quick and smooth, we can do a limited power of attorney. I would be the agent or attorney in fact. You Ross, would be the principal. The principal transfers limited financial powers to the attorney in fact, me. These powers include only those actions described by the principal, (you), and last only until the completion of the stated action. Tara, my wife, who is a notary, will be back any minute and can fill out and notarize the POA form."

"Sounds good to me. Tim, did you say there is a Capital National Bank near here?"

"Yep, right down the street, less than a ten-minute walk."

"Ok, let's see how many millionaires we have signed up on the envelope. Whoa, I didn't realize there are that many. Your old coach, Sampson, who blew up his limo getting me to the lottery yesterday, is millionaire number nine. That's calling it close. I just make in under the wire, at number ten. Hey, since we all get an equal share, last place is as good as first."

"All right, so you and Kelvin Butterworth each get a check cut off the top. The remainder is then split up at 10% for each of the lucky ten. Tim, how about making a list of all the names and addresses on the envelope, plus yours and

Butterworth's. His address is on the back of this copy of the lottery ticket. You can add the amount of your check after your name since you already know what it is. I'll work up a number for Kelvin and give it to you in a minute."

"OK starting with the number on the deposit slip and subtracting what's your check amount again Tim?" The answer comes back rapid fire. "$1,04710.88."

"Tim, what do you say, we round up your check to $123,600.00?"

"I say, I like the sound of that."

"Then, subtracting that from $34,903,600.00 leaves us $34,780,000.00. Now, if we make Kelvin's check for $280,000.00, we're left with a sort of an even number. Thirty-four and a half million dollars."

"That a whole pile of money Ross."

"Right, and according to my figures that means each of these ten people on the envelope gets a check three million four hundred and fifty thousand dollars."

"'You're going to make a lot of people happy, Ross, myself and my wife included."

There is a slight knock on the door to Tim's office which had been left open a few inches. "Tim, are you alone in there?"

"No, Tara, but please come in; there's someone I'd like for you to meet." A perky young lady with a brown ponytail seems to skate in to the room on silent wheels. Nothing below her waist seemed to have moved and yet, here she is shaking my hand. "My wife, Tara," says Tim. "Honey, this is Ross Sheehan who has come here today to free both of us from our student loans, and you from your receptionist desk."

"Nice to meet you, Ross. You will have to excuse me but I have no idea what my husband is talking about." Then, she fixes Tim with a look that demands an answer.

"Wait till you hear this, Tara. Ross has hired us to write and distribute, um, twelve, yeah, a dozen checks, ten

121

of which will make millionaires out of Ross and nine others. One, which will pay off both of our student loans, and pay a receptionist for a year. Maybe we'll even have enough left over for a down payment on that condo you like. The other check is for a guy named Kelvin Butterworth. I have no idea why he's getting a check for $280,000."

Both of them look to me for an answer, which I supply: "Gas money."

"Gas money?" Tara says sarcastically, "what's he going to fill up? The Space Shuttle?"

"Tim could have prefaced his explanation with the fact that I just won the Virginia lottery. The judge found in my favor at an arbitration hearing only a few moments ago. The reason for Kelvin's check is because he provided the necessary proof for me to win the judgement in that hearing. Two days ago, in Australia, he gave me a lift of more than three hundred miles back to my flat in Coffs Harbour. That was more than two hundred miles out of his way, and that from a guy I didn't even know. If he doesn't give me a ride and then back me up with the judge, none of this happens."

"I had to insist that he write his name and address on the back of my lottery ticket so I could send him some 'gas money.' You guys might want to tip your caps to the karma gods and mention his name. So, taking everything into consideration, two hundred and eighty thousand doesn't seem like that much, does it?"

"No, not at all," says Tara, and Tim nods in agreement. "It's all very generous of you Ross, thanks so much," says Tara, coming forward with a hug. "Sorry for being a smart ass; I get that from hanging around Tim."

"No worries. Some of my best friends are smart asses, including my best friend, me."

"Tara, we need you to perform one of your last secretarial duties by typing up a limited power of attorney form for us to sign, and then, afterwards you can notarize it."

After a few moments, Tara returns with the printed documents. We sign and Tara immediately stamps it saying, "This is now in effect and will remain so until 5:00 PM."

"Thanks, Tara, we're off to see Kenny Mallard at the bank to get the checks cut. Then we'll drop by the post office and mail them off," says Tim. He picks up his legal pad with the names and addresses on it and is moving towards the door when Tara blocks his path.

"Tim, be sure the checks are certified. Remember to sign Ross's name first, then below it write 'by' and then your signature, followed by POA. When you are ready to send them, they should go by registered mail. With registered mail, you get a receipt when you send it; and the recipient must for sign for it. They also offer additional security, like electronic chain of custody, which I don't think you need. It can be a bit slower, but it's much safer."

Tim gives Tara a peck on her facial cheek, and then a pat on her other cheeks. "Thanks, hon—back in a flash, instantly rich and momentarily debt free."

"Enjoy it while you can," says Tara, "I'm putting an ad in the paper for a paralegal tomorrow and taking a look at that condo too."

Walking down the footpath a moment later, I turn to Tim, "Mighty smart lady you got there, Tim."

"Believe me, I know it. She goes by her uncle's quote, 'At first make yourself useful, then make yourself indispensable.' She is already more than indispensable to me, but please, don't ever let her know I said that."

"Got you covered, mate."

Twenty minutes later, Tim and I are sitting with Ken Mallard in his office at the bank. After introductions and explanations, Ken uses the number on my wire transfer deposit slip to look up my new account. Suitably impressed with the figure, he then asks for two picture ID's. My passport is one, but then I have to explain about being robbed in Australia. Finally, he decides that the picture of me with the enlarged lottery check will do as a second I D. Ken apologized for being so through, but as he explains it "That's a hell of a lot of money."

Ken escorts us to a conference/waiting room. "There's coffee, a mini-fridge, and snacks on the counter; make yourselves at home. Tim, your transactions will be handled in-house and the funds will be transferred into your account, except for the cash, which I'll bring back to you. Shouldn't take longer than about twenty minutes to cut these checks. Envelopes are in the box; enjoy the snacks," says Ken.

I immediately race to the table and fill my paper plate with a Danish, two donuts and what might have been a croissant or possibly an overdeveloped fig newton. Half way through my meal I grab a coke from the fridge, add two more donuts, and finish them all off with a satisfying and almost silent burp.

"Hungry?" Asked Tim.

"You bet." I say. "Other than peanuts, which I have now sworn off for life, the only food I have had in the last three days are the two meals at Gran Nanna's.

"I have dined at Gran Nanna's table," says Tim. "You shouldn't be hungry for a week."

"You know, you're right; I'm not really hungry. It must be some kind of "peanut panic" thing. I'm better now so let's get started addressing these envelopes." I take out my battered envelope and smooth it out carefully. Tim slides a pen and half the envelopes across the table to me. "Right," I say, "Tim, you take Kelvin and the first five names, and I'll take the last five."

I had just finished writing Sampson's name on his envelope when Ken returned with the checks. I looked up, and say, "good timing. Number nine is almost done, and that leaves only one last check, for moi."

"I don't dare say small, but there is one undersized check here, for a mere two hundred and eighty thousand dollars," says Ken, picking the top one off of the stack.

"That's for Kelvin; gas money." I say as I slip the check into an envelope with Kelvin Butterworth's name and address already on it.

"Gas money?" Squawked Ken.

"Yes, and he seriously needs a new truck to put the gas in."

Ken shakes his head and says, "Tim, here's your deposit slip and cash, per your instructions. Each of the remaining ten checks is in the amount of three million four hundred and fifty thousand dollars. Pay-to-the-order-of and signatures are all that remain to be filled in."

Ken left us alone again, and all Tim and I can do is grin at each other over a stack of million dollar checks. I broke the silence by picking up a check and announcing "The first millionaire goes to my dear sister, Andy." Later finishing up Sampson's address, I notice the last envelope that's left. You say there's a post office near here?"

"Right around the corner," Tim replies.

"Remember, Tara said registered mail only. Tara, that's an unusual name; is that a family name?"

"No, it's not a family name; it's the name of the plantation," says Tim.

"She lived on a plantation?" I asked.

"No," smirks Tim, "she is named after the plantation in the movie, 'Gone with the Wind'. You know the movie where Rhett Butler says, "Frankly, my dear, I don't give a damn."

Jesus, Frankly Dear — Franklin Dearner — How could I forget my promise to Franklin, my old buddy? "Looks like we're going to need this last envelope after all," I say. I write Franklin Dearner's name on the 'Pay to the order of' line and started addressing the envelope from memory.

"Wait! . . . Whoa, Ross what are you doing? That's the last check—that's the last of the money. You can't do that; you'll be left with nothing. Slow down, let's talk this out; we need to reconsider this."

"No disrespect Tim, but there is no "we" in this; there is nothing to reconsider. However, I guess I do owe you an explanation of why I am doing, what I'm doing."

"Until your 'Frankly my dear' jogged my memory, I had all but forgotten about the promise I made eight or nine years ago to Frank Dearner. He and I had become tight buddies — just when the lottery became legal in Virginia. We'd chip in and play every week. Later on, Frank got married and moved to a state where they didn't have a lottery. Since I still played occasionally, I told Frank I'd give him 10% if I ever won a lottery, or had a windfall of a million dollars or more. He was a salesman and traveled to several other states that did have a lottery. He promised to reciprocate in kind, if he ever enjoyed such a win or windfall. Over these many years, neither one of us has won squat, but our word is as solid today as it was the day we gave it."

"Tim, I can see that my explanation did not totally satisfy you. Therefore, before you have me committed, let me tell you a bit of my history. It may give you an insight into who I am. Most people would find it hard to believe that a man, especially a broke one, would give away three and a half million dollars. I know that sounds a bit sketchy, even to me. Let me to tell you about a couple of incidents in my past; it may help explain how I don't always seem to have my own best interests at heart."

***

STORY TIME

"You probably won't find this hard to believe, Tim, but I was kind of a contrarian kid."

"You're right, Ross, I don't."

"My first experience with the power of money, (other than using it for fun tickets), came when I was 18. I was going on a surfing trip, driving from Virginia to California, the next day. At the time, I was living with my grandparents, and my grandfather stressed that I should be home early. Apparently, he didn't consider 2:30 A.M. early. The next morning, he woke me by dropping a $50-dollar check on the floor, saying, "The first one I made out was for a hundred."

"When I picked the check up, I could see that a corner had been ripped off in anger or haste. Even though I felt like the ungrateful bastard that I was, it made me smile. I saw that money was my grandfather's carrot and his stick, and that if I didn't crave the carrot or fear the stick — I was free.

"It's not that I don't appreciate what money can provide; it's just that money is not at the top of my 'things that are important' list. Much closer to the top of that list is keeping my word to others, and maybe even more important, keeping my word to myself."

"Tim, here's an example of how stubborn, I prefer resolute, I can be about keeping my word to myself.

"Three years after returning to Virginia from my California surfing trip, I went to Hawaii. After spending the winter on the North Shore, I sold my surfboard in Waikiki and flew back to LA. Once there, I called my grandmother back in Virginia, and told her I was going to hitch-hike home, and should see her in about a week. She told me not

127

to be silly, which was then — and is now — a virtual impossibility. She said they would pay for the plane ticket and I could just go to the LA airport, pick up the ticket, and fly home.

"No," I said, I knew that this situation would probably come up, and I resigned myself to hitch-hike cross country if it did. She said to hold on a second; that my grandfather wanted to speak to me.

"How much money do you have?" he asked.

I can't remember the amount I told him, but it wasn't much, maybe $20.

"I'm sending you a hundred dollars by Western Union.

"No sir," I said, "that's too much."

"I'm sending you fifty dollars," he said, "and that's final." To prevent any further discussions on the matter he hung up."

Six days later I drag myself into the house, again it's 2:30 in the morning. I awoke the next morning to find that I had three cents left in my pocket. Thanks for the carrots, granddaddy."

"I'm sure you see where this is headed, Tim."

"I do Ross; it reverts right back to you being a contrarian. You have the glibness of a 'Tom Sawyer'; and the backbone of a 'George Washington'.

"Thank you, Tim; I'll take that as a compliment, I think. It's like my friend Nicky says, "People don't change, they just get older."

"Years ago, I gave my word to Franklin Dearner. More recently, I have given my word, promised, or sworn to nine other people, that I would give each of them ten percent of the winnings. Not, eight, not eight and a half, not nine, but ten percent. And that's what I going to do.

"The first of 'The Four Agreements' is "Be impeccable with your word". I intend to follow that to the letter. Tim, you may think that I've completely run off the rails, but you're still my lawyer and we have eleven checks to send out by registered mail."

In less than forty minutes, I have divested myself of a sizeable fortune, more than thirty-four million dollars. Most of the new millionaires were complete strangers to me three days ago. That fact is hard for me to wrap my head around. As we are on the way out of the bank, Tim checks in with Ken, and tells him to close the account as soon as the last check clears. Then, the balance should be zero and the POA only had another 45 minutes of life.

Tim and I have a short, silent walk to the post office. After Tim takes care of the mailings we step outside and stop; just before we reach the steps leading away from the post office. I turn and say to Tim, "Well, it's been real."

"No, it hasn't," he says, it's been the most unreal thing I've ever been associated with. They shattered the mold with you, Ross. I'm thinking that there must be a very fine line between integrity and insanity; and you my friend, seem to be straddling that line." I'm tempted to hug but settle for a hand shake. Tim offers me his business card and says, "Call us, Ross. Anything you need, anyway we can help, call at any time, collect is fine."

"Speaking of collecting," I say, "how about our bet? You know, the two hundred bucks you bet me—that I hadn't won the lottery. I don't think that there's much doubt about that now. I mean, your check cleared, didn't it?" I grin. "I wouldn't ask, but I seem to be a bit financially embarrassed, again." Tim, a straight up fellow, handed over four of his just acquired fifty dollar bills.

After buying a two-dollar ticket for a twenty-minute ride on the Metro, I stood in the huge cavern known as Union Station. Less than an hour afterward, I sit in my reserved saver seat on the Amtrak 91 Silver Star. I'm comfy and chugging south. I finally feel at ease, at least physically. No doubt, it will be awhile before the whirlwinds whipping through my mind settle down.

I have about thirty dollars left after the buying the train ticket, plus, a hot dog and a coke for lunch. Happily, there's not a peanut in sight. Life is grand. Finally, I have the luxury of sleep to look forward to. It's seventeen hours until the train pulls into Daytona Beach, Florida.

*****

STATE SIDE

Leaving her wheelie in the hallway Marylyn goes straight to the answering machine in the kitchen of her small condo. She punches the flashing red light and holds her breath. Two calls, one from someone named Simone, with an accent (probably a telemarketer) but who strangely enough leaves a return number. The second, is a reminder notice from the landlord about the rent being late. That's it. Nothing from Ross.

Her mood switches immediately from anticipation to concern. It's been six days now since she last saw Ross, sprinting down the passenger boarding bridge in Honolulu. He was getting on the plane to Maui while I was picking up pieces of the cellular phone and my five twenties. Captain Drew Michaels caught a flight back to Honolulu and explained that he'd torn his ticket up so Ross could get on the flight to LA. Now, both he and Marylyn were on the envelope; between them, they had some serious skin in the game. They waited another day for their plane to be repaired and then flew back to Los Angeles.

After arriving home Monday evening, she had quickly left for another three-day flight on Wednesday morning. There had been no messages from Ross during her one day off. Now it's Friday, three days later and she's becoming concerned. She calls the office and checks the status of her buddy passes. Ross has not used either of the passes, from LA to Chicago, or Chicago to DC. That meant that his already slim chances have dwindled down to miniscule. Her thoughts of Ross spiral down; is he injured, in the hospital, sick—dead? She tries not to consider those options. Possibly he failed to get to the lottery office in time and is too embarrassed to talk to her. Maybe he didn't collect anything but didn't want to sell his fancy ass surfboard. No Ross isn't like that—is he? Her heart tells her Ross is a straight up, truthful guy; her head is not quite as sure.

Celebrating or being ashamed are the only two reasons she can think of why Ross hasn't called. Marylyn doesn't think anyone can stay too drunk to make a phone call for six days. Nearly a week is also a long enough time for common decency to overcome any embarrassment.

Clueless, and a bit worried she decides to call Captain Michaels.

Drew answers in a sing-song voice, "Hello there, Captain Andrew J. Michaels here."

"Drew, uh, Captain Michaels, is that you?"

"In the flesh, and with whom do I have the pleasure of speaking?"

"It's Marylyn McPherson, from work. Are you all right? I'm calling to see if you have heard anything from Ross."

"Oh, I'm better than all right! Of course, I've heard from Ross. Why else would I be drinking champagne at eleven in the morning? Didn't find the check until this morning. I had been so busy, either babysitting or visiting at the hospital that I hadn't bothered to look through the mail. I felt sure Ross would call if he'd made it in time. I was just about to give up hope when I saw the notice from the post office, for the certified letter."

The handset was already "rocketing towards the cradle" when Marylyn shouts, "I'll call you back." Out the door in a flash, she trips and almost falls over her wheelie, then she pin-balls down the two flights of stairs faster than any elevator ever did. Once in the lobby she slides to a stop at the row of mail boxes. After first dropping her keys her second attempt at extracting the mail is a success.

Buried in three days of junk mail, now on the floor, is a certified letter notification from the post office. Nine minutes later Marylyn's at the post office. She quickly signs for the letter and then carefully opens it. After looking wide-eyed at the amount, Marylyn checks the return address. CAPITAL NATIONAL BANK. She searches the envelope again. No note, no nothing. The check reveals only Ross's and a stranger's signature. The only extra is a small "Enjoy" printed on the lower left hand corner memo line.

She looked at the number again. WOW! Not being used to numbers that large she has to start with one million; she knew what that looks like. My God! It's three million four hundred and fifty thousand. Just like Ross said it would be—close to three and a half million dollars. She checks the envelope again; nothing is written on the back nor on the inside. Letdown, and a bit disappointed; Marylyn thinks that she must be the only person ever to have received a check of this size who still feels somewhat crestfallen.

Back upstairs, she sits at her kitchen table and stares at the check. Her mind is trying to process too many thoughts at once. The result is a giddy blissfulness. That ends with a stab of panic. She grabs a pen from her purse and endorses the back of the check, under which she writes DEPOSIT ONLY. This is another bit of wisdom from her grandfather.

Ross is still a mystery. Did she really know him? She certainly doesn't know where he is now or have any idea of how to get in touch with him. All she knows about him is that he has a sister named Andy, who lives in Connecticut. She remembers Ross saying that he had lived in Virginia and worked some in Florida. She also knows he is a surfer who often travels, often with a 'traveler'. None of these bits of information will help in discovering his whereabouts.

Picking up the phone she dials Drew Michaels again.

"Hello," a much straighter sounding Michaels answers.

"Drew, it's Marylyn again, you sound much better."

"You mean soberer, yeah I am. My bossy half, uh, I mean my better half cut me off. She says the airline has a zero tolerance for alcohol, and noted that I go back on call tomorrow at noon."

"Going back to work being a millionaire three times over, that's commendable, I think."

"To be honest Marylyn, I'm only going back for a few trips. Just long enough to revel in my fellow pilots' envy," says Drew.

"The reason for the call is to thank you and let you know that I got a check too. I can't find anything else except the two signatures on the check. Did you get a note or anything? Can you see if he scribbled anything on your envelope, like a phone number, or a return address? I'd really like to get in touch with Ross—to thank him—if nothing else," says Marylyn.

"Oh, I think there is something else you would like other than just a thank you Marylyn. I saw the way you two guys were looking at each other in Hawaii. Hang on, I'll check with the boss, and see if she knows anything about the envelope or the other signature."

"No envelope, but Liz, my wife, worked as a head cashier at a bank when I was flying for the Navy. She said 'that if you can get your check copied; she can locate the branch where the money actually came from.' That could narrow down Ross's location some. After you get it copied and deposited, call back for directions, and then you could stop by our house in Marina Del Ray. You two ladies can have a chat."

Marylyn makes two copies of her check in the bank waiting area; then sinks down in a sofa so plush that she isn't sure she can get back up. That is, without lying down and rolling over to get her feet back on the ground. When one of the two glass partitioned cubicles became available, Marylyn thanks the lady, but says she would rather wait. The reason being is that she wants to surprise her old high school nemesis, who is now an officer in the bank.

Preston Yeatman greets her with his ever present "Prom King" smile. He gives her his best condescending bow and says "Marylyn, delighted to see you. What can the bank do for you today?"

Armed with a quiver full of justified indignation, Marylyn began firing her verbally poisoned arrows. "I trust Tammy is doing well?" (Tammy his wife who has gained five times the five pounds Marylyn has gained since they were all in high school together. Tammy was Marylyn's immediate replacement after Marylyn wouldn't come across after the second date with Preston. Tammy was the little rich girl, until shortly after they got married and her daddy and his company ran into legal problems and both went bankrupt. It was Tammy who spread the salacious rumors about Marylyn, which if not endorsed by Yeatman, certainly were never denied by him.)

Preston nodded affirmatively, indicating that Tammy was indeed doing well.

"The kids are good too?" (Marylyn asks, knowing that both are little terrors since her cousin teaches them in school, and reports back to her on their misdeeds.)

"Yes, they're great. Thanks." A flip of his hand either a sign of surrender or wanting to change the subject, probably both. Marylyn didn't feel any sympathy but still she eases up some. She knows she has plenty of time to extract revenge for the old transgressions.

"The reason I'm here today is that I'd like to pay off the mortgage on my mother's house."

Preston cocks his head to the side and looks at the uniform she is still wearing. "You still a stewardess with the airlines?"

"Flight attendant, yes."

"One minute. Your Social?" Marylyn rattled off the nine digits so fast she has to repeat them so he can put them into his computer.

As the computer screen lights up, so does Preston's face. "Well, Ms. McPherson, it says here you have no savings account, and a total of $17.34 in your checking account. How exactly do you intend on paying off your mother's mortgage? You win a lottery or something?" Barely containing his glee, he sits up straight and beams a victory grin.

"You must be psychic, Preston. Let's talk more after you deposit this," she says, handing him the check.

Preston's eyes bulge, like a frog's eyes would on steroids.

"Is this real?" he croaks.

Trying to smile and not smirk. Marylyn says, "I think so Preston; but you're the banker, perhaps you should check."

"I'll be right back," says Preston. He takes the check and scurries over large wooden door and knocks. Apparently granted permission, he enters, and is inside for seven or eight minutes. Marylyn bathes in the warm glow of gloat for the first few minutes. Then, as time passes, she has the stomach flipping fear that maybe the whole thing was a farce. Is the check a fake? Was it all a con? Could she be charged with fraud—sent to jail? However, when Preston and another man emerged from the office, their beaming smiles confirmed the validity of the check.

Leaving Preston orphaned at his desk, the senior vice president whisks Marylyn back into his office. Thirty minutes later she leaves with five hundred dollars in cash, a new premium account, six counter checks, and the promise of two platinum credit cards. Not to mention, lots of free stuff coming within the week. She sails past a shocked Preston, saying, "Give my best to Tammy."

Back at her apartment Marylyn gives the landlord the rent check and her thirty days' notice simultaneously. Forty minutes later, after a long shower and a change of clothes, she stares at the printed copy of the check and vows that her next digs will have a bathtub, a really big bathtub. She is about to call Drew back when the phone rings.

"Hello," she says hoping that Ross is on the other end.

"Hello, is this Marylyn?" says a soft accented voice.

"Yes, can you tell me what this call is about?" As soon as this telemarketer mentions credit cards or free vacations, Marylyn will ask to be taken off their call list and hang up.

"I am Simone Alverez, and this call is from Ross, Ross Sheehan; he is your friend?"

"Yes, I'm sorry I didn't call you back, Simone. I thought you were a telemarketer."

"No, I work for Gateway Airlines here in LA. Ross wanted you to know that I got him on a plane to Chicago. He would have arrived there at 11:25 Monday morning."

"Thanks so much, Simone, at least now I know how he made it that far. By the way, did he have you write your name and address on an envelope?"

"Yes," and he said I was in with a chance for a big wind, and it could make my dreams come true.

"Simone, I'm pretty sure he said, A BIG WIN. Have you checked your mail lately?"

"No, my family, who live in LA, all have only one mail box at the post office. My brother-in-law, he has the key."

"Simone, you need to get the key and go to the mail box. You need to bring two picture ID's with you. In the mailbox, there should be a note with your name on it. Take it to a clerk behind the counter. After you sign for it, he will give you a letter. Inside that letter will be a very large check, made out to you. This is important Simone, write DEPOSIT ONLY on the back, before you even sign your name. Then take it to a bank immediately and deposit it. Call me later or I'll call you back. Thanks so much for helping Ross and all the rest of us on the envelope as well."

Now, how Ross got to Chicago is no longer a mystery, but with no buddy passes how did Ross get from Chicago to a lottery office somewhere in Virginia by 5:00 Monday afternoon? That question though pales in comparison to where is he now, and why hasn't he called? You can call it being stubborn, dedicated, or relentless but once Marylyn starts working on a problem she is there for the duration.

Drew answers the phone and says, "I was trying to tell you, the check came by certified mail, and to go to the post office, but I guess, you figured that out."

"Sorry, I got a little impatient Drew, but it's not every day a girl becomes a 'millionairess.' Is that even a word? Never mind, back to tracking down Ross. I've got a pen and paper handy so I'm ready to write down your address."

Once written down Marylyn says, "Thanks Drew, I should be there within the hour. First I have to call my mom and sister and then give the airline my thirty-second notice."

She is lucky to find a parking spot among the rows of newer and more expensive cars. After locking hers, Marylyn looks back at her dull red, seven-year-old Mustang. She thinks about getting a new one, then changes her mind and decides she likes the fact that her little red "Pony" stands out in a sea of four-wheel, foreign snobs.

After greetings and coffee, Marylyn, Drew and Liz Michaels seat themselves on the back patio. Liz wants to know how it all came together, and Marylyn, who is anxious to find— or at least get in contact with — Ross, gives her the short version.

Drew stands when she finishes saying, "Marylyn, you couldn't have found a better person to help track down Ross. It's possible that Liz has read every mystery, spy, and detective novel ever written. Her powers of deductive reasoning border on the telepathic. They also insure that I stay straight, obedient and monogamous."

"True darling. Now," Liz says, pressing the fingertips of both hands to her temples — "My psychic powers inform me that our girls need to be checked on by their father." Drew leaves with a slight bow.

"Don't know if I can live up to that billing," says Liz, "but let's see what we can find out. You have a copy of the check?" Marylyn reaches for her purse.

"Great, let's move into the kitchen where the computer is." Both girls switch to water as they sit on high stools at the island counter top. "This," says Liz, pointing to a row of numbers at the bottom left of the check, "is the American Bankers Association number, also known as the routing transit number. The first three numbers after the zero represent the institution, the next five numbers represent the branch that the money actually came from."

After a few minutes on the computer Liz announced "All right the name of the institution is Capital National and the money came from the Courthouse Capital National in Arlington Va."

"That makes sense," says Marylyn, "since it is the Virginia lottery that he won. I doubt the bank would be very forthcoming about the whereabouts of Ross Sheehan, even if they knew. How about the other signature next to Ross's, is there any help there?"

"Possibly. You see the "by" between the signatures, and the POA in parenthesis after the second name, Timothy Donald, PC?"

"Yes, I noticed that but I didn't know what it meant," says Marylyn.

"That means Timothy Donald has the power of attorney to sign checks for Ross Sheehan. The PC after Donald's name means he is a professional corporation. Usually that signifies an attorney, or a doctor, but anyone can be nominated to have power of attorney. Psychic powers aside, I would say you have two possible leads, The Arlington branch of Capital National Bank and Timothy Donald. He is no doubt an attorney; located in Northern Virginia, Arlington or Alexandria. They would be logical starting places."

"Thanks, Liz, you have given me some great pointers and inspired me. I might just buy the complete works of Sherlock Holmes and take a Pullman Sleeper Car cross country to DC and catch up on some sleuthing."

"That sounds like a wonderful trip. Would you like some company?"

"Love some, Drew can watch the girls, right?"

"Let me check," says Liz, and then in a loud voice "Honey, would you watch the girls while Marylyn and I take a train ride across the country?"

First comes the scraping and screeching of a chair across the kitchen floor. That's followed by the sound of utensils hitting the linoleum, next they hear glass shattering, and then muffled curses.

Marylyn smiles along with Liz, who says in a loud voice "Just kidding, honey."

During the ride home Marylyn thinks about the train and how relaxing it would be, but reality dictates that she finds Ross quickly. Time is of the essence. A leisurely train ride can be arranged later, maybe with Ross along for company. Checking today's mail, she is surprised to find that a new mobile phone has arrived. She had returned the smashed one back to the store in Hawaii. She hadn't held out much hope of getting it fixed, much less getting a free replacement.

The blinking red light on her telephone answering machine catches her attention as she enters the kitchen. A tingle of hope as the phone rings. Don't get your hopes up she tells herself; if he were going to call, he would have done so before now.

"Hello . . . hey Simone, I trust you have good news . . . really. I'm so happy for you and you're right, it is a very big number. I think everyone on the envelope received the same amount."

Simone goes on to explain that her brother-in-law, with the PO box key, is also an accountant. He accompanied her, and along with the bank manager, they decided to invest "the really big number" in US Treasuries. It seems like Simone is afraid to say "three million", like it would disappear if spoken out loud.

"That sounds both wise and safe; I think I may follow your lead and do the same. Simone, I'm going to do some traveling and try to catch up with Ross, so let me give you my new cellular phone number."

The first message is from her mother, making sure they are still on for dinner. The second and final message is from one "Preston Yeatman" who is overly cheerful and optimistic about their future personal and financial dealings together.

"Good luck with that!" Marylyn says out loud as she hangs up the phone.

*****

TRACKING ROSS

Vast, huge, immense and spacious are all words used to define cavernous. Which is the word Marylyn would use to describe Union Station in Washington, DC. This is where she would have been standing three days from now if she had taken the train. There are two reasons for her being at Union Station. One, from here the DC Metro can take you to just about anywhere in the area. Two, when she was here years ago, there were row after row of phone books on display. There are few public phone booths these days, and if they have phone directories, they are usually missing the page you need.

They are still here, the rows of phone books that she loved as a kid. She remembers them hanging like bats, each with its wings folded, ready to be pulled up and flopped open. Ten minutes later Marylyn has the street address of the bank in Arlington. However, finding T. Donald proves a bit more challenging. There are no discernible letters in Donald's first name other than the "T"; which is followed by what looked like a dull electrocardiogram graph.

There are fifty-one T. Donald's in the Arlington phone book alone. Marylyn dutifully purchases a small spiral notebook and copied down every number. There are an additional thirty-seven in the Alexandria phone book. Then, DC itself and the suburbs of southern Maryland enter into the landscape of possibilities. Enough she thinks—too much really. She needs a different angle of attack. Stuffing the notebook into her purse she retreats from the rows of phone books that welcomed her earlier. A few minutes of conversation at the information desk directs her to the ticket counter where she buys a ticket on the Metro.

Still armed with her wheelie, which has almost become an extension of her right arm, Marylyn departs

Union Station for the Metro Courthouse Station in Arlington. She leaves on the red line from Union Station, shortly after she transfers to the orange line at Metro Center. A quick dive under the Potomac and she pops up in Arlington at the Courthouse Station. Six minutes later she is standing right where Ross probably stood only a few days ago. She looks up at the grand steps leading to the entrance of the Capital National Bank.

Her mind has been churning ever since she got on the Metro; with a little luck, she may have found a shortcut to the location of the mysterious T. Donald. Once inside, Marylyn goes straight to the waiting area and is immediately shown into a glass paneled office cubicle. She explains to the young lady that she wants to know the interest rate for a CD in the amount of one hundred thousand dollars. As expected, the young lady excuses herself and returns momentarily with the branch manager, Kenny Mallard (according to his name tag). After introductions, Kenny leads Marylyn back to his office.

"Please, have a seat, Ms. McPherson; can I get you anything to drink?"

"No I'm fine, thanks."

"Betsy" nodding towards the cubicle "mentioned that you don't have an account with the bank. That makes one wonder why you would choose a new bank in which to deposit such a large sum? Not that I mind of course, just curious."

"That's understandable," says Marylyn. I recently received a piece of unexpected good fortune. A windfall, you might call it. I plan to be on the East Coast for a while, searching for my benefactor; and I thought this bank might help. Do you happen to remember a young man named, Ross Sheehan?"

"No," squirms Ken Mallard, "I mean, even if I did, the Bank places a high value on customer confidentiality."

"Again, I understand your position and hope that you will understand mine; that is, that even though your quote on the CD rate is ever so slightly higher than the one I now have; it's not significant enough to warrant a switch."

Marylyn stands up. "Thanks so much for your time, may I call you Kenny?"

"Certainly," he says, blushing slightly.

"Kenny, should I call a cab or can I just walk to Mr. Donald's office from here?"

"Oh, you can just walk, Tim's office is only . . ."

Ken Mallard's face goes from blushing pink to scarlet crimson in an instant. "Oh, you're good, Ms. McPherson, really good. It takes a pretty smooth operator to slick me, young lady, and you slicked me good."

"Sorry, Kenny, but you know a poor defenseless girl needs to use all her wits sometimes to get what she needs."

You hardly fit into either of those categories, Marylyn, poor or defenseless, and I have a feeling that Ro.. — whoever it is you're trying to track down is sorely overmatched."

"I hope you're right and thanks again Kenny; you've been a great help."

"Don't remind me," says Kenny, as he watches Marylyn and her wheelie depart.

A short and determined walk gets Marylyn to the storm door fronting the office of Timothy R. Donald. The 'T' mystery solved, Marylyn checks her reflection in the shimmering glass. The navy-blue skirt, cinched with a bright red belt, and topped with a white blouse seemed both patriotic and stylish. A casual finger comb and flip of her hair and she obeys the "OPEN, COME IN" sign.

A bell sounds as Marylyn crosses the threshold and she is met by a "Hello" from a woman sitting behind a work station. "If you're here about the job, I'm sorry, but the position has already been filled."

144

"No," says Marylyn chuckling to herself, "I'm not here about the job."

"Tim is in court and will be for the rest of the afternoon. I'm Tara Donald his wife, and soon to be ex-paralegal. Is there anything that I can help you with?"

"My name is Marylyn McPherson and I'm looking for a fella who did me a good turn. He apparently met with your husband just last week. Maybe you remember him, Ross Sheehan?"

Clearly, the name sent a jolt through Tara. She recovers quickly saying "I can't say if he's been here or not, you know, client confidentiality and all that. Maybe Tim would be able help you.

"Marylyn reaches into her purse, retrieves a copy of her check, and presents it to Tara. "Do you think Tim would remember signing this?"

Tara is openly surprised as she has never seen any of the checks herself. "So you're one of those?"

"If by that you mean one of "those" who helped Ross along on his journey, then yes I am."

"Well, congratulations! Tim and I also benefited from . . . oops! so much for client confidentiality," cringes Tara.

"Don't worry, I'm not going to mention this to anyone. I'm just trying to get a lead on where Ross went after he left here. Tara look, I just met Ross a week ago; spent about ten hours with him on a plane. Only a small part of that time were we alone. I know that's not enough time to really get to know someone. But there was something — a spark, a feeling, an emotion you rarely get. I can't explain it; but I want to pursue it, to see if it was real or just hormones."

"I know those feelings Marylyn; I had similar ones when I met Tim. You're sure it's something, you're just not sure what that something is." Tara closes her eyes for a moment; reaches into a desk drawer and pulls out a battered envelope. She smooths it out, "Tim picked this out of the trash at the bank after he saw Ross throw it away. It's provenance, or history of owner- ship is clear. However, whether it's part of the confidentiality pact with the client is uncertain, at least to me. This situation is making me nervous, and when I get nervous, I have to pee. You will have to excuse me for a moment while I go to the ladies."

As soon as she hears the bathroom door shut, Marylyn whips out her notebook and pen. Immediately she begins copying the information from the envelope as fast as she can.

When Tara returns, the envelope and Marylyn are exactly as they were when she left. "Sorry that I couldn't have been more help Marylyn, but there is nothing else I can tell you."

Marylyn rises and offers Tara a folded sheet of paper. "I understand Tara, really I do. Here is my new cellular phone number; if you hear from Ross please pass it on to him. I hope to have the pleasure of you and Tim's company in the future."

"Good luck," says Tara as Marylyn and her wheelie exit down the brick path back towards the Metro Station.

****

THE ENVELOPE

At the Courthouse Metro Marylyn changes modes of transportation and takes a taxi to the Key Bridge Marriott. There, with her new credit card, she books a room with a Jacuzzi tub and within minutes is submersed in soothing bubbles. The inadvertent nap, while still in the tub, made her fingers look like elongated pink prunes. Not to worry. Her hair is wrapped in a towel, her body is dry, and she's covered in a fluffy hotel robe. Pajama City! Marylyn dives under the down comforter.

After a buffet breakfast at the Hotel the next morning, Marylyn takes advantage of the courtesy van and goes to the National Mall. A long, leisurely walk leads her to the Air and Space Museum, where she is determined to complete a tour she started three years before.

Wowed by the Smithsonian as usual, she returns to the hotel refreshed and re-energized. Sitting down at the desk she takes out her notebook and carefully reads through all the names, addresses and phone numbers she had copied from the envelope in Tim's office. They seem to be in some sort of chronological order. The first one is just a single name: "Andy." Marylyn is pretty sure that Andy is Ross's sister.

The next three, John, Storkie, and Rose, all have Australian addresses and phone exchanges. The next name number 5, is her very own. Captain Drew Michaels follows at number 6, and then Simone, who is lucky number 7. Martin Maher, from Denver, is number 8 and number 9 is Sampson Samuels, who according to his 703-area code, lives nearby. Adding to the mystery are two more names, Kelvin Butterworth and Franklin Dearner. The list of numbers ends at nine — the list of names totals eleven. Ross' name is not on the list.

It would have been helpful if Ross had written down his sister's phone number an address or her last name. Obviously, he already knew them and had written the list for himself, not for her. Reality bites and sometimes it sucks. It's a bit early to call California or Denver, and it's the middle of the night in Australia. That leaves Sampson Samuels right here in Northern Virginia. The phone is picked up on the second ring by a person who sounds like he is somewhere between a man and a boy. "The Samuels' residence."

"Hello, my name is Marylyn McPherson and . . . "

"Dad!" the young man screeches, "there's a Marylyn on the phone; I think she's one of those teleprompters."

Silence, as Marylyn thinks about how she almost cut off Simone for the same wrong reason. A real pain in the ass those telemarketers are becoming.

"Yes," came the gruff reply from a deep-voiced adult male.

Quickly, Marylyn says, "I'm not a telemarketer; I'm looking for Ross Sheehan."

"Why? Why would you be looking for Ross?"

"First, are you the Sampson Samuels whose name Ross wrote on the envelope?"

"You know about that?" asks Sampson.

"Yes, and I also helped Ross as you no doubt did and like me, you probably received a humongous check last week. My name is Marylyn McPherson and I'm the flight attendant that got him from Australia to California."

"Well, says Sampson "if you got the same amount on your check as I did on mine, you're certainly not looking for money from Ross, so why are you trying to find him?"

"Are you a romantic, Sampson?"

"Me a romantic? Not now, I was once and look what it brought me, an eleven-year-old son. Speaking of him, hang-up the extension, Marcus."

"To answer your question, Sampson, I'm looking for Ross because even though our time together was short, I thought we had something special going for us. We planned to get together after the lottery, whether Ross was successful or not. He had my address and phone number; just like he, no doubt, had yours. He   hasn't gotten in contact with me; how about you, heard from him other than the check?" —silence— "didn't think so." And why did he throw the envelope with all our names and numbers on it in the trash? I don't know why but I know he did it on purpose. It's as if he wants to . . . disavow ever knowing any of us."

"That doesn't make sense; how do you know all this? And how did you get my number?'

"I met with Tara Donald today; she is the wife of Tim Donald, the lawyer who helped Ross distribute the lottery money. Tara had Ross's envelope and let me sneak a peek; I copied down everything that was on it. Tara said, Ross threw the envelope away after he and Tim had finished writing the checks. That's how I got your number along with everyone else's."

"I know Tim Donald, the lawyer," says Sampson. "Mike and I coached him in Pop Warner football. I'll ask him if he knows anything about where Ross is."

"Ross is in Daytona Beach," comes a voice, blasting forth over the phone

"I told you to hang up, Marcus!"

"Daytona Beach? Who said that?" asks Marylyn.

"That is from eleven-year-old Professor Marcus Samuels. Graduate of The University of Nowhere, majoring in Absolutely Nothing, and apparently getting his information from the Encyclopedia Brainemptia."

"Very funny Dad, but you weren't there when Ross and I were talking about surfing; and he said he would teach me how to surf over the holidays. He said if I could talk you into driving me down to Daytona Beach; he'd give me free surfing lessons. Please Dad, can we go? The Thanksgiving holidays will be here soon and I'm already packed."

"Now Marylyn, you can understand why I stopped being a romantic after just one attempt to create a normal human being," laughs Sampson.

In the background, Marylyn hears; "She sounds nice, dad, can we invite her for dinner?"

"Shush Marcus. Marylyn, you said you were at Tim's office today. Are you still in the area?"

"Yes, I'm staying at the Key Bridge Marriott."

"That's just around the corner from our house. Tonight, Gran Nanna, my mother, is cooking chicken and dumplings, same dinner as when Ross was here last week. If you're interested, Marcus and I can pick you up in say, well how about six fifteen?"

"Sounds delicious. I'll be waiting outside."

At exactly six fifteen, a small chipmunk-cheeked young male pops out of the passenger side of a Cadillac limousine, and opens the rear door. He bows and grins at Marylyn with a large sparkling smile and impossibly white teeth.

"Good evening, you must be Marcus," she says.

Sampson turns the corner around the hood, extends his hand, and says, "Sampson Samuels, father of this seemingly now mute young man. Why don't you have a seat in the back Marylyn? Marcus, you mind the door, and then get back in the front seat with me.

"Once off the grounds of the Marriott, Sampson says, "Let me guess, California?"

"Correct, how'd you know?"

"The accent, or actually, the lack of an accent."
Then in a low, whispered growl, "Turn around Marcus it's
impolite to stare."

"Marylyn, you know that romance thing you were
talking about?" He acknowledges her nod in the rearview
mirror. "Well, it's all around here now. My mother has a
crush on your friend, Ross, and my son seems to have a
crush on you."

Marcus pulls back his fist as if to punch Sampson
on the arm for the embarrassing comment. "Marcus,"
Sampson says in a stern voice, "You start thinking you're
big enough to hit me, I just might start thinking you're big
enough for me to return the favor."

"I'm sorry, dad but . . ."

"I'm sorry, too, son. I shouldn't have teased you
about having a crush on Marylyn. She is a pretty girl and
really, I wouldn't blame you if you did." Conspiratorial
grins flash between the two of them.

"So Marylyn, now that you're rich, what are you
going to do with your money?"

"Well, some of it make sure that my mom and sister
are financially secure, at least for the time being. The rest I
put in US Treasuries, except for a few "fun tickets" for
myself."

"How about you, Sampson, what are you going to
do with all that new-found loot?"

"Like you, I set aside some to take care of my
family."

"Yeah!" interjects Marcus.

"That's for college Marcus, not for games and
goofing."

"My mother and I put a substantial amount into
bank CD's for safety. The rest will be used to renovate, and
upgrade, my limousine service."

"Actually those words are a bit deceptive. I only
had one second hand limousine, and blew that up Monday

getting Ross to the lottery. This is a loaner until next week, when my new one arrives. My best friend Mike, a state trooper, is going to take early retirement and he will become a partner. The second limousine will be a stretch Lincoln Town Car, due to be delivered about a week later."

"Dad! You blew up the limo?" a stunned Marcus asks.

"Not one word to Gran Nanna! You hear. You let that slip, young man, and you won't be able to sit down until you're old enough to shave."

After their introductions Marylyn and Gran Nanna go to their neutral corners. Actually, Gran Nanna returns to the kitchen, and Marylyn sits with Marcus and Sampson in the den. At first, Sampson can't pinpoint the subtle differences in Gran Nanna, then it hits him. She actually put on a small amount of makeup and, possibly, even a hint of perfume? He turns his head, and sniffs back towards the kitchen, and realizes that Marcus is giving him a "what took you so long" look.

Dinner is mostly finished, and well deserved compliments delivered, and accepted, when Gran Nanna asks Marylyn the question. "Marylyn, why are you so fired up on finding Ross?"

"Well, Ms. Samuels, if a man sent you a check for three and a half million dollars, wouldn't you at least like to thank him? Ross had my name and information on his envelope, as he did Sampson's, and two other 'people on the envelope' that I have talked with. Other than receiving their checks, no one has heard a word from Ross. That envelope, with all our names on it, was rescued from a trash can. Ross's lawyer, Tim Donald took it out of a trash can in the bank. The fact is, I care about Ross, and now, I'm a bit concerned."

"On the flight from Australia to Hawaii, I got to know Ross, found him easy to feel close to, no doubt just as you all did when Ross was here. Tell me that the three of you don't have a warm place in your heart for him, besides the money. Don't you find it strange that you haven't heard from him? He said he would call me whether he got to the lottery in time or not. Ross also made it a point that he never breaks his word, and I believe him."

"Gran Nanna clears her throat saying, "Marylyn, please call me 'Nan.' Ms. Samuels is for the UPS driver. You're right. Ross should have called by now. Sampson, is this lawyer, Donald, is he the same little Timmy Donald that you and Mike coached in Pee Wee football?"

"Yes ma`am," says Sampson, "but you know it's called Pop Warner football, and "Little Timmy" is 6'4" now.

"Certainly I know what it's called, but saying 'Pee Wee' reminds me of how cute you little fellas were."

"Anyway yes," says Sampson, "it's the same Tim Donald. Mike took Ross by Tim's office after the arbitration hearing after he dropped me off here."

"Then," Gran Nanna says, "you call Tim Donald first thing in the morning and tell him to get busy finding Ross. Tell him there will be no more of my pecan pie for him if he doesn't help."

School nights meant homework and an early bed time for Marcus, but not before he receives a hug and goodnight kiss on the cheek from Marylyn, which rendered him catatonic.

On the drive back to the Marriott, Sampson tells Marylyn the true tale of his and Ross's adventurous charge to the lottery. He also gives her a quick synopsis of the arbitration hearing. Sampson agrees with Marylyn that Ross is a man of his word, and should have called. He also thinks that Ross is probably in Daytona Beach, just like Marcus said. The fact that Ross has not been in touch with either of them is disturbing.

Once back in her room, Marylyn realizes that it's still early on the West Coast. She decides to check with

Captain Michaels and Simone, but neither had heard from Ross. Going down the list, she finds Martin Maher's phone number in Colorado. Mountain time; it's before nine there. The phone is picked up immediately by, "Becky England!" whose voice pierces with a pitch so high, that it would have sent Cujo scurrying away like a Chihuahua. Marylyn introduces herself as a friend of a friend and explains that she is trying to get in touch with Martin Maher.

Martin, according to his aunt Becky, called two days ago saying he found a new sponsor and is now playing in a professional golf tournament in Orlando, Florida. He said he would call back again Friday evening and let Becky know if he made the weekend cut. Marylyn leaves her number and asks to have Martin call her as soon as it is convenient.

She has a good idea who Martin's new sponsor is, and that Martin probably doesn't need to play golf for a living anymore, if he chose not to. She also knows that golfers are mad, and you can never tell what they might do. After that completely befuddling conclusion, she decides to save the Jacuzzi for the morning, and to surrender to the down comforter tonight.

***

WESTERN UNION

A change in the monotonous motion of the train pokes me awake, just in time to see an elongated sign announcing our arrival in Cary, North Carolina. In answer to my questioning look, a fellow passenger informs me that we have twenty minutes in Cary to grab a snack and stretch our legs.

For the first time in three days, I wake up feeling tired. This is a welcome change from the ever-present adrenalin rush that has kept me continuously striving for the finish line. No more schedules, planes, deadlines or court appearances on the horizon. Peace . . . sort of.

The Western Union sign gives me an idea, a coward's solution. I go inside where the agent informs me that, yes, they still send telegrams, but probably not for much longer. They mostly moved money now, the telegram was going the way of the Pony Express.

I know Andy will be worried if she doesn't hear from me. If you make my sister worry then you make her mad, and you don't want to see Andy mad—hence the telegram. A solid, but mostly a cowardly defense against the screaming, berating and torrent of verbal abuse that a phone call to my sister would evoke.

Therefor I send: SUCCESS! YOU'RE RICH. I'M STOKED. RELAX SLOWLY, ROSS."

When I return to the train, my guilty feelings about Marylyn deepen. Although I've kept my financial word to her and the other participants, I know Marylyn deserves more than a check. We had an emotional bonding that was much stronger than a friendship. I'm not going anywhere near the "L" word but it was certainly heavier than a flirtation or a quick hook up.

Back in my super saver seat, I decide to call
Marylyn at the next stop. I'll apologize for my no class,
wimpy-ass, short-sighted, chicken-shit behavior and invite
her down to Florida.

The openings between cars on a stroll through the
train is a perfect weather predictor. Today is warm and
humid, with ocean breezes. The view from these
observation posts is also a great location indicator. If the
sight of wild palm trees isn't enough, the nail in the coffin
for my location is the sign we slide by that spells out
"Jacksonville, Fla." Alas, I have used up my daily
allotment of deductive reasoning powers.

Reaching for the envelope, which also doubles as an
address book, I retrieve only my passport. Then I
remember, I tossed my envelope at the bank, apparently
trying to erase those demons who have conspired to make
me feel sorry for myself. Hang on air head there is no
conspiracy; you just don't want to accept that what
happened is all your doing, your responsibility. Like a
golfer after a bad shot throwing a ball, a club, or even a
caddy into the nearest body of water. Thus, demonstrating
that it is an outside agency that caused the disaster—
certainly not the golfer himself.

Now what? Call the bank? Track down Kenny
Mallard? Ask him to sort through yesterday's trash? Wait!
Tim made a copy of the people names and their
information. Thank the Lord; I saved his card. There are
three numbers on Tim's card: office, home and cell. Tim
has hand written the last two numbers in ball point. Getting
two dollars' worth of quarters left me with only a twenty-
dollar bill. I decide to try the office first, even though it's
still a little before nine.

I'm shocked when the operator says, "Please
deposit one dollar and fifty cents for the first three
minutes." That seems outrageous, but it's been forever

since I've used a pay phone. Regardless, I have no choice but to comply.

Tim reacts as if it has been weeks, instead of hours, since we have last seen each other. He rambles on until finally, I have to interrupt. "Tim, I'm sorry, but I'm stopped in the train station in Jacksonville, Florida and time and quarters are both in short supply. I need the phone number of Marylyn McPherson, from the people on envelope; you made your own copy, right?"

"Sure. It's in your file in my office. I've just walked in the door . . . hang on a sec, I'll get it."

Time, the almost forgotten enemy rears its head again and slows its pace to a crawl. The operator interrupts the painful monotony with panic, saying, "Please deposit fifty cents for each additional minute you wish to add." After the dinging sound of the quarters dropping there is only silence, a very still silence. Fearing that the next sound heard will be that of a dial tone; I take a deep breath and sort of pray.

The prayer is answered by Tim. "Hey Ross, you know, Tara and I just might come down and . . . "

"Sorry, Tim, just the number please, I'm about out of time and quarters."

The last of Marylyn's numbers is followed immediately by the dial tone. There had been no time for "Thanks" or even a "Goodbye". Now, the porter is waving at me like a school crossing guard trying to hurry along a slow child.

Slumped in my seat, I have to fight not to feel sorry for myself. On the edge of self-pity, a subtle brain smile lifts my spirits. The smile continues to expand as the corners of my still chapped lips crack in pain. The past three or four days have been a whirlwind of unlikely, if not impossible events: a two day ten-thousand-mile journey ending in the making of ten brand new millionaires. My eyes close, and a warmth glows inside me.

This could be the story I've been looking for. This chain of luck, braided together with fate and karma could be the core of the book that I always intended to write. This actually happened and all the people are real. God knows the money is real. Can I write about something that really happened and make a book of fiction out of it? I knew instantly that I could; knew that this was my chance. Now is the time to get off my ass and write a book. When we pull into Daytona in a little less than two hours, the first thing I'm going to buy is some notebooks and pens.

*****

BOOK II

HEADING SOUTH

The next morning after a delightful Jacuzzi and a room service breakfast, Marylyn decides to make her own list.
1. Andy (Sheehan) last name? Sister? Check? No address or phone.
2. John Couldwell? Check? address and phone (yes) Australia. (find time difference)
3. Storkie (no last name) Check? address and phone (yes) Australia - call.
4. Rose Bellsome. Check? address and phone (yes) Australia.
5. Marylyn McPherson. Check 3.45m. "I like the looks of that!"
6. Capt. Drew Michaels. Check 3.45m.
7. Simone Alverez. Check 3.45m.
8. Martin Maher. address and phone? (yes) Check? (waiting return call)
9. Sampson Samuels. Check 3.45m.
10. There is no number 10, of course not — that would be Ross, and why would he write his own name down? On the other hand, why wouldn't he? I just wrote my own name down.

Then, there are two more names, without numbers.
A.) KELVIN BUTTERWORTH
B.) FRANKLIN DEARNER

This is puzzling, almost to the point of becoming a worry. She needs to find out who these last two names belong to and figure out why they're on Ross' list. Marylyn calls the front desk; tells them she is checking out and requests a cab to Union Station. Giving the down comforter a final goodbye glance, she grabs the handle of her trusty wheelie and marches out the door.

Feeling a little guilty doesn't stop Marylyn from purchasing a pricey ticket to Daytona Beach on the 97 Silver Meteor. It cost her almost as much as her air fare did to fly across country.   Once on board she finds her View-Liner bedroom to be compact but cozy. It has a bench sofa next to the window; during dinner, a conductor will fold it out into a comfortable bed. She tries her new phone with no success, unless you count a blinking "searching" message a success. Marylyn settles on the sofa.

Being cut off from the outside world is relaxing. The sun is setting; its rays of dusty light splatter through the trees and dive into the moving train so fast that it strains Marylyn's eyes. She draws the shade down and picks up her detective novel. This leads to a long an unplanned nap. Marylyn awakes to a polite knock. The knock is followed by a deep baritone voice. "Dinner is now being served in the dining car." After dinner, she is rocked to sleep by the comforting tugging, and pulling of the train.

*****

DOWN UNDER

The view from Mick O'Brien's second story General Manager's office includes the four acres of asphalt that surround "Car Mart Australia". This offers plenty of room to park and display the hundreds of automobiles for sale here. Mick looks down at his new star: a 1994 Land Rover Defender parked up on the grassy mound. Not the newest, not the fastest, nor the most expensive, but surely the one piquing the most interest. A Land Rover Defender is seen around here about as often as an albino kangaroo wearing a pair of flip flops.

Two cars, both ready for the wreckers, turn off the Pacific Highway and onto the dealership road. One car comes from the north, the other from the south. Mick watches as both of them ignore the showroom and stop instead at the grassy knoll to check out the Defender. A single young man steps out of each vehicle, and then like a pair of gunslingers, cautiously approach the Land Rover. They circle the car, remaining on opposite sides of the car. The Rover is always in between them like a boxing referee. Mick, fearing a punch-up, quickly skips down the stairs and jumps into the golf cart.

As he gets closer, Mick sees that if it comes to blows, it wouldn't look to be much of a contest. One bloke is almost half a foot above six feet and the other about same measure below that mark. Mick makes sure that the wheels chirp as he slams on the brakes to get their attention. Sliding off the seat, he stands and says, "G'day gentlemen. You blokes interested in a test drive?"

Getting small nods from both, he hands the keys to the shorter of the two and says, "Fine, the name's Mick, you know how to get Macauley's headland.

"No worries, mate, I'm Kelvin Butterworth."

"Great. I'll sit in the back. You chauffeur the two us out to Macauleys, Kelvin; the long drink of water can drive us back."

"The long drink of water looks down at Mick and says, "You can call me Storkie."

Macauleys is a craggy finger of a headland that protrudes several hundred meters out into the Pacific, forming a natural fish trap and a pretty fair surfing spot. Mick makes sure introductions are made, between the two, when they arrive. They park on the bluff overlooking the beach, where the small talk continues. After watching the local kids ride some choppy waves, Kelvin and Storkie switch seats. Mick asks Kelvin, "how did you like driving the Defender?"

"Liked it a lot," says Kelvin, "fact is, I reckon I'll take it."

"Hang on there mate," says Storkie, "I haven't had me turn at the wheel yet; nor have I had my say in who buys the car. Remember, I was the first to pull up alongside this beast."

"Look," interrupts Mick, "I'll make sure you both have an equal chance to buy this car, even if we have to toss a coin for it. First, we have to know who is serious about buying it."

"I'm serious," says Kelvin. "I'll write you a check soon as we get back."

"Bullshit! Where would you come up with that much cash?" says Storkie. Then quickly realizes that his appearance, and his mode of transportation, are no better than Kelvin's. He apologizes. "Sorry mate, I was judging a book by its cover; and my cover's no better than yours."

Kelvin can't resist. "Just so you know mate, buying this won't stretch me budget. I'll tell you a bit of a yarn. Seems a certain Yank was down on his luck and needed a ride. I give him a lift from Noosa all the way down to here, to Coffs. To show his thanks, he says he'll send me some gas money for me being such a wonderful bloke. True to his word, he sends me a very large check in US dollars. It comes to more than $300,000 Australian. Ross, ah! what a cheeky bastard."

"Ross! Did you say Ross? A yank two weeks ago? Are you kidding me?" roars Storkie. "This is crazy! This is the bloody Twilight Zone. It has to be one and the same person. This guy you gave a ride to, this yank, Ross, he has to be the same guy I flew down to Sydney — the same Ross that said he'd give me ten percent of his winnings, if he made back to the Virginia lottery in time? The same Ross Sheehan who sent me a certified check for more than three million for flying him to Sydney."

"Three million! crikey, mate," says Kelvin, "wished I'd had a plane instead of a car"

"Has to be the same guy," says Storkie "Unless there's another mad yank named Ross running around, sending off checks for three hundred thousand here, and three million there."

"I think I have just witnessed the mother of all unlikely coincidences," murmurs Mick from the back seat.

As they drive back to the dealership, Kelvin and Storkie exchange their "travels with Ross" stories. Kelvin saying what a totally hung-over, broke mess Ross was when he let him off in Coffs first thing that Saturday morning. Then Storkie recounts his and Ross's exciting flight later that same morning, down to within twenty kilometers of the Sydney Airport. The last Storkie had seen of Ross was him rolling away from the horizontal stabilizer in a gritty cloud of prop wash.

Mick has the back door open before the wheels came to a full stop. Once he is out of the car, he speaks to both of them through the driver's side window. "Right, you guys are good mates now, so let's settle this peaceably. If you both want it toss a coin for it. Either way, if one of you decides to buy the Rover, come up to the office and we'll draw up the paper work. I've got to go. I can't believe what just happened. I need a beer."

Kelvin and Storkie chat for a bit exchanging phone numbers and discover that besides both liking the Defender, they also have tennis in common. Storkie is not as dead set on having the Defender as Kelvin, but decides to flip for it anyway. When Storkie has a coin ready, he says, "You call it." When the coin becomes airborne, Kelvin barks "Heads!"

Storkie catches it in the palm of one hand and slaps it down on the opposite wrist. He peeks under the hand covering the coin. Casually he picks it up and slips it back into his pocket, saying, "Good on you mate, it's yours."

*****

DAYTONA BEACH

Once off the train, it surprises Ross how quickly his "rail legs" adapt to terra firma. The only cashier in the Daytona Beach Rail Depot is not pleased when he asks her for five dollars' worth of quarters. The grimace on her face could not have been more sour if she had been asked to crack open a Faberge Egg, rather than a roll of quarters.

Armed with plenty of silver bullets Ross chooses the only one of the three phone booths that actually has a phone in it. After dialing Marylyn's number, a recorded voice directs Ross to deposit two dollars for the first three minutes. After the eighth quarter drops into metallic limbo a phone begins to ring in far off California. It's answered after the fourth ring with Marylyn's voice, "Hi, sorry I'm not in right now . . ."

"SHIT! Answering machine." Ross hangs up as fast as he can. Then, could only listen in despair as the quarters eject from limbo land, hang silently in midair, before crashing into an empty echoing metal box. This is not the sound he had hoped for. Ross had been hoping to hear the tune of eight quarters commingling and together clanking into the coin return.

What a dork, what a nincomfocknpoop, Ross thought. Wasting forty percent of my stash of quarters while still having three minutes to leave a message. What was that, some type of financial phone panic that stripped me of all coolness, not to mention any hint of a brain cell. No choice but a redo. Each time Ross' thumb releases another quarter to join the dearly departed eight, the old ego takes another hit.

After listening to the full message, Ross apologizes for not calling sooner and leaves word that he will call back as soon as he has a contact number.

Purchasing an all-day pass on the bus gets Ross to the beach; once there it's an easy walk to his old hang out, "The Gazebo". Thinking back, Ross's means of transportation have been spiraling downhill, starting with a private jet from Chicago. then, down to a limousine, in DC, a train to Florida, a bus to the beach, and now walking.

Inside the Gazebo, Ross is welcomed like a regular on the tv show "Cheers". This is despite the fact that no one here has seen or heard from him in seven months. There are no questions about where or how he's been, just an immediate reenlistment into the family 'Gazebo'. Floridians are used to the returning snow birds, tax sliders, and those seeking, "The Endless Summer".

After being bought enough "welcome back" beers to become mellow, Ross sees his former boss, Hap, come through the door. After their first beer Ross has his old job back — surf instructor. Then, after two more beers, he has a place to stay until Hap's wife comes back from their seventh or so trial separation. Hap says that she left yesterday and that these trial separations (vacations?) last anywhere between one and three weeks. Ross is politely bombed, and super stoked at having a place to stay, and a job. The two of them finally wobble out the door at closing time.

The next day, Ross borrows Hap's three-wheeler and opens up "West Wind Surfboard Rentals and Lessons". Ross' cut is to keep thirty of the fifty dollars they charge for an hour lesson. Two late afternoon lessons put sixty bucks in his pocket, allowing him to go to the mall after work and purchase some toiletries. The first items he buys after these necessities are pens and notebooks, for his new career as a writer. It was even possible to envision a word processor, or maybe even a computer, in the future.

Ross plans to go to the bank tomorrow and see about getting his credit cards reissued; then he needs to buy one of those cellular telephones like Marylyn tried to gift him in Hawaii. He loads up on quarters again as he plans to call her at lunch tomorrow and to leave Hap's phone number on her machine. She couldn't call him back, if he didn't leave a number to call him back on. Deductive reasoning at its finest.

**

As soon as Marylyn steps off the train in Raleigh, North Carolina, she checks her phone and sees that she has service. Hoping for news of Ross, she dials Capt. Drew Matthew's number. Liz answers, noting that Drew isn't in, but that neither of them have heard anything from Ross. Liz then asks Marylyn if she knows anything about "Select Jets."

"Only that it's a popular charter jet company catering to the very rich. You pay an enormous amount, a hundred thousand dollars plus for a block of twenty-five hours and, viola` — you have your own private jet." Marylyn explains that she knew of a former pilot at Eastern who landed a job with Select Jets, and that most of the other pilots were envious.

"Well," says Liz, "add another pilot to that list. Drew just went for an interview with them. He says he can put down ten percent on a new Learjet and put it in Select Jets' pool of planes. Then, he plans to fly with them for seven years, sell the Lear, retire, play golf, and coach the girls in their chosen sports."

"Sounds like a plan, I wish you both luck," says Marylyn.

"Thanks, but I don't need a lot of luck. The girls have a half a million-dollar trust fund for their educations or rehab clinics, whichever comes first. I, have a million of my own, for fun clothes, furthering my education, or possibly a rehab clinic."

"Hey Liz, Sorry, the train is re-boarding and I've got to go. Call if you hear from Ross. Bye."

Just as she is about to step up into the train, Marylyn's phone rings. Standing on the wooden platform step the porter has placed there she searches in her purse for the phone.

"Mam, please, you must get on the train now," says the overly polite porter.

Grabbing the long silver handle, Marylyn pulls herself up between the two rail cars and hears, "Hello, Marylyn? This is Martin Maher; my aunt Becky says you called about Ross."

The porter is now crowding her with the wooden step held in front of him. "I'm sorry," says the still polite porter, "but you must be inside a rail car before the train can safely leave the station."

"Of course my fault", says Marylyn as she presses the long silver bar. The door obeys and slides open. Once inside the car she tries to continue the call to no avail. Looking at her phone she sees the dreaded "searching" marching continuously across the screen.

**

Other than the coach light over the front door, the rest of the house is completely dark. Silently, Ross let himself into Hap's house so as not to disturb his host. Guessing his way into the kitchen, he is painfully reminded that shins are the part of the human anatomy used to locate low furniture in dark places. Cracking the refrigerator door gives him enough light to see an antique rotary phone hanging on the wall. There is just enough light to copy the number from the center of the rotary wheel in to one of his new notebooks.

As Ross slides in between the fresh crisp sheets, he realizes that the night before he had never actually gotten into bed. He had merely passed out on top of the bedspread. Naked, Ross's sunburned body merges with the cool sheets to form a perfect temperature. Ross is exhausted from travel, work and being on the beach all day; these make up the ideal ingredients for immediate sleep. Even though his body feels anesthetized his mind is still wide awake. Is jet lag making him too tired to go to sleep? What is that? A double negative wrapped up in an oxymoron? He really needs some sleep to calm his mind.

His thoughts settled on Marylyn and what would happen next. If indeed, there is a next. He has really been taken by her, not just a flirt or a fling, but what is the word? Certainly, not the "L" word, maybe more like, "smitten". No, way too silly. Go to sleep stupid.

The next morning Marylyn is checking into the Residence Inn in Daytona at the same time that Ross is opening up West Wind Surfboard Rentals. Only the fate fairies are aware that, at this moment, Ross and Marylyn are less than a mile apart.

Following a quick shower, Marylyn's first call is to Martin Maher, his number having been captured by the "recent calls" memory on her phone. Martin picks before the first ring is complete, "Hello, look, whoever this is, I've got a tee time in forty minutes, so please make it quick, or I can call you back after the round."

"Hi, Martin, this is Marylyn McPherson. You called me after I left my number with your aunt and then, inadvertently, I cut you off when I got back on the train in Raleigh. The reason for the call is that I see your name on Ross Sheehan's envelope along with mine and others. Two quick questions: have you heard from Ross? and how did your name get on the envelope?"

"OK Marylyn, here's the skinny. I met Ross in Chicago, at O'Hare and together we scammed a plane ride for him to DC. Apparently, he made it to his destination on time because I've been more than suitably rewarded by a large check. Other than that, as much as I look forward to it, I have not heard a thing from him."

"Did your check start with a three and have two commas in it?"

"Hold on, I'll have to write it down; I'm not used to numbers that big. Yep two commas, never thought of it that way. So, Marylyn, did you help Ross get to DC, too? I mean, he had no money and he came all the way from Australia.

"I did help Ross. Being a flight attendant, my buddy passes got him from Sydney to Honolulu. Then, sent him to Maui with passes all the way through to DC, which he only used until LA. On the flight from Sydney, we formed sort of a personal bond and I would really like to catch up with him again.

"Sorry, Marylyn, that's my phone alarm. I've got to run. I'll call you back his evening."

***

Hap, ninety percent friend and ten percent boss, pulls up to "West Wind Surfboards" to relieve Ross for his lunch break. A quick word of thanks for the lodging and the job, then sand spits from under the rear wheels of the ATV and Ross roars off. First stop is the phone booth at the mall, where last night he foolishly squandered a gaggle of silver bullets.

This time he felt much better when the quarters joined hands, and together made their suicidal leap into their tin grave. This time, he left a message saying that, again he was sorry for being a petulant jerk and hoped to hear from her soon. He quoted Hap's phone number, twice. It was lame but hopefully it would be sufficient.

Arriving at the bank he'd used in the past, he barely has the $50 needed to open a new account. Then, he explains that his credit cards had been stolen and he needs them both replaced. Thankfully, since both the Visa and MasterCard have been issued by this bank, he can pick up his new cards in three business days. A drive through burger and fries accompany Ross back to the beach with not a peanut in sight.

West Wind Surfboards is actually a seven-foot-wide, sixteen-foot-long enclosed contractor's trailer. It is a tandem axle that's towed to and from the beach by Hap's '89 Bronco. When Ross pulls up next to "the business," he sees Hap standing by one of the two plastic Adirondack chairs talking to a girl. Across the card table sits her husband or boyfriend in the other Adirondack. He is staring up, at the bottom of the umbrella, the only other piece of furniture in the sandy showroom.

Ross bides his time, watching the pelicans skim along just in front of the long swells; they pull up just before the small walls of water snap shut, crashing on the sandbar. It reminds him of Storkie and their near 'plane surfing' catastrophe. He looks at his empty wrist, a causality of his skin in the game; now a newly pinked band of skin replaces his watch. Hap calls Ross over and introduces him to the couple, each of whom will be taking a lesson later in the afternoon. The guy wanted a surfing lesson, followed by his wife on a stand-up paddle board. Then added a stand-up lesson for himself. Cool. Almost a C-note all up.

**

After breakfast Marylyn calls the rent-a-car company; the one that "will come and pick you up." Forty-five minutes later she drives back to the hotel in a new 2000 Jeep Cherokee. Four-Wheel drive is probably overkill for Daytona but she has already seen one car get stuck in the sand from her balcony. Better safe than sorry.

A tip from the assistant manager guides her to an outlet mall, where she purchases some summer clothes, sandals and two bathing suits. The only item she purchased that is a bit excessive is an "Akubra Snowy River Australian" hat. She has tried on a few of them, during her lay-overs in Sydney, but never had the extra cash to buy one.

After stashing her stash, she slips into a new swimsuit and her new beach cover-up, and heads for the pool. The new suit is a bit on the skimpy side; but even after some vigorous laps, nothing fell out and nothing fell off. The bare minimum, pun intended, for her not-so-strict modesty code. A pool side triple-decker sandwich, almost leads to a food induced nap. That could have been disastrous to Marylyn's already rose-colored skin.

Back in her room, and back on her phone. Martin Maher didn't answer, but he did have a new message: "Hey, I made the cut for a change, so I'm playing the weekend. I need to be focused, so the phone's off until Sunday evening. Leave a number and I'll call you back then."

Next on the list is Simone, who answers on the second ring and sounds genuinely sorry that Marylyn has not heard from Ross. Taking that as a sign, Marylyn asks Simone if she can ask a favor of her. Simone's answer is "Sure, anything."

Marylyn continues, if she wasn't too busy, could Simone stop by Marylyn's apartment in Playa Del Rey, check the answering machine and see if Ross had left any messages?

"Certainly, says Simone, but explains that it might take a while as she has loaned her car to her aunt and bus schedules are sketchy around Lincoln Heights in East LA, where she lives.

"Simone, get with it girl, you're a millionaire! No car, no problem; take a cab. Once you get to Salt Marsh Towers, go up one flight to number 206. There's a fire extinguisher on the wall directly opposite my door; taped to the bottom of it is a key to my apartment. Let yourself in, the answering machine is in the kitchen and I hope you'll see a blinking red light. There's stuff to write with there, so you can jot down any phone numbers or addresses that Ross might have left. Thanks so much, and please call me back right away on my phone and let me know if there's any news."

**

The lady at the beach access booth took Marylyn's money in exchange for a beach pass. She said the pass is good for the day, and includes all of the beach accesses down to Ponce de Leon Inlet. There are however, several areas of "pedestrian only" beaches. Here, she informs Marylyn, she would have to exit the beach and make a small detour, before returning to the beach on the other side of the pedestrian only beaches.

Marylyn found riding next to the ocean thrilling as she saw- toothed her way between the beach and the highway all the way to the inlet. She parked in a row of cars on the beach and watches as the surfers ride wave after wave. It looks to be both challenging and way fun; she knows she will have to try it soon. Marylyn's phone rings, and when she answers, Simone begins talking so fast, it is hard to understand her. After she calms down, Simone repeats the two messages from Ross, including repeating his phone number twice, just as Ross had done.

After thanking Simone, an idea pops into Marylyn's head.

"Simone, do you like convertibles, as in a Mustang convertible?"

"Si, I mean yes, who wouldn't?"

"Great, and you have a driver's license, right?"

"Yes, I have a California driver's license for three years," says Simone.

"Cool, look, there's a set of car keys hanging by the phone; grab them and go down to the parking garage. There, in parking spot #206, you will find a red Mustang convertible. Take it. Use it as your own car for as long as you like. The insurance is paid up and . . ."

Simone interrupts with, "No, I can't, I can't take your car."

"Yes, yes you can. Look, Simone, I'm three thousand miles away in Florida, and I already have a rent-a-car to use while I'm here. Just take the car, put the top down, and give the boys a thrill as you cruise down the Coast Highway. Drive it for long as you like." Cutting Simone off before she has a chance to say no, Marylyn adds, "Thanks again for the phone number; I'm going back to my room and call him right now. I'll let you know as soon as Ross and I hook up. No! Wait, I mean when we meet up or talk on the phone." Giggling, Marylyn hangs up.

Simone wants to protest, but Marylyn hangs up too quickly. She feels more confident when she sees that the Mustang is an automatic. At the stop sign marking an end Salt Marsh's property, Simone takes a deep breath for courage, and puts the top down. The waves and honks start almost immediately, and by the time she slows down for the Venice Beach traffic, she has had enough. The parking lot of a KFC is a good place to grab a soda, and put the top back up.

****

LONG DISTANCE

On the way back to her room, Marylyn stops off and buys an international phone card. Work as a flight attendant had shown her how expensive long distance calls could be. Especially when they were placed from a hotel room. Her cellular phone, she had no doubt, would be expensive too.

Wealth is one thing; wasting it is another.

"Andy," (no doubt Ross's sister) is the first name listed on the envelope. Since there is no phone number or address associated with it, "Andy" is for now a dead end. Next is John Couldwell. Marylyn knows who he is from Ross' story. He lives in an apartment in Coffs where Ross sometimes stayed; and were together when Ross found out he had the winning numbers. Dialing the phone card's 800 number she is instructed to enter her pin number, and then dial John's fourteen-digit number, which includes, country, city, and area codes.

"John Couldwell," a gruff sounding voice answers.

"Hi, my name is Marylyn and I'm the stewardess who helped Ross get from Sydney to the US. I was wondering if you had heard anything from Ross, or did you just get a check?"

"I've heard nothing from the ungrateful bastard; just a big bloody check, one that's well deserved I might add. If I hadn't loaned him the $50, the last of me emergency money, it would have been a non-event from the start. Then I went and borrowed a car to get him up to Storkie's. Ross wouldn't have gotten a foot off the ground if it hadn't been a for me."

"Seems Ross needed more than just a ride to Sydney, John. It took the help of quite a few people to get him the 10,000 miles to Virginia. It's a shame you had to go to all that trouble plus loan Ross $50 bucks. And all you got was a check for three million; more's the pity, John. Have you got Andy's number?"

"I should have her number; she's called here often enough. I've changed phone companies since Ross left, and I've tossed all me old phone bills."

"Could you call your old phone company and get her phone number, or copies of your old bills, and then call me back with Andy's number?" asks Marylyn.

"Yeah, I reckon," says John, sounding like a heavy burden has been laid upon his shoulders.

Hanging up after leaving her number with John, Marylyn moves down to the third name on her list, one Norbert Krautheinie. Translation (cabbage ass?) After following all the instructions and dialing a total of twenty-nine digits, success. "Big Hat Station. Storkie speaking."

"Hi, my name is Marylyn and I'm looking for Norbert, is he around?"

The silence is long enough for Marylyn to wonder if the connection had been broken. Finally, "where in the bloody hell did you get that name?"

Bingo! "I got it off an envelope on which Ross Sheehan wrote down a list of people, me included, who helped him succeed in a recent journey. This is the phone number written next to Norbert Krautheinie's name."

"This is Norbert Krautheinie; I usually go by me nickname of Storkie. Yeah, I did help Ross out all right, 'bout got both our asses killed flying him to Sydney. Didn't think he'd ever make it in time, but that big check proved me wrong. Don't like the name 'Norbert'; it's a pain, but it sure looked good sitting on that check. So, Marylyn you helped Ross and got a check too?"

"Yes, but I haven't seen or heard from Ross since I sent him off to Maui with buddy passes more than a week ago. I just talked to John Couldwell and he hasn't heard from Ross either. Have you, or anyone you know heard from Ross?"

"I only just met Ross with John this past Saturday, but I did meet another bloke, Kelvin Butterworth. He's the one gave Ross a ride from Noosa, some three hundred kilometers, to Coffs Harbour. This was the very same Saturday that I flew Ross down to Sydney. Ross sent Kelvin a check, too, but only for three hundred thousand dollars. 'ONLY' Jesus . . . would you listen to me, apparently it doesn't take a body long to get snooty about money. A fortnight ago, three hundred thousand dollars was a bloody fortune."

"Thanks for that information, Storkie. Here's my number—let's call one another, if we hear any news of Ross."

It is still mid-morning of the next day in Australia, so Marylyn decides to try Rose Belsome in Campbelltown, New South Wales. Marylyn's second try at dialing is slow and methodical after putting in 29 digits the first time only to hear, "You have dialed an incorrect number." It seems that calling to Australia can be not only expensive but also tedious.

Her carefulness pays off as the ringing is interrupted by a soft Australian lilt, "Hello."

"Hi, is this Rose?" When answered in the affirmative Marylyn continues, "Let me guess. You recently met a yank, and helped him along on his journey. Now you are rich beyond your wildest dreams."

"Now let me guess," says Rose. "First, you're not a psychic. Second, you have also recently had a similar experience."

"Now who's the psychic, Rose? You're right. My name is Marylyn and, yes I did help Ross with buddy passes from Sydney to the US. And, you're right again — I also got a check. My limited psychic powers tell me that both of us are luckier than we are psychic."

"I'll take luck any day" says Rose. "Although, I suppose there was a bit of fate involved in that day, too. I had already set aside $50 for the "pokies", that's slot machines to you, and had called a taxi to take me to the hotel. Those two coincidences were already in play when Ross turned up on my door step. Him needing a ride to the airport and being short the fifty bucks to pay for a taxi — and me having both at hand. Which is why I took a punt on Ross and his almost impossible trek."

"Well, Rose, speaking for myself, and I'm sure everyone else on the envelope, we're sure glad you did. Have you heard anything from Ross since that day?"

"Not a word, other than the check. I find it a bit strange, but no, I haven't heard a thing," says Rose.

"I'll leave you my telephone number, and I would appreciate it if you'll let me know if you hear from Ross."

**

With this new information Marylyn decided to update her envelope list.

1. Andy???

2. John Couldwell Gave Ross $50 and a ride to Storkie's for a flight to Sydney. Check 3.45$

3. Norbert Krautheinie (Storkie) Flew Ross near Sydney Airport Check 3.45$

4. Rose Belsome Gave Ross taxi fare from Campbelltown to the Sydney Airport Check 3.45$

5. Marylyn (Me) Buddy passes from Sydney through to DC. Check 3.45$

6. Captain Drew Michaels Gave Ross his plane seat from Maui to LA check 3.45$

7. Simone Alverez Gave Ross her work mileage for ticket from LA to Chicago   Check 3.45$

8. Martin Maher Somehow, hoodwinked Ross a plane ride from Chicago to DC. check 3.45$

9. Sampson Samuels Blew up his limousine getting Ross to the Lottery Office check 3.45$

10. Ross??? Marylyn penciled in along with the new number she had gotten from Simone.

A. Kelvin Butterworth Gave Ross a ride from Noosa to Coffs Harbour $300,000

B. Franklin Dearner??? Address only.

Ross had apparently figured out the cash amount of the winning ticket almost exactly. Eight checks accounted for and two more @ 3.45$ million would make thirty-four and a half million. Ross, who always said he was good with numbers, had picked the cash payout at about thirty-five million dollars.

It is unsettling though: three names left, and only two 3.45$ million dollar checks left. Surely, his sister, Andy, would get one, and it's impossible to think that Ross would not include himself. It must be that this Frank Dearner is an old friend and maybe Ross gave him a couple of hundred thousand dollars, like he did with Kelvin Butterworth.

Having Franklin Dearner's address, she quickly gets his phone number in Tarheel, North Carolina. Before she has a chance to call him, her phone rings. She picks it up on the first ring.

"Give it to me over the phone, they did!"

"What? who is this?" asks Marylyn.

"John Couldwell. Is this the stewardess who helped Ross Sheehan get to Ameriker?"

"Yes. Sorry John, It's Marylyn McPherson Ross' friend; what is it you were saying?"

"I said, they, being the phone company, gave me Andy's phone number over the phone."

"Terrific, thanks, John. I've got a pen handy so fire when ready."

As soon as John utters the last number, he hangs up.

Now, armed with three important phone numbers, Marylyn feels a bit apprehensive about who to call first.

She feels like smacking herself in the forehead and muttering, "I should have had a V8." Silly girl she has Ross's phone number now. Just call him and he will clear up everything.

She is still holding her breath when she heard three disparaging beeps, and then the recording, "We're sorry, you have reached a number that is disconnected or no longer in service. If you feel you have reached this recording in error, please check the number and try your call again." Dialing extra carefully the second time nets the same result. The third time is no charm, and she hangs up after she hears "We're sorry . . ."

Stunned, Marylyn carries on as if on auto pilot, and dials the number she has for Franklin Dearner. He answers with a jovial, "Hello, Frank Dearner speaking." His voice has a hint of a southern drawl.

Marylyn was about to go on with her canned speech about being a stewardess, helping Ross, and then finding Franklin's name on the envelope, but as soon as she mentions Ross's name Franklin Dearner explodes.

"Ross Sheehan! My main man! He saved me from a plight worse than death; poverty. Hang on; I have to tell my wife."

Marylyn can still hear Franklin's muffled voice, "Misty. . . honey, the phone—it's about Ross Sheehan."

Franklin Dearner returns to the phone obviously out of breath. "Sorry, I got so amped up hearing about Ross, I've lost my wife and forgotten your name."

"Marylyn, it's nice to speak with you, Franklin."

"That's it, Marylyn. You know Marylyn, you're the only person other than Ross and my wife that calls me Franklin."

"Would you prefer Frank?"

"No, I like the way it sounds when you say Franklin."

"Easy, big fella, you're married remember?" she scolds.

"Not anymore, I just told you—I lost my wife."

After a joint chuckle, Marylyn got back to her intended line of dialogue. "Franklin, as far as I know Ross only sent out checks to people who helped him in his travels from Australia to the lottery office in Virginia. Eight of us on the envelope got identical checks for $3.45 million. May I ask if you got one for the same amount?"

"Exactly the same," says Franklin. "But my check wasn't for helping Ross in his travels, with money or anything else. I've been in no shape to help Ross or anyone for the better part of a year. Both Misty and I have been working part time just to keep our heads above water."

"Why would you get a check? What was the check for then, if you didn't help Ross in his travels?"

"You're right I didn't help him a bit. I wasn't even aware of anything until the check came. There was a note scribbled at the bottom of my check that read: "As always, men of our word" I knew then that Ross had either won a lottery or had a huge windfall. I'm guessing that whichever one it was, it came to about thirty-four and a half million. That would mean my $3.45 million check would represent a ten percent of the windfall. I'll tell you the story. Years ago, Ross and I made kind of a pact, you know, gave our word that if either of us ever had a huge windfall or won a lottery worth more than a million dollars; we'd give the other guy ten percent of the winnings. Now, since one of those miracles has apparently happened, I'd really like to thank Ross for saving my marriage, my house, my kids' educations and last and least, my ass."

"Well then . . . shit," says Marylyn, "You know Franklin, if your figures are correct, and I have no doubt that they are, then we have a dilemma. Yours is the ninth check for three point four five million that Ross sent out. That means there's only one 3.45$ million check left, which would make a total thirty-four point five million. Problem is, there are still two people on the envelope. Andy, who I'm pretty sure is Ross' sister, and Ross."

"Well then . . . shit, you're right," says Franklin. "Andy is Ross' sister and they were real close growing up. She is a couple of years older than Ross; she got married and moved up north shortly after Ross and I started hanging out together. He thinks the world of her and she would definitely have been at the top of his list — before anyone, even himself."

"Look, Franklin, I'm kind of at my wits' end. I don't have a phone number, address or a last name for Andy. Then there's the phone number Ross left for me on my answering machine. It's area code is for Daytona Beach, but it's no longer in service. You got any ideas?"

"Matter of fact, I do. If I can find my wife, Misty, she might can help. She was two years ahead of me in high school and in the same class as Andy. Hopefully she knows someone who has stayed in contact with Andy over the years. Hang on — if the kidnappers haven't taken her away in the trunk of their car, I should be able to find her."

A few moments, later Franklin returns to the phone; he is again breathless. "OK, found her. I couldn't pay the ransom but they gave her back anyway. Misty knows the girl who was Andy's best friend in high school. She'll call her now but needs to use this phone. Give me your number and I'll call you right back."

"Make it twenty minutes;" said Marylyn, "I'm going to the bar and get the biggest rum drink they make."

As Marylyn waits at the bar for her 'Haitian Libation' she looks out the sliding glass doors, past the deck, down towards the ocean. The day's light is dimming but she sees a man driving an ATV down on the beach; cruising the water's edge. What a life, she thinks. I could learn to adapt to and maybe even live that life-style.

Ross, unaware that Marylyn is following his progress through the sliding glass doors, continues along the shore line checking out the surf. It's is getting bigger, thanks to three days of a relentless north east wind. While a Nor'easter is good for building a swell, it is in fact, a total disaster for business.

Another crap fact: Ross has never seen the red light on Hap's answering machine ever blinking, signifying that a message is waiting. So, either Marylyn and Andy have both decided never to speak to him again or, more likely, Hap has forgotten to relay any messages. Ross is bummed. Perhaps a few medicinal beers at the Gazebo would buoy his sinking spirits.

Two hours later, and if anything, the medicine is having the opposite effect than the one intended. No wonder they call alcohol a depressant. Ross is tired of hearing people expressing their personal opinions with pathetic attempts at political or ethnic so-called jokes. Jokes which inevitably reveal more about the person telling the joke, than about the people they are trying to demean.

Hap is entering just as Ross is getting ready to leave, and he talks Ross into having "one for the road". Hap slides a beer over and remarks that he and his wife are back on speaking terms, so perhaps, Ross should consider looking for new digs in the near future. "No worries," says Ross "I'm out of there tomorrow, and by the way, I left your home number with my sister and a girl I met. So, if they had left a number or a message on your answering machine — you'd have let me know, right?"

"That's highly" (a long, echoing belch) "unlikely to occur," says Hap.

Thinking that Hap means that Andy and Marylyn wouldn't care enough to call. Ross challenges him; "Yeah, why's that?"

"Land line been disconnected for months. June and I both just use cell phones, now."

**

Back from the Conch Key Lounge and half of Marylyn's "Haitian Libation" has been enough to still the waters. The other half sits on a plastic table out on the balcony. Now, sitting at the desk armed with the number for Ross' sister, Marylyn takes a breath and starts punching numbers.

Andy is delighted to hear from her. Marylyn fills her in on Ross's itinerant travels from Australia to Virginia. She explains that she got Andy's number from Franklin and Misty Dearner. The small talk was over. Marylyn asks, "Have you heard from Ross?"

"He called me more than a week ago from an airplane; he was somewhere near DC and still on his way. Then, I received a telegram from North Carolina saying he'd call. Two days ago, I got a phone message and Ross left a number to call him on. That led to a disconnected number. I don't know if that qualifies as hearing from him or not. But other than that, no, I haven't talked to him in over a week. The only clue was that useless phone number. I thought it seemed familiar; it's the same one that I already had in my address book. It's for Hap Velzy, his old boss in a surfboard rental business in Daytona Beach. I checked; it's been disconnected."

"Which is where I am now," says Marylyn, "trying to track him down. I thought that Ross and I really clicked; we had planned to reconnect, whether he was successful with the lottery ticket or not. Now, Ross is in the wind and I'm left with a half-assed apology and probably the same bogus number that you have." She went on to tell Andy about the list, and that nine of the people on the envelope had already received their ten percent. Had she?

She had indeed — almost three and a half million dollars.

"I'm not sure," says Marylyn, "but Ross may have inadvertently cut himself out of the money, out of any of the money. If the ten people on the envelope have each received ten percent of the winnings, then, even with my limited math skills, it's obvious, 100% of the winnings have been given out. Ross was not one of the ten people on the envelope. I don't think Ross got any of the money. He may be embarrassed, broke, and in hiding."

"That silly soft-hearted bastard, he always was too generous for his own good. If you're right, then he will be too proud to ask for anything, let alone take any money, even from his sister. Now, we need to find that boy and straighten him out," says Andy.

After agreeing, Marylyn says, "the weather has been too windy for the beach lately, but the weather man is calling for a nice forecast this coming week. I plan to check out all the surfboard rental places, north and south."

"Marylyn, it might go smoother if you use an indirect or a sneakier approach; might even go easier with a partner?"

"You mean you'd come down here and help me find Ross and bring him to his senses?"

"Sure, my daughter is visiting her grandmother for a week up in Canada. "Right now I've got plenty of time and money. It's beginning to get cool up here and I could be there tomorrow afternoon. Give me the name and number where you're staying in Daytona, and Marylyn, spell your last name for me please."

After giving Andy the information, Marylyn says "this is going to be so cool, two wily women ganging up on one poor, unsuspecting male; he doesn't stand a chance."

After punching off the phone, Marylyn steps out onto her balcony and reintroduces herself to her rum drink. The wind seems to have followed the sun over the horizon, leaving only a dark stillness. She can make out the long slashes of white foam on the ocean, courtesy of the

breaking waves parading in from far out in the ocean. It is
both mesmerizing and relaxing. Just before falling asleep in
her chair, Marylyn gets up and heads back inside.

The next morning the phone jars her awake at eight-o-five
in the morning. Simone is halfway through her apology for
calling early when Marylyn stopped her. "Simone, it's fine
really, just give me a minute to throw some water on my
face and grab myself a cup of coffee. I'll call you right
back—five minutes."

The previously soft spoken Simone is full of energy
when they reconnect. "Marylyn, remember when you said
for me to use your car like it is my car, for as long as I
wanted?"

"Sure, and I meant every word of it."

"Well, my new car, which is really your old car,
needs an inspection sticker. It also needs some lights to be
replaced, brake 'chose', and new tires." Simone steps on
Marylyn's attempted interruption by saying, "No it's fine, I
don't mind paying at all. This is for the best, because now
the car is very safe; and if it's OK with you, my cousin,
Gloria and I would like to take it for a trip across the
United States. She is from Columbia, like me, and is an
exchange student at the University of Florida. Her vacation
is for a week, and we would like to use the car to drive
cross country to Gainesville, Florida. We have both flown
over the US, but you can't see much from a plane. So, is it
all right if we use the car? We both love it, and maybe we
could even stop in and see you, and hopefully Ross?"

"Of course it's all right; I think that's a fantastic
idea. Call me when you get close."

"Cool! Gloria says we will be like 'Thelma and
Louise' —without the cliff. First, I will go by your
apartment and check for messages from Ross."

There are no new messages from Ross so, Simone
leaves, re-taping Marylyn's key to the bottom of the fire

extinguisher. Just as the elevator doors close Simone in silence — Marylyn's phone begins to ring.

"Damn," Ross says as the ringing switches over to the answering machine. Most of the time he makes more sense when he hasn't rehearsed what he is going to say; he hopes this is one of those times. "Marylyn, it's Ross again with another apology. You may already know this but the phone number I left for you to call me on no longer works. Sorry about that. I just bought a cell phone and here is the number." He carefully reads it off the receipt and then repeats it."

"Which reminds me, thanks for trying to pass me that cell phone in Hawaii; I should have made a better catch. You probably have a new cellular phone by now; it seems as if everyone in Florida does. Please, call me as soon as you get this number and maybe . . ."

It is probably a good thing that the recording time ran out, because he felt as if he was on the verge of committing verbal suicide. He had used up the majority of his lunch hour retrieving his re-issued credit cards from the bank and then using the good one to buy the cell phone. Now he had just enough battery to call Andy, and give her his new number.

The phone fairies remained in their contrarian cycle, and Ross's cell phone call began ringing in Andy's house thirty minutes after she had left for the airport. He left another apology and his new number.

Ross gets back to work just in time to help Hap load two stand up paddle boards onto the roof rack of a SUV. As the smiling renters drive away he remarks to Hap that his arms are a little sore from their early morning surf.

"Yeah me too," says Hap, rolling his shoulders. "Used to drink all night, surf in the morning, work all day, surf till dark, and then go out and drink and chase the ladies. Used to! That's what old age is: looking back on all the crazy stuff we used to do. Now, I'm not saying we can't rock and roll anymore Ross. We might just need to slow down a bit, be a little more selective with what we chase, ride and drink."

**

Marylyn is excited about the prospect of teaming up with Andy to locate Ross, but that doesn't solve the financial enigma. Is Ross really broke — or is there more money than she is aware of? Did he just take his share off the top and then give ten percent to each of the ten people on the envelope? She hopes so, but that wouldn't explain his apparent reclusiveness.

There is one way to find out. Shuffling through the pages of her note book she finds the card Tara had given her. On it was the number for the law office of "Timothy R. Donald". The female voice that answers isn't Tara's, so Marylyn introduces herself as "a friend of Ross Sheehan" who would like to speak to Tim Donald. That produced quick results and Tim is on the line in seconds.

"This is Tim Donald; may I ask who is calling?"

Marylyn gives her name, and the short version of her brief but meaningful relationship with Ross.

"Yes, I know who you are. My wife Tara told me that you stopped by and that the two of you had a chat. Have you heard from Ross?"

"Only two phone messages: one was an apology for not calling; the second one, he left a number which is now out of service." replied Marylyn.

"I haven't fared any better," said Tim, "one quick call, and then he only wanted your phone number." Marylyn feels an emotional twinge. It's like a small static electrical tingle that shoots right through her. She recovers and asks her question: "I know that you helped Ross with the distribution of the lottery money and signed the checks with him. Can you tell me the total amount of cash Ross received? Isn't that in the public records? That isn't under any type of client confidentiality, is it?" she asks, crossing her fingers.

"No, it isn't; you're right. Wait. I have the file right here. Ross received a total of thirty-four million nine hundred and three thousand six hundred dollars. Marylyn, so that we're clear on the amount that we dealt with; two checks totaling a little more than $400,000 came off the top, leaving, $34,450.000.

Stunned into silence Marylyn can barely utter "Thanks" before hanging up.

Well, as her granddaddy use to say, "that tears it," meaning it's done, over, finished. There is no doubt about it now. The total amount that was awarded to Ross has all been doled out. Ten lucky souls are now multi-millionaires, and Ross Sheehan is not among them.

Marylyn calls Franklin and explains about the lawyer and the money. The fact that she now knows that Ross is broke doesn't deter her. The search for him will only intensify, but when she stands face to face with him again, then what? After talking with Andy, she knows that Ross is way too independent, too stubborn really, to take any money from anyone. Does Franklin have any ideas?

"Well it sounds like our buddy done painted his butt into a corner. You know, my wife Misty talked me into buying her a new Toyota SUV, a Lexass, I think it's called, and Daytona Beach, well that seems as good a place as any to test out the four-wheel drive. I'm sure both of us would enjoy seeing Andy again and I'm looking forward to the pleasure of meeting you. Then, there's a big hugging thank you, that I want to deliver to Ross in person. We need to find that boy; pull his head out and clear up his thinking. If he's broke, we need to fix up his finances. Don't seem fair, him winning all that money and ending up with nothing."

"Well, as they say on TV Franklin, 'Come on down!' By the way, I think your wife's new car is called a Lexus."

"Whatever," replies Franklin.

After a room service club sandwich and two hours of mindless TV, Marylyn is getting ready for bed. Glancing at the clock it occurs to her that 11:00 at night here is a good time to call Australia. Talk about time differences, with daylight savings off, Australia is now sixteen hours ahead. It's now three o'clock in the afternoon in Sydney; tomorrow afternoon.

Rose answers her phone with the same lilting Aussie "Hello."

"Hi Rose. It's Marylyn again. I'm afraid I've got some unsettling news. There's still no word from Ross; I'm in Daytona Beach, Florida trying to find him. After checking with his sister and the lawyer who co-signed the checks with Ross, it's a fact — Ross is broke. He may not be completely penniless but the numbers don't lie. He gave away 10% ten times. That equals a 100%. Apparently, he didn't get any of the lottery winnings."

"Bloody hell, how can that happen?"

"I don't know, Rose, but if I give you their phone numbers, could you call the other Aussies who are on the envelope and let them know what's happened? See if they've heard any news. I'm up to my chin here, trying to keep the US contingent informed."

"No worries, I'll ring them up straight away. We'll see to it that Ross gets "a fair go.""

No sooner had she pushed the off button, than the phone rings, vibrating in her hand. It gives her nerves a bit of a jolt. "Hello," she says cautiously.

"Marylyn, it's Martin Maher. Hope I didn't wake you, but I did a bit of celebrating after the tournament this afternoon, and I'm behind in returning my calls. Placing sixth in the tournament qualifies me for the Jacksonville tournament next week. I was thinking about flying home to Colorado for a couple of days, but then, I didn't want to miss a chance of catching up with Ross."

"I'm happy for your success Martin, but don't worry about missing Ross. He's still in the wind; and I'm still in Daytona trying to find him. Tell your Aunt Becky I said, "Hi" and call me when you get back to Florida."

The queen-sized bed looked mighty tempting but then she thought back on what Tim said. "Ross was only interested in your phone number." A mini aftershock zips through her and produces enough energy for her to pick up the phone and dial Captain Drew Michaels in California.

Drew answers on the first ring and Marylyn doesn't waste any time either. "Hey Drew, its Marylyn. I'm just calling on the off chance that perhaps you or Liz might have heard something, anything, from Ross?"

"Sorry, not a word. You know Marylyn, thanks to Ross my wish list is almost complete. Of course, that list of is subject to change if Liz divorces me. Seriously, the item at the top of my bucket list now is to thank Ross in person and express my gratitude in words."

"Well Drew, Ross may need more than words of thanks; he's broke!"

"Broke? What broke? What are you talking about?" asks Drew.

"It seems Ross gave away 10% one too many times — ten; and that left him with nothing. I've talked with all ten people and each of them got a check for $3,450,000. The lawyer Ross used to distribute the checks said that two smaller checks were made out to other people and taken off the top. The total cash amount Ross received and distributed was thirty-four million, five hundred thousand dollars. That leaves ten other people with 3.45 million each; and one broke surfer whose claim to fame was; "I'm pretty good with numbers.""

"Speaking for myself, I would like to help Ross in any way that I can, financial or otherwise." says Drew.

"So would I," says Marylyn, "but we have a couple of problems. One, Ross is in the wind. He's probably around here, in Daytona Beach, but no one has heard from him in over a week. The second problem: his sister Andy says, and I agree, is that Ross is too proud to take any money from anybody. She actually said 'pig headed.' Anyway, first we need to find him, then we need to hold him down and give him a mental enema."

"Hold on, Liz is pawing at me. I think she wants to have sex. 'SMACK!' Ouch! Sorry! Honey . . . now I see; it's the phone that she wants. Here's Liz; bye."

Marylyn retells her the story of Ross's apparent financial suicide. After they catch up on the health and happiness of Liz's girls, Liz launches into the career change that Drew has made. Not only had he been in talks with Select Jets, he bought a plane and secured a contract with them. A fellow pilot Drew went to the Naval Academy with had taken medical retirement and could no longer fly for Select Jets. Drew put down what he calls "a small down payment" three quarters of a million dollars, on his friend's plane. Now, like it or not, we own a Learjet 60.

"It's not as bad as it sounds," says Liz. "Select Jets has been making all the payments and paying the maintenance bills out of the profits the plane has generated. If everything goes according to plan and recent history repeats itself; we should own our own personal jet in seven years. Options included, that's the length of Drew's flying contract with Select Jets."

"Say, Marylyn, if you locate Ross before the weekend, Drew is dead-heading his new plane to Miami on Friday. Maybe you, Ross, and Drew can grab lunch in Florida."

"As they say, from your lips to God's ears."

Marylyn is picking up her order at the McDonald's drive through window when her cell phone rings. Trying to manage a coffee, an Egg McMuffin, and a phone is too much. After securing her breakfast she finally punches the answer button. Then tries to talk over her own message to be heard. Just as the message ends, Andy says, "Hey, It's me." An irritated beep comes from the vehicle behind Marylyn. Salt spray from the northeaster has coated her rear window; the result being that all she can make out in her rearview mirror is a guy on a motor-cycle. He is just a blurry figure in sunglasses and a ball cap.

She considers flipping the dude off. Instead, she humbly gives an apologetic surrender, by holding up the coffee in one hand and phone in the other. Finding places for them both, Marylyn managed to make a U-turn at the exit sign and pulls into a spot on the other side of Mickey D's.

"Andy . . . Andy, are you still there?"

"Yeah, I'm here in Atlanta and should arrive in Daytona on United at two thirty-five."

"Great, I'll pick you up. I'll be wearing an 'Akubra'; that's an Australian cowboy hat."

Leaning out to look at her side view mirror for a bit of lip McMuffin, she notices that the guy who was behind her is on a three-wheeler and not a motorcycle. He's at the exit sign and then he looks to the left to check for traffic.

"It's Ross! My God Andy! It's Ross. He's here. Right here at McDonalds. I've got to go."

"OK, but don't spook him, don't let him see you. He sees you, he's liable to rabbit."

The half-eaten McMuffin and the phone jointly disappear into the breakfast bag as Marylyn starts the car. She almost backs into a car coming in the entrance. Then she has to stop, pull back up into her parking place and to let the other car pass. Craning her head around, she glimpses Ross heading north a block away. Backing out again, she successfully circles around the building and slows at the exit sign. Marylyn hangs a left on the main drag and going a bit over the speed limit searches the road ahead for Ross.

A couple of minutes pass, and still no sign of Ross. She comes to a stoplight. To the right is a beach access; to the left a substantial highway headed across the intracoastal waterway. Which way? It's a little before ten; he works on the beach; it must be the beach. She turns right.

Damn, the day pass. She has to stop at the shed and get one. She knows it's trouble when the gate lady looks sadly at the twenty-dollar bill and squeaks, "Sweetie, is that the smallest you have?"

Marylyn franticly searches for "something smaller" and is ready to tell her to keep the change; when the elderly lady says, "I've got it dear." Then takes forever to count out two fives and five ones. The day pass and the bills join the McMuffin and the phone in the Mickey D's bag. Immediately Marylyn faces the same decision again: left, or right? As with most right-handed people, Marylyn chooses right; which is wrong.

Moments earlier, Ross waved his way through the same beach access and turns left. He drives north and parks behind the rental trailer in order to keep the bike in the shade for the first half of the day. He learned the hard way that it is excruciatingly painful to hop on a sunbaked leather seat wearing nothing but a bathing suit. He has some early lessons this morning and needs the Mickey D's breakfast for energy. The last of the hash browns have just been devoured when the young Canadian couple turns up for their lessons.

Marylyn searches the beach south for two miles and still no sightings. When she comes to a "pedestrian only" blockade of cars on the beach, she is forced to turn right and get off the beach. A half a mile on the highway and she returns to the beach. She sawtooths her way to the jetty at Ponce Inlet. Marylyn stops there after making a U-turn and reaches into the breakfast bag for the phone to call Andy.

"Andy, it's me. I lost him and . . . great, now I've got ketchup all over my hands, my phone; it's probably in my ears. Never mind, I'll keep searching. I'm going to look north from where I got on the beach, but really he could be anywhere."

"Not to worry," says Andy, "Now that we definitely know that he's in Daytona, we'll find him easy enough. The name of the surfboard place where he used to work, has been dancing on the tip of my tongue all morning. Wait, they just called my group number. I've got to go; see you at two-thirty."

Marylyn becomes vigilant once she passes the old bat in the shed; now that she is covering new territory. She slows when she sees a trailer with the name, "West Wind Surfboards" underneath the name it reads," Sales, Rentals, and Lessons." No three-wheelers in sight, and she's sure the guy under the umbrella isn't Ross. He looks like an Egyptian mummy, wrapped up from head to toe in towels.

She turns the Jeep and her attention towards the ocean — just in time to see a girl escape from the blinding rays of the sun. The girl is surfing; sliding across the ocean on a shimmering glassy wave. Marylyn lets the car stop and continues to watch as the girl fights for her balance. She rides across the face of the wave, arms flailing, torso bobbing, barely maintaining her stance until the wave brakes and takes her down with it.

She pops up quickly in the waist deep water; looks back directly into the sun behind her, and gives someone a smile as her thumb points to the sky. Ross is that someone, but he is invisible to Marylyn behind the glare of the sun. He returns the salute of happiness the girl has given him. It makes Ross feel good that she turns to him for approval.

She shares her joy with Ross, even as her husband sits under the shop's umbrella, mummified as he is with a terrible sunburn.

The next mile and a half of Marylyn's beach search ends with two dead ends: one, no Ross, and two, another "pedestrian only" blockade of the beach. Marylyn decides it's time to go back to the hotel and freshen up. She wants to make a good impression on Ross's sister.

Marylyn is naked. It is twenty minutes later and she is admiring the demarcation lines that separate her creamy white skin from the new reddish pink. The startling contrast between what everyone sees and what only she sees. Maybe later, she'll chose to let someone see, what only she saw. (Funny what words say).

The ringing phone injects her with a panicky sense of false modesty and she grabs a hotel robe from the back of the bathroom door and walks to the night stand. "Hello."

"G'Day Marylyn. It's Rose, here in Sydney. Have you found our boy Ross yet?"

"Hey Rose. No, not yet, but I did see him this morning. I was trying to follow him to find out where he works or lives, but he gave me the slip. No worries, as you Aussies say. Andy, Ross's sister is on her way down here and between the two of us, we should be able to track him down in no time."

"Well, love, let us know when you've got that scoundrel cornered. We're five of us now, and everyone is ready to jump on a plane to Ameriker as soon as you give us the word. We'd all like to thank Ross in person, and talk, or as John says, beat some sense into him about taking a bit of money."

"Five?" questions Marylyn. "I thought it was just you, John, and Storkie?"

"Right, but I've acquired a new friend and business partner, name of Woodrow, that I'll be bringing along. And the Stork, well, he's found himself a new mate by the name of Kelvin and he's shouting him a trip to Ameriker. Kelvin's the bloke gave Ross the ride that started all this."

"Yeah, Storkie told me about meeting him, and Kelvin's name is on the envelope; I'm sure he'll be welcome. I'll let you know as soon as we drop the net on Ross. Got to run. Bye.

***

As soon as Andy enters the arrival area, there is Marylyn standing out like a tall poppy in her Australian cattleman's hat. After their initial greeting Andy stands back and looks at the hat. "That's quite the fashion statement. I love it. That hat's so hot it's cool. I have to have one."

"I just bought it here in Daytona," says Marylyn, "even though it was made in Australia. I'd be happy to take you to the shop that sells them anytime you like."

"Thanks, but first I'd like to get out of these clothes and into the ocean. It's been years, and all I thought about on the plane is how much I missed it. I need some vitamin 'SEA' as Ross calls it. You're at the Marriott, right? I should have called and made a reservation. You think there are any vacancies?"

"I feel sure that there are. It's not the tourist season yet and the parking lot is not near full. The hotel itself doesn't seem that crowded either."

Ten minutes after registering and going to own her room, Andy is back, knocking on Marylyn's door and ready to hit the beach. Her only request is to go to an unpopulated section of the beach. Andy lacks a bathing suit and is only wearing shorts and a bra under her cover up. They stay north on A1A and bypass two beach accesses in order to save time. In doing so, Marylyn unknowingly passes within a block of Ross. Close again for the second time today.

Marylyn and Andy park up near the dune line and stroll down to the water's edge. They smile at one another when the surf laps at their ankles; both take off running and then simultaneously dive under an oncoming wave. After a few strokes, Marylyn is content to rollover and float, while Andy powers on for another thirty yards. After resting a minute, she swims vigorously back towards Marylyn. Stopping short, she dives and pops up spitting salt water, "I've got the name. 'West Wind Surfboard Rentals' that's where Ross worked."

They body surf into the beach and walk up to the car. Marylyn says, "I'm pretty sure I passed 'West Winds' earlier today." They take the beach back to check. They find West Winds easily enough, but it is closed for the day.

The next morning finds the girls sitting in the Jeep picking at their McMuffins. Marylyn is better prepared today; she's backed into a parking spot on the exit side of the building. Ready to launch into action at the first sight of Ross. Earlier in the morning, they purchased some straw hats and cheap oversized sunglasses for disguises. Ready to test their sleuthing skills, they keep a vigilant eye on the drive through lane.

Twenty minutes later the boredom is broken by Marylyn's phone ringing. Seeing that the call is from Simone, she quickly explains to Andy who Simone is and puts the phone on speaker. "Hey, Simone, I'm here in Daytona with Andy, Ross's sister and I've got you on speaker phone, OK?"

"Yes, that's fine, I'm with Gloria and wait, now we're on speaker phone too. Have you found Ross?"

"Not yet," says Marylyn, "but we", looking at Andy, "feel confident we'll find him today. Hang on a second," she says handing the phone to Andy.

"Hi, Simone, I'm Andy, Ross's sister, and I'd like to thank you for helping Ross and well, all of us really. Marylyn saw Ross yesterday but couldn't catch up to him;

but now that we know where he works, finding him shouldn't be a problem."

"Where he works? Why would Ross work? He has millions and millions of dollars."

"Simone, Marylyn hadn't told you because we've just figured it out. Ross has given away all of the money and now he's broke," says Marylyn.

"Oh no! Gloria and I are in Fort Walton Beach, Florida on the Gulf of Mexico. The desk clerk tells us that Jacksonville Beach is a 'straight shot', and less than five hours away. He said we could be in Daytona Beach by this evening. When I get there, I will give Ross ever how much money he needs."

Marylyn takes the phone back. "That's very generous of you Simone. It's likely that all ten of us would be more than willing to help Ross financially. First, we have to find him; then try to convince him to accept some money. According to Andy, getting him to accept money from anyone is going to be a problem. He hasn't reached out to anyone for help or money, not me, or even his sister. Call us back when you and Gloria get to Jacksonville."

Not even a minute after clicking it off, the phone chirps again. This time, it's Martin Maher, the golf professional. After explaining to Andy that Martin is responsible for the "Chicago to DC" part of the puzzle, Marylyn puts the phone on speaker. "Hey, Martin, still no Ross but we've almost got him corralled. You're on speaker — Ross's sister, Andy, is with me."

"I look forward to meeting you both. That's good news about Ross and I have some of my own; I'm still playing well and that means a late tee time today. It will be after six when I finish and I probably won't feel like renting a car and driving down tonight so . . ."

"Wait," interrupts Marylyn. "I may have just the solution for you. There are two young ladies, Simone, who helped Ross get from LA to Chicago, and Gloria her cousin, who are driving to Daytona by way of Jacksonville Beach. They could give you a ride, or you guys can just hang out and come down tomorrow."

"Sounds great. Give them my number and I'll let them know where I'm staying."

"Right. Good luck to you Martin; I hope you win."

*****

SLEUTHING

Simone answers the phone and Marylyn explains that Martin is like them; in that he assisted Ross and is now a member of the envelope crew. Marylyn also tells the girls that he is a professional golfer, presently in Jacksonville Beach. Could they give him a lift to Daytona? This coincidence piques the girl's interest, especially Gloria, a "walk-on" member of the University of Florida golf team. They agree enthusiastically.

It's ten-thirty at McDonalds and breakfast time is finished; toast, as they say. They stash their trash and head out. Halted again by the beach access shed; Marylyn makes "the old bat" inside happy, by presenting her with the correct change.

They drive south on the beach, zigging off to the road when they come to a pedestrian only section, and then zagging back onto the beach at the next beach access. They know that 'West Wind Surfboards' is north of the Marriott, but need some time to prepare. The beach dead ends at the jetty and Ponce Inlet; their stopping there leads to a refreshing dip in the Atlantic. They follow that with a walk on the jetty; where they can gaze out across the Inlet and see New Smyrna Beach.

Back in the Jeep they slip on t-shirts, then try on different hats and oversized sunglasses. Afterwards, they sit in the car and watch the surfers riding waves. Some ride right up next to the jetty and Marylyn thought that was dangerous. Andy, who use to surf, explains that it 'wasn't really'. Today's detective action, they decide, will involve only observation and identification.

They drive back on A1A, until Marylyn takes 'her' exit to the beach, and is waved through at "the old bats shack". They continue north and Marylyn spots the trailer she had seen twice the day before. Driving slowly, she holds down the brim of her hat to shield her face. Since she is the closest to the trailer, she whispers to Andy. "Look, Andy, can you see? It says West Wind, right? Do you see Ross? Look, Andy. What do you see?" Andy leans forward in order to see around Marylyn.

Marylyn hisses at her, "Get back! Don't look, don't look, he'll see you!"

Andy collapses forward, her head down on her knees, and explodes in laughter. Marylyn speeds up as if to escape danger, and then slows back down. She looks over at Andy, who is still laugh-gagging and trying to regain control by inhaling huge gulps of air.

"What in the hell is so funny? I didn't see anything funny," says Marylyn.

This causes another laughing fit from Andy, who finally chokes out a response. "You . . . you kept saying. 'Look, look!' and then when I leaned up to try to look — you scream, 'no, don't look, don't look! He'll see you.'"

Andy rocks forward again covering her mouth, in a vain attempt to stem the imploding laughter. Then, Marylyn re-creates and visualizes the scene from Andy's point of view. This forces her to bring the jeep to a halt. Seconds later, she joins Andy in convulsive laughter. The laughter from both, though still uncontrollable, slows to intermittent sputters. It would almost come to a stop, and then one or the other would say, "Look!" followed by "Don't look!", and the laughing eruptions would continue again even harder. Finally, suffering from empty tear ducts and aching stomachs, they regain some composure. Both are still gasping and gulping for air instead of breathing.

A mile further north, they pull up to and stop at the base of the dunes. Although they have only known each other a short while; a comfort bond has formed between them. Like with any two good friends, words are not always necessary in decision making. By mutual and silent consent, the girls walk slowly down to the water's edge and slip into its soothing peace.

No diving in or sprinting out this time, just leisurely back and breast strokes interrupted only by the pair of them attempting to float, which neither could do, for long. With the slightest of nods, they exit the ocean. They walk a further half-mile north to dry off some and then return to the jeep.

A new plan is "talked out" and agreed upon. This time Andy will ride in the back seat and make the identification. Marylyn will drive; this time holding down the right side of her hat brim, since they're coming from the opposite direction. Once their disguises are in place, they trundle off south to find Ross. Windows up, AC on, everything is quiet and cool. Coming from this direction, Marylyn can see that the trailer is angled a little towards the north-east. That should make the lettering on the trailer easy to read at a steady speed of 10 miles an hour. Steering with her left hand and holding down the side brim of her hat with her right, Marylyn says, "OK, here we go, ready?"

Andy holding a mock salute, half for the shade and half for concealment, says, "you bet!"

They haven't quite passed the entire trailer when, from the backseat, Andy says, "West Wind Surfboards, and there sits my baby brother, hard at work, napping under an umbrella."

"Really?" questions Marylyn, who keeps her head straight ahead.

"Big sisters are never wrong, Marylyn. All right mission accomplished, now I'm getting up front. I don't like the feeling of being chauffeured," says Andy, as she crabs over the console and plops down in the passenger seat.

Andy takes off her over-sized sun glasses and checks them out. "These things make me look like a cartoon character. Not so with you, Marylyn, they look fine on you but I need my own.

After putting on her own glasses, Andy powers down the window and leans her head out to check herself in the side view mirror.

"Shit! Stop, STOP! My glasses flew off."

That startles Marylyn so, that she swerves out the hard-packed, rutted tracks they had been in, and comes to an abrupt stop in the softer sand.

Andy jumps out quickly, muttering to herself, "I hope we didn't run over them." She finds them by the rear tire, in a mound of sand, which was pushed up by the hard stop. As she holds the glasses out towards the ocean, and away from the sun to check for damage, she notices a person coming towards her. Even with only her peripheral vision, she can tell that it's a man, that is walking in her direction. Andy knows that walk, knows that man, knows—it's Ross.

Andy spins around, then quickly steps back to the jeep, jumps in and slams the door. "Go! Go! It's Ross, he's close and he's coming this way."

Marylyn checks the rearview mirror, apparently to see if it really is Ross.

"Goddamn it, it is Ross; now Go, Go! get us out of here!"

Startled, Marylyn mashes hard on the accelerator causing the right rear tire to spin and drop down another inch.

"Stop!" says Andy, causing Marylyn to give her an exasperated look.

"Sorry, my fault," says Andy, "put the car in reverse and go back slowly."

Marylyn does as she is told and the jeep creeps backwards up the hill of sand that she's just built, but then,

205

at the top, the wheels loses traction and spin their way back down deeper into the gully they had just created.

"Doesn't this have four-wheel drive?" Andy shouts.

"Yes, I think so. I remember I asked for it. Yes, it does; it definitely has four-wheel drive."

Andy scours the dash and console, "There!" she jabs a button on the console. "Now go." Marylyn jams her foot down on the accelerator, and the jeep dropped down for half a second, then lunges forward with all four wheels spewing rooster tails of sand out behind the jeep. Marylyn has to let off the gas quickly as they are already well over the 10-mph speed limit. Each one looks out at their own side-view mirror to see who or what they left behind in their wake.

There stands Ross; wet from his dip and now plastered in sand. His arms are outstretched, palms facing up questioning the heavens. It is man's well-known interplanetary pose for, "What in the Hell just happened here"?

"We can never, ever tell him," says Andy, "Never!"

Marylyn nods in silent agreement and their bond grows even closer.

Back at the hotel a dip in the pool is followed by lunch at an umbrella-covered picnic table. A cool ocean breeze helps calm their emotions from the earlier near catastrophe. After lunch the girls split up in the hallway and go to their separate rooms to chill out and wind down.

Marylyn wakes up from her nap at a little past four in the afternoon. The clock reminds her that it's early morning down under, and it might be a good time to call Rose in Australia and give her the latest news about Ross.

Rose is overjoyed about Ross being located and excited about coming to the US, with her new friend, Woodrow. She says she'll get in touch with the blokes up north and call Marylyn back as soon as the Aussie contingent makes a flight plan.

Marylyn reminds her that if they can get to Los Angeles by Friday, Capt. Drew Michaels can meet them there and give them a free ride to Miami in his Learjet. Once there, they can rent a car for the four-hour drive to Daytona. Marylyn smiles, as she thinks about all the coming possibilities.

A knock on her door brings Marylyn to the peephole. After she lets her in, Andy suggests that they cruise the beach again. Perhaps they can follow Ross after he closes up and find out where he's staying.

"No way," says Marylyn, "After the stunt we pulled, he'd recognize that jeep right away."

"Hence," says Andy, dangling a set of keys, "a white Camaro."

"Very. . . what would you say? Enterprising?" asks Marylyn."

"Enterprising indeed, I got the idea from your rent-a-car key ring. I knew the jeep had been burned, or made, or whatever they say on TV, so voila` — a car disguise."

Marylyn agrees to another surveillance trip, but only under rigid stipulations: long range observations only, and absolutely no contact or close encounters of any kind. Her phone rings and Marylyn checks the caller ID; then she waves Andy to an upholstered chair; and sits herself down at the writing desk.

"Hello Sampson, you were next on my list to call and give the good news to. We found Ross. He's here in Daytona; just like Marcus predicted. By we, I mean Andy, Ross's sister, and myself. She's here with me now. May I put you on speaker phone?"

"Sure Marylyn, that would suite me just fine. Glad to hear the good news about Ross, and it couldn't come at a better time. Marcus and Gran Nanna have joined forces, insisting that I promised them a trip to Florida. Now, Mike, my partner, takes an early retirement and he's ready for a vacation. Plus, there's been a delay and now neither one of the limousines will be delivered for another two weeks. However, I've got a loaner and three antsy folks raring to go to Daytona. We're all just waiting for you to drop the green flag."

"Sampson, you're the last person on the envelope puzzle, and now all ten people and all the money is accounted for. It's turned into something like 'hide and seek.' Ross has been hiding, and Andy and I seeking. Now that we've found him; it's time for the big showdown. The trouble is, Ross still has zero money and isn't likely to be agreeable to take any. Now comes the hard part, carving out some of his stubborn pride and force feeding him some common sense."

"Well," Sampson says, "when you talk about people who can apply enormous amounts of pressure. I can't come up with two better candidates than Marcus and Gran Nanna. They have sent me around the bend countless times. Thanks for the news; we'll be leaving for Florida in the AM."

**

As the Camaro approaches the trailer, they can tell by the missing umbrella and chairs that 'West Winds' has closed for the day. Andy is parallel with the trailer and ready to turn back when a three-wheeler burst out from behind the trailer. Ross spins up a wall of sand as he bat-turns back towards the beach access. Andy is unable to turn around right away without being way too obvious. She has to wait until Ross is far down the beach before making her own sand spinning reversal.

With no sign of Ross when they get back to the stoplight on the highway, and no clue as to which direction he went; the girls do what most women do when confronted with a baffling situation — they go shopping.

After countless stores and hours of searching, sizing, and trying on, Marylyn returns to her room exhausted and empty handed. Maybe, the fact that you can buy anything you want, takes away the desire to actually buy anything. Andy, however, did find herself an 'Aussie' hat. The phone rings and Marylyn uses it as an excuse to stretch out on the bed. "Hello."

"G'day Mate. It's Rose here. Ready or not here we come!"

"That's great. Is everyone on board?"

"Yep, the three of us '10 percenters'. That sounds a bit more modest than saying 'millionaires.' Plus, two more hanging off the outriggers: Woodrow, my friend, and Kelvin, Storkie's mate."

"Kelvin, he's the guy who gave Ross a lift that started this all off?" Marylyn asks.

"Right, we call him 'the one percenter' because of the smaller amount he got. No worries; he's not complaining. The lot of us are booked on Qantas flight 783, and God willing we should turn up this coming Friday morning at 9:40, at LAX."

"Sounds super. I'll call our pilot buddy Drew Michaels, and make sure everything is still a go with the ride on the Learjet."

Ten minutes later Marylyn called Rose back. "Everything is a go; either Drew or his wife, Liz, will be there to meet your flight. Look for a sign that says, 'C'MON AUSSIE!'

**

The next day, Martin, Simone, and Gloria walk up to the reception desk at the Marriott in Daytona. Being the oldest at twenty-seven, Martin speaks up. "We'd like two rooms on the second floor please." Turning to the girls, he says, "Marylyn told me she's in room 216," then back to the clerk, "I take it that room 216 is on the second floor?" A slight nod from the clerk proves him correct.

"Excuse me," the voice comes from the male half of a middle-aged couple standing behind them. "Didn't mean to eavesdrop, but does that 'Marylyn' in #216, have a friend named Ross Sheehan?"

Turning to face the questioner, Martin says, "yes; who's asking?"

"I'm Frank Dearner and this is my wife, Misty. We're friends with Ross. Marylyn called us and the news about Ross being here is the reason we drove down from Carolina. We're here to meet up with her and hopefully Ross."

"Martin Maher, pleased to meet you both; this is Simone, and her friend Gloria, who is on her way back to school in Gainesville. Simone and I are also here to meet up with Marylyn, Andy, and Ross. Apparently, you haven't heard the good news Frank: Andy is here, and she and Marylyn have found Ross."

The clerk interrupts with: "We have rooms #223 and #213 available sir. Just sign here, and we'll need a credit card."

"I'll pay for our room," says Simone, who offers her card to the clerk, and nods at Gloria.

"After we all get checked in, Martin, why don't we go over to that bar for a stand-up beer. My ass is on fire; driving twelve straight hours will do that." Says Frank.

"I know the feeling," says Martin, rubbing an empathetic hand over his butt.

"Franklin!" scolded Misty.

"Oops, sorry about the language, hon."

"It's not the language, Franklin, it's the beer. It's only just after 11:00 in the morning."

"Misty, can I help it if my liver is still on daylight savings time?"

Their butts apparently resuscitated, Martin and Franklin join the girls at the table as soon as their second beers arrive. Martin and Simone tell their stories of helping Ross get closer to the finish line, and Franklin fills them in on his history with Ross, and their promise to one another years ago. That is the reason for Franklin's check and the reason for their being here. Misty explains that she and Andy were friends in high school, but lost touch once Andy married and moved away.

As they wait in the lobby for the elevator; Martin calls Marylyn on his new cell phone. After a brief explanation of who is there with him, Martin mostly just nods in agreement, saying little other than "right, sure, . . . OK."

Boarding the elevator last, Martin informs the captured crowd, "How cool! Marylyn and Andy are down near the jetty getting ready to take a surfing lesson. She says to just chill out, that she and Andy will meet us for lunch by the pool at about 2:30.

Driven by hunger rather than any previous agreement, all five recent travelers assemble poolside an hour before the appointed 2:30. Pushing two tables together, they order and get to know each other better over lunch. They are listening to yet another one of Franklin's stories about his and Ross's exploits when Andy and Marylyn turn up.

Andy is immediately engaged in a hug fest, first with Misty, then by Franklin. After introducing himself to Marylyn, Martin allows himself to be embraced too. Simone and Gloria are next; which calls for more hugs. Andy and Marylyn switch places and the introductions and hugs continue their round robin format. With everyone introduced and seated, Marylyn orders sandwiches for herself and Andy. They are more than ravenous after their surfing lessons.

Marylyn's cheeks are bulging with the final bite of her sandwich when her phone rings. Checking the caller ID, she stands up, mimes the sorry sign and steps away from the table and the noise. There isn't much of a pause before the chatter resumes.

When she returns to her seat, Marylyn explains that it had been Captain Drew Michaels on the phone. He, also being one of the ten percenters, told Marylyn that he had just loaded five loaded Australians onto his Learjet. Now, he's about to whisk them off to Miami. Seeing the confused looks of her audience, Marylyn elaborates "Drew, Captain Michaels, used part of his windfall to buy a plane and partner with Select Jets. The plan is for Select Jets to pay off his plane by charging other people to charter it. Since Drew is new to the job, he'll deliver his plane to Select Jets headquarters by dead heading it from LA to Miami. He also gets 'stick' hours in that type of jet, to qualify to fly for Select Jets. The Aussies are hitching a ride."

"Whoa, hang on a second that doesn't add up," says Martin. "There are five of the ten percenters right here at this table, Simone, you, Andy, Franklin and myself now if .
. . "

"No," interrupts Marylyn, "I see where you're going Martin but only three of the Australians are 'envelopers' or 'ten percenters' as you call them. The other two are just friends, tagging along. Drew, the pilot plus the three Aussies makes a total four 'envelopers' on the plane. Add in the five of us and you get nine. That leaves only Sampson, the limousine driver, who has already left DC and should be here tomorrow. I hope that's right — no, I'm sure that's right — we all have certified checks to prove it. The only one who didn't get a check is Ross, who is more deserving of one than anyone else."

**

The same group gets together in the morning for breakfast. The buffet smells delicious and most take larger portions than they should. But hey, it is sort of free, isn't it? After filling their plates, they peel off the end of the buffet line like ducks; circling and then landing at a large corner table.

Once everyone is seated Marylyn speaks up: "I received two phone calls this morning; one was from Sampson, the man who gave Ross his last-minute limousine ride to the lottery. Thirty minutes ago, Sampson and his family had just crossed the Georgia state line and should be here by this afternoon. The second caller was Captain Michaels, the pilot, saying that he and the Aussie contingent arrived in Miami, rented a car and should be here in about four or five hours. Drew says he's doing the driving because he's the only one who could possibly pass a sobriety test.

"Since all the beneficiaries should be here by this evening, we (glancing at Andy) have reserved and closed off a section of the Conch Key Bar for 7:30 tonight. Then, with all hands on deck tomorrow evening, we'll prepare our plan to ensnare our quarry and perform the necessary exorcisms."

Martin raises his hand and is acknowledged by Marylyn. "Gloria has to get back for classes at the University of Florida, can I borrow your Mustang to take her to Gainesville?"

"It's not my Mustang; I gave it to Simone. Ask her. Matter of fact, I have the title right here" Marylyn says, rummaging in her bag. "I just paid that car off for the third and final time a week ago. Marylyn signs the title and slides it over Simone who is sitting next to her, "Just sign and it's yours."

Before signing, Simon and Marylyn put their heads together; whispering and giggling for a moment. After agreeing with double nods, Simone takes the title and walks it over to Martin. After handing him the folded title she leans down and whispers, "You can rent a car to get back from Gainesville?" When Martin's head bobbles a "yes," she says, "When you get Gloria to her school, you get her to sign this title, then the Mustang will be hers. I will keep paying the insurance but don't tell her until you leave her at school. I will get a newer one."

*****

CONCH KEY LOUNGE

The room dividers separating the Conch Key
Lounge in half are of a Japanese design, made with rice
paper and framed in spruce lattice. This allows for privacy
without blocking out the light. The half of the lounge that
Marylyn reserved has access to the L-shaped corner of the
bar, along with a pair of restrooms and a side door.
Everyone enters through the center of the dividers where
two panels have been folded back. This half of the lounge
is also reserved for the next evening when Ross will be in
attendance, hopefully.

It is now 8:45, and behind the room dividers the
scene is more like Mardi Gras than a meeting. After
introductions, drinks flow and strangers quickly become
friends. As they feast on shrimp and blackened scallops,
voices become louder and inhibitions lower. Marylyn sees
where this get together is headed and steps away from the
group. She gives a loud, shrill, penetrating two-fingered
whistle. That brings about an abrupt and shocked silence.

Straightening her back against the bar, Marylyn
faces the more than the dozen people present. "I always
knew that would come in handy; I just never knew when.
Now, even though no one has nominated, voted for, or
elected me as the spokesperson, I feel some responsibility.
Assuming that no one else wants the job—I accept."

A mumbled, "Here, here," and several, "You go
girl" cheers secure her position.

"First, let me say it's been a pleasure meeting every
one of you. Regardless of tomorrow evening's outcome, I
think we should all stay in touch with one another and have
an annual get together. Now on to the business at hand. By
showing up here I think we have all demonstrated a

concern for Ross and his welfare. To this end, we need to come up with an idea or a plan that would persuade Ross to accept some money.

"Andy is first on the envelope list. As Ross's sister and as a sort of a partner in previous lotteries with Ross, she thinks she might be able to convince him to split her winnings. However, Ross has never mentioned money in any of his correspondences with Andy. Andy can explain more when she returns from picking up her daughter, Anna, at the airport."

"How about if, before we try to solve that problem, we each give a short explanation of how each one of us helped Ross get to the lottery in time. Kelvin, you are second on the list, and even though I know you didn't get millions, I understand Ross sent you some gas money for your part."

Kelvin walks up and stands a chaste three feet from Marylyn. Facing the group, he says, "Yeah, Ross did send me some gas money. In fact, he sent enough for the next thirty years. Anyway, I never knew Ross. I was up surfing in Noosa when Ross got all his gear knocked off. He had to sell his car to the wreckers for, I think forty bucks, and he used that to 'shout the bar'. Naturally, everyone shouted him a drink back. Just before he passed out, he mentioned he needed a ride to Coffs. When the bar closed, I lifted him up over me shoulder and poured him into me truck."

Kelvin is returning to his seat when Marylyn says, "Kelvin forgot to mention that Coffs Harbour is four hours and a couple of hundred miles out of his way."

"John, who Ross stays with while he is in Australia is up next chronologically"

Once up to the bar, John turns to Marylyn and says, "You make it sound like I have a disease. Just kidding. I know it's a time line of when things occur."

"Ross shows up on me doorstep that morning; he's crook from drink and broke as a swagman. First thing, we call his sister back in the U S; she has been ringing my house at all hours for days. She tells him, if he has the ticket, he's won the lottery. Ross finds the ticket and the two of them confirm the numbers. Then, right away, Ross finds out that he has less than two days to get the ticket to Virginia. That's when the bloody phone service ran out of money and me bloody phone shit itself."

"We knew Ross's only chance was to get on a plane to the States that afternoon. I loan him me last fifty dollars, me bloody emergency fund, so we can buy petrol for the bloody car; which I had to borrow. Then there's petrol for the bloody plane. After, I race him up to Storkie's so he can fly Ross to bloody Sydney."

"Next up 'Storkie' the amazing Aussie fly boy!" announces Marylyn.

"Don't know about amazing, lucky is the word I'd use for myself. Anyone was amazing, it was Ross. He's the one had the ba — ah, guts to jump into the rear seat, behind an unlicensed pilot, in a sort of a stolen 1943 Ryan PT-22 Recruit airplane. Ah—you don't need to mention that last bit, about the lack of a license and the sort of a stolen plane, to Ross. After nearly dumping us into the Pacific, it looks like I managed to get him close enough to airport in Sydney to catch a flight out in time."

Marylyn continues on with her job as mistress of ceremonies. "Rose, would you come up and tell us how an Aussie damsel saved a surf dude in distress?"

"There's way too many coincidences love; the fate fairies had it all lined up. I had already called a taxi to take me to the hotel. The fifty-dollar note in me bag was ready to give the poker machines a hiding. I thought the knock on the door was the taxi driver, but no, it's Ross. What are the odds? You find a young good looking bloke standing on your door step; then, he offers you a chance to win millions? In exchange for what? A ride to the airport, which I had, as in a cab on the way, and the fifty dollars at hand to cover his fare. Fate, mate. It had to be."

"Thanks Rose, I'm next on the list," says Marylyn. "I think most all of you know that Ross is a silver-tongued devil. It shouldn't come as a surprise then, that he talked me into giving him companion passes from Sydney all the way to DC. That didn't work according to plan, and I had to get him a ticket to Maui from Oahu. After that, I had to leave it in the hands of Rose's fate fairies, and our pilot friend, Captain Drew Michaels, who took the flight to Maui with Ross. I'll hand the baton over to you, Drew"

As Marylyn watches him walk up to the bar, she realizes how totally different he looked out of his uniform. He has a natural grace and seems very much at ease.

Drew nods his thanks. "Like you, Marylyn, I fell under the persuasive lip service of one Ross Sheehan. Ladies, you better hide your daughters; this man could talk the panty girdle off the Statue of Liberty.

It took him less than the twenty-five- minute flight to Maui to convince me that I should give up my chance to see the birth of my second daughter, so that he could challenge extremely long odds, and get to a Virginia lottery office in time. I knew his chances were slim at best, yet, Ross made it sound like a sure thing. Even as I tore up my ticket, which meant I was giving up my seat, I felt hypnotized. As I watched Ross board the plane to LA, I was sure that my marriage, and my life as I knew it, were over. Needless to say, the check came just in time."

Simone is next; her gait approaching the bar makes it seem as if she were gliding on roller blades. Like Irish dancers, nothing above her waist moves.

"Ross and I bump into each other outside the airport chapel. I see a lost look on his face and I say for him to go inside and to ask for whatever he needs. This chapel has no special religions, so all people are welcome. I see him again when he comes out, and he says he feels better. I tell him I would pray that his hopes would come true."

"Later at the other end of the airport, Ross and another man knock a thief to the floor. The police come and take the thief away. Ross explains to me that the thief stole his property and now that he has it back, he needs to get to Washington DC. I give him my work mileage to get him a stand-by ticket to Chicago. That is as far as I can help him."

"Martin Maher, a soon to be member of the PGA Tour, COME ON DOWN!"

"Thanks, Marylyn, but that's more of a wish than a fact. However, I do feel very much at home with this crowd. Being a golfer I'm used to people who talk loud and dress bad. Just kidding . . . everyone here seems nice. That might be because most of them are loaded, and rich too. OK, enough golf jokes."

"It's strange, when I first saw Ross at the airport in Chicago, I planned to ask him to loan me money for a ticket to Denver. He looked like a guy who would give you the shirt off his back. He would have too, except for the fact that the shirt on his back wasn't his. He was broker than I was. Ross told me about the lottery ticket and his need to get to DC. Somehow, with a pretty much a useless private jet card, possibly some of Simone's prayers, (a nod to her) and a double load of Irish BS, we tricked and cajoled Ross onto a private jet to DC."

"The final hero in the, "Mr. Sheehan goes to Washington" saga is Sampson Samuels."

"No hero here, Marylyn, just a fortunate guy being in the right place at the right time. I was sitting in the coffee shop at general aviation, wondering how I was going to pay for my transmission to get repaired. That's when Ross came flying in; looked at the clock, and commenced to rant.

I told him, that clock was wrong. That they had forgot to set that clock back when daylight savings time ended, early on Sunday morning — that he had another hour. Then he told me about the winning lottery ticket, and lickety-split we're out the door. No doubt about it: we used every drop of engine oil and transmission fluid and every pound of compression, but we got that old screaming, smoking Caddy to the church on time."

"Indeed you did Sampson, and for that we all owe you. No, actually, we all owe each other the exact same debt of gratitude. Each one of us had an equal and indispensable part in Ross's success; without the actions of any one of us, none of us would be here.

"And now," Marylyn says, "to the last name on the envelope, Franklin Dearner."

"You know, Marylyn," Franklin says, "there is one person who is on that envelope and who did receive ten percent and yet wasn't indispensable in Ross's success — me. There's also one person who isn't on the envelope, didn't get a check, but was indispensable, and that person is Ross Sheehan. I feel kind of like a street-hobo dining at a nice family's Christmas feast. Hey, I'm eating well and I'm not sending the check back, but I am determined to see that Ross gets his fair share."

Later, the "ten percenters" and their friends splinter into smaller pods. Andy, who has quietly rejoined the party, brings her daughter Anna over and introduces her to the first pod. It consists of Frank and Misty Dearner, along with Gran Nanna, Sampson, and Marcus, his eleven-year-old son. When Anna smiles at Marcus and offers her hand, he freezes and instantly becomes a statue. Marcus finally manages to nod his head in a barely noticeable up and down motion.

Sampson tries to come to the rescue. "What Marcus means is that he is pleased to meet you, Anna. Isn't that right, Marcus?" Another robotic attempt at a nod. After Andy and Anna walk away, Marcus glares at his father with a grimace that would usually be associated with one being extremely constipated.

Wisely, Sampson steps away and moves up to the bar to talk to Marylyn. "Sorry to bring you bad news, but I'm afraid my son's love interests have switched to a younger woman. It looks like he's already decided to drop you for Andy's daughter. 'Love is so fleeting.' Now all I have to do is convince Gran Nanna that she's not Ross's dream girl. Lately, she's been acting crazy. She's dressing up for breakfast, no old bathrobe and a head scarf for her anymore. Tonight, there's makeup and even a hint of perfume; the kind of perfume she only ever wears when she has a "dinner date with the deacon."

Meanwhile Gran Nanna has sidled up behind Sampson and is standing there, listening. Marylyn can't warn Sampson because Gran Nanna is keeping her eyes locked on Marylyn's.

"Sampson, you don't know from nothing," Gran Nanna spits. "Ross said, he thought I favored, ARETHA!" She emphasizes that with a snap of her generous hips slamming into Sampson.

"Lord, give me shelter," moans a tottering Sampson.

A spoon being tapped on the side of an empty carafe is enough for Marylyn to quiet the crowd for a second time. "Remember everyone, we'll meet in Andy's room # 208, at 5:30 tomorrow evening."

*****

SNARE

Marylyn replaces the Merriam-Webster pocket dictionary on the shelf, and walks out of the drugstore. Just as she thought, the word "snare" is a kinder, more gentle word than "trap." 'Snare: a position or situation from which it is difficult to escape from. b (1) something by which one is entangled involved in difficulties or impeded: (2) something deceptively attractive.' It sounds just like her and Andy's plan. She didn't care for the term "trap" which to her conjured up images of small furry animals with their legs pinned in the steel jaws of a spring-loaded weapon.

Marylyn and Andy's plan involves a seductive, enticing setting, with the loving intention of helping Ross. And from which, he damn well better not try to evade or escape.

She waves her pass at her (now) friend in the beach access shed. Marylyn is getting used to, and welcomes, the slush-like feel of the loose sand fronting the ramp. Minutes later she passes "West Winds" with a casual glance. Armed with sunglasses, a scarf and driving the undercover Camaro, Marylyn has no fear of discovery. She sees Ross, who is helping two guys unload their stand-up paddle boards.

She parks several hundred yards up the beach, backing in, so she can face the ocean. From this vantage point, she can also see the umbrella and will know the minute Ross takes it down. That's probably one of the last things he would do when he's closing up for the day.

Dusk. It's the first hint of nature's dimmer switch at work.
It has just begun to do its thing when the umbrella at "West Winds" flops down and disappears from her sight.

Marylyn is watching and is instantly on the move. She rolls up to the trailer and slides out of the Camaro. Ross, who is just locking up the trailer, turns and says, "Sorry ma'am, were closed for the day."

Marylyn takes off her sunglasses, the scarf, shakes out her hair and then puts her hands on her hips in a show of defiance. Silence, then an awkward smile appears on Ross' face. His head tilts to the side and his eyes sparkle with recognition.

"Is that? . . . Marylyn, is that you?"

"In the flesh, whatever flesh I have left; I've been peeling for two days."

"You look great, Marylyn, tan and fit."

"No, you're the one who is tan and fit, Ross; I'm sunburned and sore."

"Well, you look terrific. I don't know how you found me, but I'm really happy that you did."

Another awkward silence, then they each take tiny steps forward and come together in sort of a wooden, platonic hug. That is followed by an equally clumsy kiss: half lip, half cheek. Who knew who aimed where? Both smile, in sort of a nervous embarrassment. This isn't the comfortable feeling of slipping into a pair of old shoes; it felt more like a first date at the junior prom.

"Back at work, I see. Would it break your rules if a lady bought you a beer or two?"

"No — not as long as I can return the favor. If I remember correctly, I already owe you a favor from the plane."

"Really," chuckles Marylyn, "Well, I've retired from flying so I'd have to check back in my day planner to be sure. Before the return of any favors though, it seems apparent that we are both out of practice in the art of hugging and kissing."

"I agree. The window for improvement in that area seems to be wide open," says Ross. "Should we try again?"

They did, and slowly, with teasing tongues and a full-on embrace.

"Wow," said Marylyn, "that is quite an improvement." Ross leans forward for another kiss, but Marylyn put him off by saying, "Why don't we delay the practice session until after we get the sand off? How about we meet for a beer in about an hour. You know the Conch Key Lounge in the Marriott?"

"Sure, I'll be there."

**

Ross's mind is traveling at warp speed — however, like a scud missile it has no guidance system. Nervous impulses flash aimlessly from one neuron to another. Twice, people behind him have blasted Ross with angry beeps and honks. These were to urge him through green traffic lights, where he had remained stopped.

Pulling into his sub-leased beach cottage, his mind is still spinning. He takes the key out of the bike and just sits there, taking in some soothing breaths. "Back at work, I see", she had said. Did she know he was broke? If so, she didn't seem to be stressing over it. Still, he felt very defensive about any hint of gifts or charity. Ross still felt— made my bed and...

Anyway, I'm just going out for a couple of beers with a chick. Even as that thought flashes by, he knows it isn't true.

Once inside the cottage, a glance at his notebooks calms him a bit. Writing, for just for a few nights, has given him an insight into a new purpose in life. It isn't ingrained yet, far from it, but he feels that writing could be a meaningful pathway forward. The pages of his first notebook are almost full of what his grandmother called "scribbleigraphy," his hand writing.

Back to the present, first a shower and a shave. Then hope that Rusty, the sub-lessee, left some clothes he can use for the evening. After a shower, he finds that Rusty's clothing tastes range from retro salvation army to nouveau salvation army. Although he does find a decent pair of khakis to go with the new "West Winds" sweatshirt Hap had given him. Ross combs his hair, brushes his teeth (again), and is out the door.

All the way to the Marriott he can't get that old piano solo by Floyd Cramer out of his mind. He can hear the melody, but the name? Is it "First Date" or is it "Last Date?" Sometimes, they are one and the same.

**

Standing in the doorway of the Conch Key Lounge, Ross feels like the two sides of his brain are having a tug of war over his sanity. One side is anxious to follow up on his and Marylyn's initial encounter; the other side wants to call in sick and delay tonight's date until mañana, some indefinite time in the future. Conflict and interest are conflicting. Before he can put his cold feet into reverse, Marylyn spins her barstool around and chirps, "Hey, sailor, over here!"

The bartender greets him as he is sitting down with, "Hey, Ross, you having a draft?"

Glancing at Marylyn's nearly full beer he says, "A draft is fine thanks." As the bartender walks away Ross leans over and whispers to Marylyn, "Did you catch his name?"

"It's Bruce. I told him I knew you, and he talked like you two were old friends?"

"No, seen him surfing, didn't even know he worked here."

When his beer is delivered, Ross says, "Hey Bruce, you got some good waves out there Friday."

"Thanks, but you caught the wave of the day, Ross. Every-one in the water was stoked about that giant left you caught."

After Bruce leaves, Ross turns to see a puzzled look on Marylyn's face.

Ross answers her look with: "Surfers like compliments, so they throw bouquets; that way you're sure to get one back."

"The bouquet he threw you was bigger than the bouquet you threw him," says Marylyn.

Ross shrugs, "My wave was bigger."

Three couples come in and sit down at the bar and almost immediately the atmosphere in the bar changes. It goes from secluded and private, to noisy and crowded. The couples are a bit loud; when Bruce offers Ross and Marylyn refills, she opts for a pitcher. and asks if they can drink it on the other side of the room dividers.

"Sure," says Bruce, "just slide open up a couple of panels and I'll be there with the beer."

Bruce walks back behind the bar through the open flap at the other end and brings them their beer just as they are sitting down, "Enjoy" he says.

Marylyn, who puts her Australian hat on for the short trip through the partitions; takes it off upon arrival and places it on the table. "Nice hat," remarks Ross.

"Thanks, I always wanted an original Australian Akubra. It seems ironic, all those trips Down Under, and I end up buying this one in Daytona Beach."

Marylyn has inconspicuously seated herself so that she faced the side entrance door. "So Ross, you made it; that's pretty obvious, I mean the check was good. I knew you got there in time but when I didn't hear from you, I got worried."

"Jeeze, that makes me feel even worse than I already do. Truthfully, I was embarrassed, I was sure I'd done something really stupid; and I felt sorry for myself.

226

The messages were late and lame. Then the number I left for you to call— well, I didn't know Hap's phone had been disconnected.

Then, after some much needed rest and a couple of surf sessions, I returned to normal. Granted, my normal is not very normal. Looking back, I can't believe the timing, the people, how things lined up. Could it have been coincidence, fate, luck, a combination — who knows? Everyone was an essential part of the end result, except Franklin Dearner, who got his check for a promise I made to him, years ago. As you may have guessed, my word is essential to me. So, I'm good with all of it now. I'm especially good with having you sitting here with me."

Marylyn starts to thank Ross for the compliment, but the noise of the pressure vacuum escaping from the side door jolts both of them. Marylyn grabs Ross's hands to keep him from turning around, saying, "That's just some misguided tourist."

She keeps Ross's attention with the story of how she tracked him down, As Andy moves silently across the floor.

"As I was saying, tracking you down was a simple matter of deductive reasoning. I have a friend who worked in a bank, and she knew that the routing number would tell me the name and location of the bank the check was drawn on. We figured the other name on the check is likely an attorney, the POA being the hint. Kenny Mallard, the bank manager, is a very nice man, but he should never play poker. When fibbing, his face lights up like a ripe tomato. After I tricked the truth out of him, it was an easy walk to Tim Donald's office. There, I had an enlightening twenty-minute talk with Tara, Tim's wife. After that came a sixteen-hour train ride, and here I am."

"Your turn Ross. How about the last half of your trip? I lost track after Maui; when Drew gave you his seat, making it possible for you to fly on to LA. What then?"

"Well, in LA, I met a young woman, Simone, who gifted me a standby ticket to Chicago. There, I met a broke golf pro, Martin Maher, and somehow between the two of us, we BS'd and scammed a seat for me on a private jet to DC. There I met Sampson, the nicest two- legged-t-rex, taxi driving, law bruising guy you'd ever find. He gave me the most exciting and terrifying forty-five-minute taxi ride in four-wheel history. We made it easy; had maybe two, three minutes to spare."

"I'm sure there's more to it than that," says Marylyn.

Ross decides to lay his cards on the table. "Well, I did manage to make ten new millionaires along the way."

"But not you."

"No, not me — how's that for a guy who says he's good with numbers."

Ten red tipped, ivory fingers appear from behind Ross' head and softly cup themselves over his eyes. He is half out of his chair when Andy's voice croons, "Guess whoooo?"

"My God," he says re-seating himself; his head moves slightly from side to side. "Well, it can't be — no wait. I know who it is; It's Eleanor Roosevelt."

"No, silly, it's your sister!"

He stands and they share an awkward embrace with the chair between them.

As soon as they are all sitting again Ross looks from one to the other. "So, it seems like you guys have met previously and arranged this surprise."

"Guilty," says Marylyn, "but I didn't know she is going to pull that 'guess who?' thing."

"She did that all the time when we are kids," says Ross, smiling at Andy. "It seems, she was most fond of doing it when we are the only two people in the house; it was really baffling. I'd be sitting there by myself, reading or writing, and up would come the hands and then I'd hear the Guess who?"

"And you know what Marylyn," Andy grins, "he never once guessed it was me."

"Speaking of writing, Ross, on the plane from Australia you said that you needed to find the right storyline or plot. It seems to me that this last adventure of yours would make a great book."

"I agree with Marylyn." Says Andy. "Ross has always been a gifted story teller and now that he has a suitable vehicle, he needs to get in to writing like he got into surfing. Strange how this might play out — 'Surf holiday convinces man to write book.' As they say: truth is sometimes stranger than fiction."

"Thank you ladies for your input and your concern. It must be true that great minds think alike, because, of my own accord, I have decided to pursue writing. In keeping with that goal, I have purchased the most rudimentary tools, pen and paper. I have already started writing about my recent journey."

Both ladies heap verbal applause on Ross's decision and the evening seem headed towards a glorious ending — until Andy mentions giving Ross some money.

That's when Ross drops the depth charge that burst the bliss bubble. He tells them in no uncertain terms that he will not accept any money, under any circumstances, from anybody.

Andy stands up so violently that her chair screeches backwards and tips over. It seems that Ross is not the only member of the Sheehan family who is stubborn. As Andy marches past the opening in the dividers, Marylyn gets up and replaces Andy's chair. Ross is staring down at the table when Marylyn says, "I need to make sure she's all right." Then she follows Andy's path out through the partitions, and back into the other half of the bar.

"Absolutely not! That's what Ross said the minute I even mentioned chipping in some money," Andy says standing by Franklin's and Misty's table. She is explaining what just took place in the next room. Martin Maher, seeing that this is personal, stands and offers Andy his seat. He and Simone leave, saying that they need to talk to Drew Michaels about Select Jets.

Then Marylyn turns up and takes the empty seat next to Misty. Andy and Marylyn recount how everything was going along swimmingly, until Ross erupts and becomes adamant about not accepting any money— from anyone, under any circumstances.

"Really? We'll see about that," says Franklin. "Misty, hand me that check book; you know the big one, the one with all the cash in it. What's it called? Money Market Funds?"

"Yes, here it is," says Misty, handing him the checkbook "What are you going to do Franklin?"

"As Marlon Brando said, 'I'm going to make him an offer he can't refuse," Franklin says, as he exits the room— checkbook in hand.

*****

SOMEONE ELSE'S SHOES

For a large guy, Franklin is almost silent as he passes through the dividers. He remains unnoticed until he pulls back the chair opposite Ross. Startled, Ross jerks his head up first in surprise and then in recognition.

"Jesus, H. — Franklin, you about gave me the big one!" says Ross, placing his hand over his heart. "What in the world are you doing here?" Then Ross is up, steps around the table, and smoothers Franklin in a two-armed bear hug. A three-handed, hand shake (two hands by Ross) is followed by another hug, finally Franklin says, "Let's sit."

"You know Ross, your check, along with all the other million dollar checks that I've gotten, could not have come at a better time. Seriously, Misty, the kids and I all thank you. Now, concerning this situation about money."

"Look," Ross says, "I made my bed . . ."

Franklin holds up his hand like a white gloved traffic cop. "I'm having my say now Ross; when I finish, you can have yours." Franklin was the older of the two, and used to having the dominate role. "Time being, I talk and you listen, OK?"

Ross nods.

"You know, Ross, you were always pretty much a horse's ass. Life to you was just one E ticket ride at Disney World after another. No wife, no job to speak of, no responsibilities. That's cool, ASAP, (always surf and party) a lot of guys envy that life style. What I'm saying is this: being a horse's ass is not such a bad thing; now being a jackass, that's a whole different animal. Allow me to help you not to become a complete jackass."

"Apparently, you remembered the promise we made to each other years ago; and that's why I got the check, right? The promise was that if either of us won a lottery or had a windfall of more than a million dollars we would give the other guy ten percent? Right?"

Ross, says, "Yes, that was it exactly, but ..."

Franklin cuts off Ross's attempt at a rebuttal with another hand signal, and continues on.

"Recently, I was fortunate enough to receive a windfall of almost three and a half million dollars. Like you, I keep my promises; and I know you wouldn't ask me to go back on a promise or break my word. Therefore, I'm going to keep that promise, and my word, by giving you ten percent of my recent windfall." Staring hard at Ross, Franklin says, "you wouldn't ask a man to break his word, would you?" Franklin starts filling out the check, saying, "that's Sheehan with two E's, right?"

All Ross can say is, "Yes, two E's."

Turning Marylyn's Aussie hat upside down, Franklin drops his folded check into it. "Now let's have a toast to being undeservedly wealthy."

Picking up his glass to clink against the pitcher already in Franklin's hand, Ross says, "you snookered me pal."

"You made the rules buddy; therefore, you were easily snooked."

Like all good bartenders, Bruce seems to be able to read minds, or livers as the case may be. He picks up the now empty pitcher, replaces it with a full one, and adds two frosted glasses.

After Bruce leaves, Franklin resumes his serious demeanor. "I'm sure you had a lot of terrific and rewarding things happen to you, since you found out that you won the lottery. Let me ask you this: from the start of your trip, until this very moment, what was the most fun? What gave you the absolute, best feeling?"

After a long moment of deliberation, Ross smiles and says, "Writing those checks — writing those ten, actually twelve, checks. That was by far the best feeling I've ever had."

"I thought it might be. Know why I thought that?"

"No why?" says Ross.

"Because just now, writing that check to you is one of the best feelings I've ever had. It doesn't top marriage and kids, but it sure feels great," says Franklin.

"Don't you think that Andy, Marylyn, Martin, and the rest of the people who helped you, deserve to get that same feeling of happiness that we've had. They've earned the right to get that feeling, Ross. Put yourself in their shoes. They just want to share some of their good fortune with you; after all, you shared your good fortune with them. They deserve the right to return the favor, and to feel good about it. Let them give as freely and receive as much pleasure from it as we have."

"And finally. If anyone in this group does decide to give you anything, don't mumble any horse shit about, 'you not needing anything' or 'them not having to do this.' Just fake being humble, and say thank you."

*****

PAYBACKS

Before Ross can fully recover from Franklin's verbal spanking, a loud "G'DAY MATE!" comes bellowing in from the partitions. He is stunned to see John and Storkie, beers in hand, sauntering towards him. "I've come for me fifty bucks mate," John says. "Just kidding mate, heard you are a bit short so I'm letting you off the hook. I have recently become a man of some means, and as such, I am no longer in need of such a pittance." Delighted with his verbal high road, John slides a check into the hat and says "I really mean this Ross, thanks mate."

Ross is so stunned, he's speechless. His eyes glisten and he doesn't trust his voice; instead, he gives John a 'thumbs up'. Then it's Storkie's turn. "Your pilot friend, Drew, let me spell the second seat guy for a bit on our flight across the US. I had a seat in the 'mayor's office', mate. I learned a lot. I even offered to fly us back to LA when the time comes, but Captain Michaels said, no way. He said, in Ameriker you actually need a pilot's license to fly a airoplane. Imagine that. Seriously, when I get back home, I'm getting a proper commercial flying license. Once I get it, John might come in with me and buy a small private jet plane to charter. You might want to come in on it with us Ross, maybe start up a Select Jet franchise in Australia." Storkie looks to John for support, who nods in the affirmative.

"You did a better than ordinary job of keeping your end of our bargain, Ross. I'm here to show you that I, too, am a man who keeps his word. Here's your watch back; piece of crap mate, but it did keep good time."

"Easy Storkie, or I'll tell the others that your surname translates into "CABBAGE ASS.""

"Hang on there, mate! Let's keep that between us and I won't tell how you let a bloke who has no flying license take you on a near death flight of sky surfing — with pelicans, no less. Plus, the fact that he did it in a semi-stolen World War Two pilot training plane with a wooden propeller."

A deal of mutual blackmail is struck. After flying a very small paper airplane check into Marylyn's Aussie hat, Storkie grabs John and they leave the same way they have entered. They step aside at the partition opening to allow Simone through.

Walking towards Ross, she possesses an aura about her that says she already has one foot in heaven. He doesn't know who is shadowing Simone, until he recognizes Kelvin's goofy grin.

"Simone, it's wonderful to see you again." Ross stands, and gives her cheek a kiss. "Kelvin, you're also a surprise, a happy one to be sure, and I'm glad to see you too."

"Is that right?" says Kelvin, and offers his own cheek for kissing.

"Not that happy," Ross says, shaking his hand. "How'd you end up with this mob?"

"Ran into Storkie down in Coffs whilst buying a car— actually, with the money you sent. The Stork and I started off on opposing sides, trying to buy the same car, but we ended up as mates. We've met for tennis a few times, and then he decides to shout me a ticket to come see you, in Ameriker. I'm finding things here in the States very attractive," says Kelvin, as his eyeballs flash a left flank at Simone, and his infectious grin grows even bigger.

Simone speaks softly as she drops her check into the center of the "Snowy River" hat vault. "Ross, always you will be in my thoughts; you have given many people, more people than you know, a chance for a better future."

"She's something, aye Ross? Today was her first time on a surfboard. After we figured out that she was left-handed and a goofy foot, she caught on real quick. Tomorrow, we're at it again; I'm giving Simone surfing lessons, and she going to teach me how to speak Spanish."

"It's easy to see who got the short end of that stick," says Ross. "Kelvin, I'm sure you'll keep a keen eye on Simone, in and out of the water."

"They'll be no worries on that matter, mate." Simone and Kelvin turn into each other as they leave, lightly touching hands as they walk away.

Rose shows up next, with a man Ross doesn't recognize. He is not a young man but he's wiry and fit; a bald head and rimless glasses add years to his appearance. Ross stands, "A Rose by any other name is still a beauty."

"Not exactly Shakespeare, Ross Sheehan, but I'll take that compliment along with a hug and a kiss, thank you very much," says Rose.

After the hug, Rose holds him at arms-length and says: "Never did I think I'd see you again, mate. It seems you've met with some friendly leprechauns who have kept you traveling under some very lucky stars.

"Sorry, let me introduce you to Woodrow Truman, my good friend, and now business partner. After I cashed that check of yours Ross, I was determined not to give it all to the poker machines, so I bought the hotel where I play them. Now, even when I lose, I win. Right, Woodrow?"

"Right, and it's Woody, if you don't mind, Rose."

"Woody it is love," says Rose. "Woody is the manager of the hotel that I bought; now since I sign his pay checks, he fancies himself a gigolo." Ross looks over at Woody, who beams with pride, and gives Ross a big 'thumbs up'. In a show of male support, Ross fires a big wiggling thumbs up back at Woody.

Rose clears her throat. "Can't say I was too surprised to hear that your heart was bigger than your purse, Ross. Well, you've a good group of friends here, so take our kindness graciously, just as we did yours. The next time you're Down Under mate, drop in on us at The Great Southern Hotel in Liverpool." She gives Ross a card, adds a swift peck on the cheek, and drops her check into the hat, all in one fluid motion.

"Come on Woodrow, Rose says, "let's go find us a night cap."

As they're leaving, Rose and Woody stop and chat briefly with Captain Drew Michaels. Drew sits down and looks back towards the departing couple. "Two of the soberer members of the Australian Olympic Drinking Team that boarded my plane in LA. They all were pretty much under the influence when got on the plane, and amazingly, walked off in Miami unaided, after six more hours of partying. Hell, I suspect they had been drinking for the whole fourteen hours from Sydney. Speaking of drinking, here, I brought you a fresh one," Drew says, as he slides a beer over to Ross.

"Thanks Drew. Marylyn says your new baby girl is doing fine and that your wife has forgiven you."

"Yep, all the girls are doing great, and I wanted to let you know that I've named my newest daughter in your honor. Although, I still don't know how you convinced me to take such a long shot. Right now, we call her Chancy, but when she gets older she may like her real name, Chance."

"Chance Michaels, sounds cool; she seems to already be lucky. Christened with a name like that, and we already know that she's smart, look who she chose for a dad."

"This." Says Drew, dropping his check into the hat, "is just chump change compared to the wealth of character you have shown, Ross. Here's my card; your name is on a very short list. My service will put you straight through, any time. You ever need anything, I got you covered front to back — head to toe."

Drew walks away. Marylyn who has silently snuck back in by way of the bar, comes up behind Ross and cups her hands over his eyes. She smushes her boobs on either side of Ross's head and cradling it in her bosom clouds she leaned down and whispers "Guess whose?"

"Well, says Ross, I'm just guessing, but I'm pretty sure they're not Eleanor Roosevelts."

Marylyn chuckles and says, "I thought you could use a bathroom break and then maybe you would like to meet me on the patio deck for some fresh air? I told the others we might take a breather, and I'd let them know when you're ready for your next audience. First though, we need to put these, (Marylyn flattens out the checks) some place safe. She folds them in half, pulls out the top of her scoop neck t-shirt, and slides the checks down her well-defined cleavage highway. Ross watches in astonishment, not sure that he has seen what he just saw.

"There," says Marylyn, "they should be safe in there for a while."

"How long is a while?" asks Ross, with a lecherous grin.

Marylyn arches her eyebrows in tandem and smiles, "Only time will tell, and time will only tell me."

Placing her now empty Aussie hat back on her head, Marylyn walks east towards the patio door; Ross pivots west towards the men's room.

*****

SUNSET

Ross walks out on the patio deck and joins Marylyn, who's looking out at the ocean. Mr. Sun is watching traces of daylight disappear in his rearview mirror, as he continues to arch his way west across the country. There is still enough ambient light to see that the evening glass off has left a good chance for rideable waves in the morning. Ross thinks a lot about waves. He thinks waves are like snowflakes; no two are ever exactly the same. Looking at Marylyn, "you want to go surfing tomorrow?"

"I'd love to, but I'm just beginning. Would you happen to know of a good surf instructor?"

"Must be your lucky night, lady, because I do actually. Yeah, I know a guy."

"Then," says Marylyn, turning to Ross, "we have a date." She seals that statement with a kiss, which started politely and then steadily increases in length and passion. A breathless halt brings them to a silent agreement that they should go back inside.

Marylyn takes one last giant breath of ocean air, as if she wants to keep it forever. "I love breathing salt air; it makes my lungs feel exhilarated."

"Looks like they're exhilarated too," Ross says, nodding at the two distinct buttons that suddenly appear — protruding from Marylyn's white cotton tee-shirt.

"There they go misbehaving again, bad girls. I guess if we were in Australia, they would be called "traveletts." One final canoodle at the patio door, and they stroll back into the 'Conch.'

Marylyn leaves Ross at the table, saying that she is going to the ladies and would bring them back a couple of beers.

Almost immediately after Ross sits down he is joined by none other than Martin Maher, the Chicago connection.

"Man," Martin says, as he sits down across from Ross, "am I glad I found you!"

"Yeah, why's that?" Asks Ross.

"Because you owe me fifty thousand dollars," says Martin.

Ross's face crinkles up into a question, "I do?"

"Absolutely. You remember that kid named Sidney who worked behind the counter at Select Jets in Chicago?"

A nod from Ross. "Sure, I remember Sidney; without his help, we would both still be sitting in 'the windy city.'"

"Well then Ross, you should remember this: just before you got on the plane to DC you said to get Sidney's information, and if you got to the lottery in time, I should make sure that Sidney was suitably compensated. When the check showed up, I knew you had made it. I deemed that a hundred thousand dollars would be suitable compensation for young Sidney, and I thought you'd be happy to chip in half."

"Delighted to. Sidney has crossed my mind more than a few times since Chicago. He showed great imagination and some very smooth fabrication in saving our bacon. How about you give me Sidney's information and if any of these checks (glancing at the stack) are good, I'll send him another hundred thousand, rather than pay you the fifty?"

"Excellent! You know, Ross, that check took a lot of the pressure off me. Not being worried about money has freed me up; I'm playing loose. I've finished solo seventh and tied twelfth on the PGA tour in the last two weeks. Meaning, enough money won for full time status on the 2001 Nike Tour and probably get me somewhere between six to ten starts on the PGA Tour."

"Then, there's Gloria, Simone's cousin, she's gorgeous and she plays golf for the University of Florida. They have a match this Friday, and I'll be there. This," says Martin, releasing his check over the now empty hat 'is just a drop in the bucket', pun intended."

Marylyn returns with the beers and Ross starts to introduce Martin, when Marylyn says, "Oh, we've met; how you doing Martin?"

"I was wondering," says Ross, "and now I know. I'm being conned by the very people I thought I was conning."

Marylyn walks out with Martin, saying they had to find some insurance papers to give to Gloria.

When Ross looks up, Sampson, all 6'1, 243 lbs. of him, is striding towards him. He is all straight lines, squares, and rectangles. A square head sits on a straight shoulder line. Two heavily pumped rectangular arms hang on either side of a square trunk. All of this mass rests on two stout rectangular legs. One might think that Sampson's gait, with his physique, would be a bit stiff. Not so. Walking towards Ross, his carriage is fluid — almost graceful. He's a phone booth, gliding on roller blades.

As he gets closer, tiny, flashing meteors of light from above ricochet off his clean-shaven head, and some of Sampson's straight lines began to quiver. The skin around his eyes begins to crinkle, and tiny parentheses bloom around his lips, forming a smile. "Surf Dude, you've put me in a bit of a pickle, my man."

Ignoring that for a moment, Ross says, "Well, if it isn't the Mario Andretti of Arlington, Virginia."

Ross steps around the table; he gives Sampson a handshake and a tentative embrace. A bear hug from Sampson might break a couple of ribs. "New threads man! You're looking good! Now, what's this about a pickle I supposedly put you in?"

241

"First my son. Marcus is so 'stoked', is that the word?" A nod from Ross. "Well, he's so stoked that all he talks about is surfing. It's surfing clothes, surfing magazines, surfing videos, and now that we're here in Florida, it's even worse; he's begging me to buy him a surfboard. He's even threatened to run away, leave home, and come live with you. It would serve you right if I let him. Ross, he's so amped; he's driving me crazy. He says you promised him free surfing lessons."

"I did, and I will give him lessons, first chance I get. I'll teach him how to catch a wave, and how to stand up. He will learn to wipeout on his own. I'll give him a board to use for the whole day. My prediction is, that by the end of the day, he'll be so tired, his ass so worn out, he won't be a bother to anyone. You just keep a close eye on him when he's in the water. And on land, if he gets too stoked, you might just have to remind him to eat. The only thing he might bug you about: getting his butt and the board to the beach the next day."

"Thanks, I appreciate that," says Sampson. "Good news! Mike is taking early retirement from the state police and joining me in the limousine business. Plus, I've been talking with Drew Michaels, the pilot, and he says he'll speak to Select Jets about using our limousine service for their customers at Dulles and Reagan National."

"Great, it sounds like your business is getting off to a flying start."

"Ross, come on now, if you're going to be a writer, you'll need better material than that."

"Everyone's a critic," smiles Ross.

"Now if I can just keep Gran Nanna's delusions in check," says Sampson.

"She's here?" asks Ross.

A small cough from behind Sampson causes both men to look towards the opening in the panels. Gran Nanna, in a dress and a hat more suited for the Kentucky

Derby than a hotel bar, struts her way closer. She keeps
Marcus reigned in beside her with a vice grip on his bicep.

Ross stands and salutes the glare out of his eyes.
"Nan, so good to see you again. For a moment, I thought it
was Aretha, herself."

Now standing next to Sampson, Gran Nanna
flashes her eyes triumphantly at her son; then lashes out
with a lateral hip shot that actually unbalances Sampson
and makes him take a step to the side. After giving Ross a
hard look, Sampson rolls his eyes up towards the heavens.

"Hey Ross, when do I get my free surfing lesson?"
chirps Marcus.

"Tomorrow morning, my man, under one
condition."

"What's the condition?" asks Marcus timidly.

"Lose the hat," says Ross.

Marcus snatches off his Frank Sinatra style
Budweiser logo hat with one hand and hides it behind his
back. He uses his other hand to dunk a check into the
Aussie hat, and smiles. "Done."

Less than a minute after the Samuel's clan leaves,
Marylyn returns. She gives Ross a kiss on the cheek, slides
him a beer, and sits down. Reaching into the hat, she fishes
out the two checks. "These should make a total of ten; let's
see," and with that she wedges out the secreted checks from
her bosom bank and counts. "Yep ten. Now do you have a
deposit slip handy?"

"No. Wait, actually I do. The lady at the bank typed
up some checks and deposit slips for me until my
personalized ones arrive."

Marylyn grabs a pen from her bag and says, "I'm
going to write 'deposit only' on the back of each check, then
you sign your name under 'deposit only' — that way,
you're protected, the money can only be deposited into
your account, OK?" Ross nods yes, and when they have

finished their respective duties Marylyn says, "Deposit slip?"

Ross plucks it from the inside of his meager cash stash and hands it over. "Thanks," says Marylyn and then flashes her dynamic duo again as the checks, and the deposit slip, disappear again down the front of her scoop neck t-shirt.

Ross continues to stare at Marylyn's chest saying "Your girls have apparently always been healthy, now you've just made them wealthy; could wise be far off?"

Marylyn gives a non-committal shrug.

"Maybe, I could teach them to how to read," says Ross.

"What? What are you talking about? Don't be silly."

"Braille?" queries Ross.

"My God, you're hopeless; let's get out of here." But, she is smiling.

Not a word is spoken, but by silent and mutual agreement they stop at the partition opening and embrace. Lips merge and hands roam over new and unexplored territory. Arms around the other's waist, they wave goodnight to Bruce as they head out the door and into the lobby.

They wait for the elevator, and after another passionate clutch and release, Ross's lips are nuzzling Marylyn's ear, "Remember, I owe you one from the plane?"

"I don't know," murmurs Marylyn, "with penalty and interest, I think it's more like two now."

"There you have it, fans; on top of everything else she also possesses a great mathematical mind." That seems to be cause for a celebration, and what better way to celebrate than another embrace and another reciprocal grope.

Just at that moment, Marcus, two strides in front of his father, comes around the corner and stops dead in his tracks. Marylyn and Ross are engaged in a full bodied, limb entwining, breath snorting, passionate struggle. His hand is caressing her butt cheeks, and, from her arm position, she is no doubt returning the favor.

Marcus turns back and squeals, "Dad! Ross is gonna to get himself some."

"You hush son," says Sampson, and he gently pulls his son back around the corner. Holding Marcus there, Sampson pokes his head around the corner; takes in the scene, and says, "Why don't you two get a room?"

Marylyn removes her hand from Ross's ass and uses it to remove Ross's hand from her ass. Now that she has access, she removes her room key card from her back pocket, holds it up in the air, waggles it around few times, and then shoves it back in her pocket. Immediately, she grabs Ross's hand and replaces it back on her ass. Then puts her hand back on his.

The elevator dings its arrival and the doors slide open.

***

SUNRISE

The laser rays of the sun skip off the ocean, through a gap in the curtains and pummel Ross's eyes. He scrunches his eyes even tighter, but to no avail. Slowly his Beachwood aged brain solves the problem by telling Ross's neck muscles to turn his head. Ross treats himself to a four-limbed dog stretch and then scoots his back up against the headboard. He assesses the situation and finds that he's a little hungover, tired, sore, and a bit hungry. Surprisingly, he has never felt better in his life.

Possibly because of the presence of the young lady sitting at the writing desk, at the foot of the bed. Even better than how he feels is the view. The lower vertical slat, the two sides of the chair and the seat itself, form a perfect rectangular picture frame. The picture inside that frame is the top of two perfect ass cheek cupcakes, centered with a dimple of cleavage. This magnificent piece of live art sits cuddled in a pair of tiny light blue panties.

As Marylyn leans back in her chair the curtain of her t-shirt drops over the portrait. "Ross, is everything OK?"

He looks up and their eyes meet in the mirror. He feels like a kid with his hand caught in the "Peeping Tom" jar. That guilt vanishes when Marylyn smiles and says, "Glad you're enjoying the view, but we've got things to do."

"Things. What things?"

"Well, it's now nine twenty and you have a surfing lesson with Marcus at ten. I have to deposit these checks into your account, and at noon, I meet you for my surfing lesson.

"I hope this sounds more inquisitive than greedy, but how much is the deposit?" asks Ross.

"What a strange coincidence: everyone chipped in ten percent of the amount that they received from you. That means you will now have the same amount that we all started with. Three million, four hundred and fifty thousand dollars."

"Wow, looks like I'll be giving West Winds my two weeks' notice. But, to be fair to Hap, I'll stay on until he finds a replacement."

"Good, now you have everything you need to write your book: time, money, and a terrific story. One thing occurs to me though — didn't you tell me on the plane that you told a lady neighbor in Australia that you were going to write a bestseller?"

"That's right, I did. When I was leaving, Margaret asked me what kind of a book I was going to write. Then, before I could pick a genre or a category," I blurted out — "It's going to be a bestseller."

"Ross, I know that you say you never break your word, so how can you be sure that the book you're going to write will be a bestseller?"

Giving Marylyn his cockiest wink and a grin, Ross says, "Oh I'll think of something."

THE END

Made in the USA
Middletown, DE
26 August 2019